THE FUTURIST

JAMES P. OTHMER

ALMA BOOKS

ALMA BOOKS LTD
London House
243–253 Lower Mortlake Road
Richmond
Surrey TW9 2LL
United Kingdom
www.almabooks.com

The Futurist first published in US by Doubleday in 2006
First published in UK by Alma Books Limited in 2007

Printed in Jordan by the National Press

ISBN-13: 978-1-84688-026-1
ISBN-10: 1-84688-026-2

For Judy

In memory of Richard T. Othmer

"The source of fear is in the future, and a person freed of the future has nothing to fear."

– Milan Kundera, *Slowness*

"If I am lonely in a foreign country, I search for ruins."

– Christopher Isherwood, *In Ruins*

"Our show is about not knowing what the truth is."

– John Stewart

THE FUTURIST

Futureworld

The Futurist never saw it coming. But now that he thinks of it, it's not surprising. Not surprising that she's telling him in the most intentionally archaic way: a pen-and-ink note slipped into his state-of-the-art carry-on. Written in past tense. The only ways Lauren could have topped the irony of this is to have told him via foot messenger. Or carrier pigeon. Or smoke signals. All of which would be hard to do right now since he's thirty-seven thousand feet in the air somewhere between New York and Johannesburg. But she does top this. Right after a passage that begins with *Among the many reasons I can suffer you no longer* and concludes with *delusional, sociopathic prognosticator,* she tells Yates – the Futurist – that she's leaving him for a sixth-grade history teacher.

"Healing."

"What?" Yates asks.

"It's blue-flame hot. Everyone thought it would be Revenge. Or some crippling Mass Anxiety. But it's Healing." Blevins is sitting beside Yates in First Class. He consults part time for Yates and moonlights as a class-reunion designer.

"What, are 'Kick-boxing for Healers' classes suddenly popping up at the Soho Equinox? Has Miramax optioned the rights to the word?"

"I'm just saying..."

"Tonight on the Healing Channel..."

Blevins presses on. "Anything Celtic, for some reason, is still hot. The charming-little-people part, not the warring hordes. Ancient disasters continue to fascinate. Mountaineering tragedies and/or nautical disasters, with the fascination value of said disaster increasing relative to its respective depth or height."

"With an underwater mountaineering tragedy being the ultimate." Yates reaches for his glass of Maker's Mark.

"Angels were hot, but now you can't give them away. Buddhism, we are thinking, is due to break through in the US in a big way."

"Is that related to the Healing?"

"Buddhism and Unprotected Sex. The I-don't-give-a-fuck factor has never been so mainstreamed."

"I hear Turkey's still hot. Despite..."

"Yeah. But it's never just a place. It's the combination of extreme American activity and obscure locale."

"Skateboarding in Mongolia."

"Boogie-boarding the Yangtze."

"Fucking in outer space."

"Exactly." Blevins smacks his hands together, waking the British resin-furniture mogul in seat 4D. "So?"

Yates stares at the small screen on the seat back in front of him. The progress of the flight is charted by a flashing dot on a map of the hemisphere. Eight hours from refuelling in Cape Verde, another four from the Futureworld Conference in Johannesburg.

"Hardly H.G. Wellsian."

"Pardon?"

"William Gibsonian."

"I agree. Which is why... did you get a chance to look at the other stuff?"

"What?"

"The insights with a little more substance."

"The Future of Racism? The Invisible Poor?"

"Yeah. What'd you think?"

"I didn't get a chance to read them. In fact, I left them home."

"For Africa alone I have tons of stuff on AIDS, famine, education."

"This shouldn't be news to you: nobody wants to hear a bleak futurist, Blevins. And it's not like I haven't tried."

"But you haven't tried in a while."

Yates lowers his drink, stares at Blevins and thinks, *You're picking a bad time to lay a guilt trip on me.*

"Besides, it doesn't have to be so bleak if you spin it right. If you serve it up as an opportunity rather than an indictment."

Yates yawns. Blevins takes a breath, pushes on. "There's a lot more. I just beamed it onto your laptop."

Yates looks down at his crotch, feeling more than a little violated knowing that part of Blevins has got so close. And it's the worst part of Blevins at that; the well-intentioned part. He looks back at the tiny screen map. For a moment the flashing dot seems to go in reverse, one hundredth of a degree latitude back towards America.

He tries to picture her planning it. He imagines her curling up on the couch and listing the best ways to push his forward-thinking buttons with the most humiliating results. *Let's see. Whom to leave him for? An archaeologist? Genealogist? Antiques dealer? Presidential biographer? Or – this is perfect – a history teacher.* He closes his eyes – and there she is in the apartment of a lanky, bearded vegan with body odour, coupling on the floor, atop a suede-elbowed tweed jacket and thirty-two scattered, internet-plagiarized essays on the Battle of Hastings.

From the seat pocket in front of him he removes the folder containing the outline of his unfinished speech and, somehow, the emergency evacuation instructions for the Boeing 747. Most in his field would kill just to be able to network at something like Futureworld, but Yates is even more privileged. He is a VIP Speaker, a bona-fide A-list player in the culture of expectation, a highly compensated observer of the global soul with press clippings a yard long to prove it. Indeed, he's been in constant demand since the day four years ago when he coined the phrase that for fifteen minutes became the rallying cry of a generation. Ball-players worked it into post-game clichés. The President used it in a speech before both Houses of Congress. Even a pornographic movie was named after it. In many ways Yates's star has never been brighter, but now he feels a crisis of faith coursing through him, a waning confidence in the very future he sells. After so many years of it – several books (mostly ghostwritten), commencement speeches (all ghostwritten), a fawning Charlie Rose, conferences like TED, Davos, Tomorrow-a-Go-Go – after repeated optimistic promises of a better world yet to come, he's convinced that none of it will ever be. He no longer feels excitement for the future, but a deep nostalgia for it. As if the future is something already lost.

A young white man with a placard bearing Yates's name greets him at the international-arrivals gate in Johannesburg. "I'm David, your chaperone," he says, handing Yates a business card. "Whatever you need. Transportation, shopping – anything, anytime." At customs, David goes to a special line, nods to the agent and Yates is waved through. At the terminal exit, Yates glances back and sees Blevins still fumbling with his documents, scanning the ceiling for a sign that might make sense of the chaos.

Chattel houses in primary colours. Smoking heaps of sidewalk trash. Barefoot children in the shadow of Colonel

Sanders. High-rises and corporate parks inhabited by squatters. The shucked shell of a city. Yates observes the world through windows that only roll a third of the way down. Through black-tinted, bulletproof glass. He sits alone in back seats and attempts candid conversations with drivers paid to accommodate. He gleans local lore from chatty bellboys, from *Condé Nast Traveler*. From the top steps of grand hotels he elicits profound sociological insights. From a parting in the curtains of eighteenth-floor executive suites he absorbs geopolitical expertise. He gets it with his healthy choice breakfast from English-speaking room-service waiters. From gratis newspapers dropped outside his door. From Spectravision. Then he chronicles it, rolls it around in his head, and distills it down to anecdote, to conversation-starter, to pithy one-liner and finally he turns it into a highly proprietary, singularly respected worldly expertise that is utter and complete bullshit.

Outside the window, thousands in the morning fog, walking. "Where are they going, David?"

"The bus terminal, sir. To jobs in the suburbs. Sandton. Fourways. There's no work in the city. In places like Soweto. The business and the money surround the real city now. But the core is hollow."

"How can it survive?"

"Exactly sir. This is an issue the Ministry of Business Development is addressing. And why they lobbied to have a conference with the prestige of Futureworld here. To have people like you stimulate thought, progress. The economy."

Yates looks at Lauren's letter, runs his finger along the blue veins of her cursive script as if searching for a pulse. His phone vibrates and Blevins's number comes up. Blevins, last seen drowning in a rip tide of humanity. Should have offered him a ride. But, after seventeen hours of his earnest babbling... Still, the poor bastard.

"Hey, David. Why don't you pull over, let me hop up front."

"I can't, sir."

"Why not? It'll be easier to talk."

"I would love to, sir. But it's not safe to stop here. Besides, if you're seen up front with me I will lose my job."

He once did a trust fall at an anarchist's convention. He once gave the keynote address at a sports mascots' seminar, including a Q&A session that touched upon costuming, mime-bashing and health care. He once was a replacement judge at the Miss Crete Contest. He once addressed the sales force of a failing dot-com and a rollicking Luddite symposium in the same week and received standing ovations at both.

At registration they give him a canvas bag filled with corporate goodies, the latest digital gadgets, a menagerie of mahogany African animals, a leather Futureworld bomber jacket and two bottles of Cape Town Merlot. He scans the lobby for familiar faces. The preliminary materials had promised the likes of Jobs, Bezos and Spielberg, the Google guys, Angelina Jolie and a recently defeated presidential candidate. He sees none of them. But he does see Faith B. Popcorn, mother of all legitimate futurists. Faith B. Popcorn, Yates feels, can see more than the future. She can see through him. His sycophantic projections, his scientifically lewd dance with plagiarism. He's certain she's on to all of it and is itching to bring him down. Which is why he lowers his head, turns away and moves towards the elevators.

In his room at 10 a.m. he uncorks the first bottle of complimentary Merlot, turns on Sky News and opens his laptop. At every conference Yates answers to two sponsors. One is the true host whose name appears on the posters. The second is almost always a corporate or political sponsor that pays him to subtly and sometimes not so subtly disseminate its message. This time it's the Johannesburg CBD or Central Business District. Struggling economically, racially divided, ravaged by AIDS, poverty and violence, Jo'burg wants to be a player on a global scale once more. The speech-writing task is somehow to ignore the desperate reality, take the existing recipe and replace it with what the corporate world wants to hear. Insert name of relevant construction project here. Next cite the top-notch leadership team in place and of course the passionate people who work for them. Then sprinkle generous amounts of quotes from Thoreau, Verne and – for tomorrow – Mandela. Throw in a dash of the best one-liners, with apologies to everyone from Black Elk and John Lennon to Marshall McLuhan and the tabs of wisdom tied to Celestial Seasons tea bags. Be sure to suck up to the panelists, especially those who detest you most. Now add an uplifting regional anecdote about a local who overcame great odds, perhaps something from the *Jo'burg Times* or whatever it's called, or maybe allude to a profound scene witnessed en route from the airport. Then end on a note of pure optimistic adrenaline. Paint a vivid picture of what can be. Describe it in absolutes. A day when every South African will be wirelessly connected to the free world. When Jo'burg will again be synonymous with the world's great capitals. A corporate renaissance. A health-care miracle. Racial harmony...

Yates used to believe it. Used to think things like this were possible, or were at least admirable goals. He used to do his homework and think things through. He actually would talk to the locals, research the region, eschew partisan money. And he would earnestly try to come up with conscientious, albeit undoable and improbably quick solutions to ancient problems. But now...

* * *

He emails Lauren, suggesting that they talk, but it gets kicked back. Next he tries her home number, which has been disconnected. Finally he dials her cell and lets it ring, for fifteen minutes. Here's an observation that won't make it into his next telcom speech: right now it is possible to be dumped in real time from another continent, to careen into a digital wall of resentment and hostility, at the speed of light.

A knock on the door. A young black woman in a tight red dress. Joani from Swaziland. Courtesy of the CBD. He gives her 100 rands and the commemorative Futureworld bomber jacket and sends her away. He sits back down and drinks. Channel-surfs. Procrastinates. An hour later, another knock. David the chaperone.

"I thought you were another complimentary hooker."

"Sir?"

"Nothing. Glass of wine?"

David looks at his watch. "I'm here to take you to the soccer match."

"Pardon?"

"It's on your itinerary. It is an important game."

"I really can't deal with soccer right now."

"It's part of your appearance contract."

Yates has never been to a soccer game, and this is a big one. Ellis Park Stadium is filled beyond capacity. The crowd rocks and sways with a tidal grace and magnitude, a singing, chanting force of nature. Looking around, he wonders if he's the only white man in the stadium. The riot begins soon after he's seated, but it will be a while before he notices. A player receives a yellow card. Yates receives a gin-and-tonic. A teenage boy is stabbed in general admission. A joke is cracked in the VIP box. Blood flows on the hot concrete of section 214 and people start running for the tunnels. But the game continues. When the tunnels clog, a rush is made towards the field, which is caged off with thick wire. Yates notices none of it. The primal roar and collective groan that comes when flesh presses upon itself to the point of bursting he chalks up to raucous enthusiasm. The gunshots he assumes are fireworks, and cheap, third-world ones at that. The men scrambling up the barrier wire he sees as performing some kind of regional sporting ritual, like the wave, not clawing for their lives. To Yates, it's all a spectacle performed on his behalf, and when he's handed his second drink he's already wondering how he can integrate this into tomorrow's speech. Such passionate people!

The first clue that something's wrong occurs to Yates when an aide grimly whispers into the ear of the Minister of Business Development. The second hint is the dozens of policemen wading into the crowd. But instead of stopping the stampede, they inflame it. Far above the fray, surrounded by security guards, Yates watches the shiver and press of the mob. Black clubs strobe across the sun-blasted sky and plunge into the multitude. Gunshots. Bodies compacting against barrier wire. A young man in green face paint atop the cage is shot in the chest by someone in red face paint and falls back upon the others.

At midfield, the referees huddle with players from both clubs. They've become the spectators, watching the life-and-death competition in the grandstands.

Half an hour later they walk Yates onto the field, towards the stiffening dead, past the stunned next of kin, faces pressed against the wire, waiting for permission to mourn. They certainly would prefer that Yates were not here, but there's nothing they can do about it now. A man lays unattended on a stretcher, splintered tibia exposed through a bloody gash in his trousers. Two policemen are removing film from a journalist's camera. All Yates hears is the sound of sirens going the other way. All he sees are the privileged and the dead. Body bags in the goal mouth. Some zipped, others empty, waiting to be filled. He stares at the faces of the dead, painted just hours ago with ritual strokes for the opposite of death. A child of five, alone, looks at Yates. Yates cannot hold his stare.

"How many?" asks the Minister of Business Development.

"Forty-three," answers a policeman. "More heading to the hospital." The policeman looks at Yates, as if he thinks Yates can actually do something to change any of this. Yates looks down, sees blood drops on the white dust of the goal line.

"Tell me," the Minister of Business Development asks Yates. "In your opinion, what can be done to minimize the fallout, to ensure that this will not diminish our chances of hosting the World Cup here in ten years?"

Brand America

Message light flashing on the hotel phone. Faxes slipped under the door. A new complimentary goodie basket on the desk. Moans of the dying or the tantrically gifted in the next room. There will be a cocktail reception in the De Beers Parlour in an hour, but Yates is too tired, too close to drunk to drink any more, at least in public. And then there's still the speech waiting to be written. With a hotel pen he peels the foil from the neck of the second bottle of complimentary Merlot.

He once consulted for a firm that designed edgy logos and teen-centric merchandise for fictitious companies. He recently shared a $350 bottle of Krug Clos du Mesnil on a red-eye with the CFO of a company that makes antivirus software, who revealed to him in an unguarded moment that they are also the foremost creator of viruses. Last year he was paid five figures by an undisclosed government agency to go to Kauai to play golf and brainstorm random acts of terrorism.

Nothing on the news about the riot. Just a mention that the game's been rescheduled. And nothing from Lauren anywhere. He remembers one of their last conversations. She asked where he was with the novel she'd recommended. He said the part where the guy leaves

Brooklyn to go to a liberal arts college in Vermont. She just nodded, smiled, and that was that. She didn't want to discuss theme or structure, or whether he liked it. She only wanted to know where he stood on ground she'd long ago covered.

At cocktail hour, again at David's insistence. Sponsored by Grey Goose. Catering by Emeril. He hasn't shaved or eaten a proper meal in thirty-six hours, and the drinks – now it's bourbon again – continue to go down smoothly. He stays off to the side of the room, close to a bar and an exit. While others proudly display their name tags, Yates pins his beneath his blazer, down by his appendix; whenever someone leans forwards to try to steal a glimpse, he shifts his glass in a blocking manoeuvre. Here's the thing: at Futureworld, none of the official panelists actually respects Yates. But because he's appearing here as an official speaker, he will be respected and legitimized everywhere else. And it is in the mainstream of everywhere else that the big money flows. So several times a year he endures the sniggers of the intellectual elite, the dismissive sneers of the fallen and reinvented digerati, the cold shoulders of physicists and philosophers, in order to thrive elsewhere.

Here's an eminent cognitive psychologist in a coonskin cap; here's the biotech tsar whose lecture topic is caveman sex; here's Bono, Condi and some kind of Kennedy offspring. There's the Tiananmen tank kid who's no longer a kid. The born-again doomsday economist who once wrote a best-selling book called *Dow 40,000*. That's the woman who says she can teach string theory to a six-year-old. Make way for Amanda Glowers, the sixty-two-year-old advertising legend appointed by the president to raise the favourability rating of Brand America in the eyes of the world. The way she thrusts out her hand, there's no way that Yates can choose not to shake it.

"Amanda Glowers." She squeezes with exaggerated vigour, anything to conceal her true age. She cuts off Yates before he begins. "I know you. You spoke in Monterrey. You look wiped out. I never drink on the plane. Did you drink on the plane?"

"From the strip search in JFK until... now."

"What's your topic tomorrow?"

"I'm not sure. Either something like *Rebirth. Redemption. Resilience.* Or: *Fear. Paranoia. Hopelessness.* Maybe I'll write it two ways and take the audience's temperature during my introduction."

"Lovely." Amanda Glowers adjusts her signature scarf, if scarf is what you call an eight-foot length of embroidered silk. She considers Yates, contemplating whether or not she wants to play. Yates reads the three-line title on her name tag:

US Undersecretary
of Public Diplomacy
and Public Affairs.

"How about you? You all set?"

"Still the same. Transform the down-with-America issue into the repositioning of a brand."

"How's that going?"

"Some polls have us doing better by a click or two. Perception-wise."

"And perception matters?"

"A poor one leads to unrest, which can threaten national security. We're an open and tolerant society. They should know."

Yates finishes his bourbon and motions for another. "I thought that's precisely why they hated us. I thought the problem wasn't *their* understanding of Brand America, but *our* lack of understanding of Brand Third World. Brand Eastern Bumfuckistan. I thought the sharing of cultural knowledge would be better if it was reciprocal."

Amanda Glowers rolls her eyes.

"You just rolled your eyes."

"Right now we're conducting focus groups in five of the markets that despise us most."

"Wow. I didn't know they had two-way mirrors in Fallujah. Have some more M&Ms, Mohammed, and tell me how you really feel about democracy."

"Funny."

"How do you know if it works?"

"A thirty per cent conversion rate for Muslims would represent a sales spike any *Fortune* 500 company would kill for."

"Conversion to liking us, or conversion to Christianity?"

"We're launching a global Brand USA news channel. A print campaign. Webisodes. Outdoor. TV."

"How do you place the media? Cave walls in the Khyber Pass? The back cover of *Jihad Quarterly*? During a very special episode of *Survivor* on Channel 28 in Uzbekistan?"

"How'd you know?"

"Can you do subliminal stuff? Find the Nike swish in the hide of a camel. Or more blatant: slip the first amendment onto page 728 of the Koran. Get the next winner of *American Idol* to lip-sync during half-time of the biggest infidel stoning of the year."

"You're just trying to be an asshole now, aren't you?" Before Yates can answer, someone else does: Faith B. Popcorn.

"Of course he is. It's a lot easier than being original."

"I think he's just drunk, Faith." Yates looks at Amanda Glowers and thinks of her with something akin to affection. He imagines a montage of a late-night tryst with Amanda. Her personal-trainer-sculpted sixty-two-year-old frame astride him in a red, white and blue thong. Sharing swigs of a sparkling American white right out of the bottle. The imprint of her bridgework upon his left earlobe. Primal moans. Martial thrusts. A faint cry of *Mommy*.

A man in a pink tuxedo and white spats whom both women apparently know interrupts them. The only writing on his name tag says *Genius*. Now two men in silver sweatsuits converge on the bar from opposite sides of the room on next year's can't-miss Segway models. They hop off with the nonchalance of Huntington Beach skateboarders and belly up to the bar. One orders two dirty martinis while the other passes a comment about the afternoon's soccer match at Ellis Park, which sparks a burst of laughter from all within earshot, except Yates and the bartender. Across the room, Blevins is standing on his toes, presumably looking for Yates, who ducks his head and slips away from the others.

He stops at the table outside the grand ballroom that displays the seating cards for tonight's welcome gala. A jazz combo is warming up behind the doors inside. *Something Blue*. He finds the seating card with his name, in between Yanni and Yoko. After looking left then right, he crumbles the card and puts it in his pocket.

"Looks like someone's not properly embracing the future." Blevins, expressing his purported brilliance with a white linen suit and a red bow tie the size of a piece of Trident gum.

"Tonight it will have to begin without me."

"Heard about the game."

A waiter passes with a tray of fluted champagne glasses. Yates grabs two.

"Having a bit of a party, then?"

"Gotta write my speech. Gotta get out of here before I get penalized for Unnecessary Pragmatism."

"Do you need help? I've..."

"I'm fine."

"Uh-huh."

"Don't start."

"Some guys were looking for you earlier. Government types."

"US?"

"I think."

Yates empties the first glass, briefly considers offering the other to Blevins before drinking it too. Blevins steps closer. "Look. I don't know what's bothering you, but I'd kill to have your gig. To have the opportunity to talk some kind of sense to all of these supposed movers and shakers. To add a touch of morality to the intellectual elite. Not that you have to abandon the other stuff. Just integrate a conscience into it. Shit. You make nice-nice here, drop a few sound bites that may actually provoke rather than affirm, and you'll still be golden on the lecture circuit."

"Tell me when I should be overwhelmed with emotion and hug you."

"I think I've figured out a way to do it, to weave in some of the more socially responsible insights without seeming maudlin."

Yates doesn't answer.

"So if you don't need anything substantial from me, why bring me?"

"Because it's in my contract, and I thought you'd appreciate the day rate."

In the elevator, he sees a writer from a tech magazine on an all-expenses-paid trip courtesy of the CBD. "Yates."

"Cartmann, right?"

"Close. It's Hartmann." Hartmann seems to be even more inebriated than Yates. "You get a chance to sample the local flavours, yet?"

"Pardon?"

"I just paid a visit to *Swaziland.*"

"Jesus, Hartmann."

"Cut me some slack. I'd never been with an African-American woman before."

"She's not African-American. She's African-African." Yates shakes his head, then looks back up at Hartmann. "What was she wearing?"

Hartmann puts his hand on his chin, makes a big show of thinking. "A commemorative Futureworld bomber jacket, and not a hell of a lot else."

The Phenomenon of Me

In his room he breaks every corporate travel-expense rule and loses himself in the high prices and tiny portions of the minibar. Macadamia nuts. M&Ms. A 20-cl Heineken. A Dewar's mini bottle. Cape Town taffy. While he checks his email he calls Lauren on his cell and lets it ring for ever. The room phone rings and he dives across the bed. Kurt Monicker, Chairman of Futureworld.

"Just ensuring that you're alright, since you're not joining us for dinner."

"I'm fine, Kurt. Less than, actually. But fine for tomorrow. The travel. The soccer." He twists open a tiny bottle of Absolut. "I'm not much of a drinker, Kurt, but that champagne hit me like a riot stick. Thought I'd rest up, polish my speech."

"Anything you need?"

Yates looks at the open minibar. Most of the booze is gone. He thinks better of it. "No thanks, Kurt. I'm all set here."

On the news there's something about endangered tourists on the space station. No big deal, really, other than the fact that Yates is partially responsible for some of them being on the space station to begin with. He presses mute and tries to think of something else. More moans in the next room. Still no answer on Lauren's cell. He tries to imagine the history-teacher friend. Wonders if maybe he'd had him back when he was in sixth grade. If this is some kind of sinister payback for a twenty-five-year-old wisecrack. He wonders if he and Lauren were ever in love, or just two people who were really good at avoiding it. As he contemplates this, he fixes a gin-and-grape soda and Googles himself. In seconds the browser searches the complete archives of the digital universe for all things Yates and comes up with 3,468 responses. All but five begin with "Coiner of the phrase..." One is the text of a speech he gave to a marketing class at Yale. The second is an excerpt from a four-year-old *Wired* magazine article that ordained him the Codifier of Cool. The third, a *Who's Who*-like entry, defines him as a futurist; prognosticator; seer; shaman; snake-oil salesman and coiner of the ubiquitous phrase... The fourth is a website for a Yates from Peabody, Mass., who likes NASCAR, the Sox and the music of the Kings of Leon. The final response is for a mature-women sex site that has nothing to do with Yates, unless you count the Amanda Glowers thing.

At 9 p.m. the room phone rings. David, asking if Yates is okay.

At ten Blevins calls, drunk in the ballroom, rambling about American memes and the future of altruism and the doomed space hotel. Yates goes to the window, parts the curtains and looks at the sky for stars, for the space hotel, for a guilt-tinged form of comfort. Some people write letters or make phone calls when they are alone and far from home, when they yearn for something or someone that matters. Yates looks at the sky. He looks for the familiar constellations of his youth, the stars that his father once took great pains to identify for him. As he grew older, he would take great pains to show indifference for those same stars, just to piss his father off. Even so, no matter where he's been, and no matter how he feels about his father, he never can stop himself from looking at the night sky and wondering what his father would make of it, and of the men they have each become. He wonders now what his father, a man who never said or did an embarrassing thing in his life, thinks of his son's involvement, albeit limited, in this celestial catastrophe in the making. Probably something like, *He's compromised every bit of his earthly reputation, why not shoot for the stars?* Yates looks for stars, but if they are up there they are hidden by the paranoid glow of the lights of the broken city, and the impression that whatever sentences he writes in the next several hours can actually make the slightest difference.

At eleven, a quiet tapping at the door. A tall, blonde white woman.

"Marjorie," she says. "Howzit."

"Fine, thanks. Come in." He steps back and waves at what's left of the minibar. Marjorie grabs a can of Coke and opens it. She stands near the TV, considering the wreckage. Snack wrappers, empty cans and tiny bottles. The laptop. His scattered notes. All spread out upon the bed, the floor, the desk. Earlier he'd slipped Lauren's letter inside the lower-right corner of the mirror frame because he liked the symmetry when he looked at himself. Marjorie goes right to it, reads it.

"So do you knock on doors until someone invites you in? Or did they send you specifically to me?"

"Specifically to you."

"Nice of you to say, even if you're lying."

Marjorie tilts her head from side to side, puts the Coke on the desk and stretches her arms over her head. Her blouse rises, revealing a flat, tanned belly. Yates considers her legs, long and strong, partially covered by a skirt two generations too matronly for her age, which he puts at about twenty-five. Now her face. Blue eyes, long interesting nose. Tanned and unblemished. Maybe closer to twenty. "You're beautiful."

She shrugs, changes the channel to a music station. Percussive world beat. Chanting. Soweto hip-hoppers with gold teeth and American baseball caps. Who says the Tampa Bay Devil Rays don't have a broad fan base? Marjorie turns towards Yates, swaying awkwardly to the music, betraying her elegance, perhaps purposely undermining any hint of heartfelt sexuality. With her right hand she picks up the soda. With her left she starts undoing her blouse. By the second button, Yates is laughing, shaking his head, waving. No, no, no. "How do they pay you?"

"By the visit. The overall length."

"How will they know?"

"Sorry?"

"Whether or not we did anything. So if you were to stay a while?"

"They'll just assume."

"Then, get comfortable. Watch me make an ass of myself. Unless you'd rather knock on doors."

Even though he's being nice, she gives him a look. Like she distrusts good more than evil. Then her jaw unclenches and her face softens.

"Interesting profession, in a country with a gazillion per cent incidence of HIV."

"Slightly less than. Besides, I'm a virgin. At least this aspect of it."

"Of course. And I've never had alcohol before."

"My commitment is exclusively for this event. As a favour. The CBD promised me a job."

Yates opens a bottle of Namibian lager, Windhoek. "A job as what?"

"As something fundamentally different than this. An executive job." She looks at his cellphone on the bed. He dialled Lauren two hours ago and it's still on redial.

"What's that noise?"

"It's my cellphone. I'm making a call."

"To whom? How long do you plan on letting it ring?"

"It's personal."

"I see." Marjorie nods towards the note on the mirror. "Why did she break off with you?"

"Break off. She broke off with me two days ago. Basically because she changed. Because her tolerance level for my self-absorption diminished precipitously over the years. At first she was thrilled to be immersed in the phenomenon of me, but slowly she lost interest, occasionally even thinking of herself and then, inexcusably, others."

Marjorie sighs, kneels in front of the minibar. "Maybe I will have a wettie."

"A what."

She points at the minibar. "A drink."

"So then, what do you think?"

"Sorry? Think of what?"

"Me, of course. No faking it."

"So it is sex you're after, after all." Marjorie opens a mini Bacardi and pours it into the Coke. "So, do you want me to masturbate you, to affirm your self-diagnosis, or honestly wing it and take you to blissful new heights of self-loathing?"

"Lucky me. The heretofore-undiscovered call girl with a Ph.D. You know, you can leave at any time. And if you want to stay but don't want to indulge a heartbroken drunk, that's fine too."

She stares at him for a moment and takes an exaggerated breath. "I see. I think you're currently pathetic, potentially interesting. Cute in a rather odd way."

"Very good. But what I'm after is how, you know, after you meet someone, you go, *I wonder what his deal is?* Or, *His deal is he's a liar, and he's bold only because he's really insecure.* Or, *He's keeping something in, some secret pain.* Or, maybe, *He's just a fool.*"

"Fine. Then your *deal* is you're drunk. Self-destructive. In all likelihood a nihilist. I wonder if you're truly so full of your own piss or you just used to be and are in the latter stages of denial. I sense you're superficially arrogant, mostly because you like tweaking people with it, your pretend arrogance. What else? You're not at all comfortable in your well-to-do skin. And beneath the surface may lie the most miniscule mite of a half-decent soul."

"So what you're saying then is you think I'm really, really hot."

She wants to smile, but won't allow it. Instead she lights a cigarette and walks to the window. "Lekker."

"Translate, please."

She affects a male American voice. "*Rilly, rilly hot.*"

Yates sits up. "What about you?"

She turns from the window. He wonders if she'd been looking for stars, too. She considers him before talking. For a moment it seems as if she won't answer, but then she starts to speak without pause. "I'm not from Johannesburg. I grew up well off and white on a farm in Greylingstad. An Afrikaner. My family came to South Africa in 1669 with the Dutch East India Company, and when the Brits took over they were part of the voortrekkers, or pioneers, who felt that it was their divine right to settle and farm in the hinterlands. After apartheid some of the blacks who lived nearby and worked for Afrikaner families for hundreds of years apparently felt that it was their divine right to claim the land back. One day, when we came back from the funeral of another farmer, they were waiting in our home. My father, a racist, who no doubt had had some run-in with his workers over the years, resisted. They killed him. Then they killed my mother, a nice person but aider and abettor to a racist. Then they helped me lose the first part of my virginity. The only reason I lived is because there had been gunshots and they heard cars coming in the distance. Relatives in Sandton took me in until I was eighteen, and now I'm on my own. This, as I said, is temporary."

Yates doesn't know what to say, so he drinks. Then, "Did they catch them?"

"I don't even know. The government said it was a robbery. They wouldn't admit that it was racially or politically motivated. As you can imagine, being a white victim in post-apartheid South Africa can be rather complicated." She pauses and cocks her ear to the wall. The neighbours' moans have picked up in volume and rhythm.

Yates points his thumb in the direction of the moans. "At least somebody likes living in the future."

Marjorie changes the channel to an American show about spectacular car wrecks. Yates pours a $23 cognac mini bottle into his toothbrush cup and looks at his speech, which seems more trivial than ever now. The more he tries to change it, the more false it – and by association, he – appears.

"What are you so dramatically toiling over?"

"My speech. For tomorrow. It seems like so much... bullshit."

"Then tell the truth," she says, and to this he has no answer.

A few minutes later he turns to tell Marjorie that it's okay if she spends the night, especially if it will keep her from having to sleep with geniuses, but she's already asleep. He takes the remote from her lap and changes the channel just as a minivan is about to careen into a gasoline tanker.

He turns back to her and wonders what her real name is, if her story, her past, is true. Then, as if flicked by the finger of a Hollywood poltergeist, Lauren's letter slips from the mirror and drifts onto the floor. For the first time in his life, Yates feels old. As he thinks of them now, pieces of his past seem so long ago, distant the way incidents from his grandparent's childhood once sounded when described to him. Not just of another time, but another era. Where he had always been a free spirit, never afraid of or angry at anything, he now cynically critiques the world each day and resents his lack of ability or desire to change it. Blevins, he grudgingly admits, may have a point.

After a while he puts down his drink and goes through the poses of grief, clutching knees to chest, rocking. He wants to cry. Is trying to, but can't. He looks at the sleeping Marjorie and tries to summon the most maudlin, sentimental memories. At first, they're the clichés of an inebriated cynic. Funerals and beach walks. The death of his first dog. Then they're not. The boy near the body bags. Sunday-morning sex with Lauren. And his last failed visit home with the strained conversations with his father who, more than anyone, more than Lauren, or Blevins or even Faith B. Popcorn, truly knows Yates, his weaknesses and disappointments and especially those parts of himself that he refuses to acknowledge. He thinks of his mother's desperate, uncomfortably obvious ploys to bring father and son back together and their feeble attempt to satisfy her, for her sake only. Now he tries without success to imagine the last time he was truly excited, about anything. He thinks of all this in the hope that a rush of tears will come, leading to some kind of epiphany, some kind of catharsis. As if that's the way it really works.

He looks back at Marjorie, then the speech. He clicks the cursor to the left of the title – "Kinetic Tomorrowland", whatever that means – and drags down through eight pages of lies. He deletes it all and begins to type.

* * *

The thrum of the shower wakes him up. At first he's confused. At first he thinks he's home, and that's Lauren singing in the cloud of steam. But slowly it registers. Johannesburg. The future. The semi-virginal call girl shaving her legs with his Mach3. If he was any more hung-over, there would be blood seeping from some combination of ears, eyes and nose. He needs to hydrate, but the minibar offers nothing except Jägermeister and a cherry-flavoured, carbonated drink that may or may not be alcoholic. In the bathroom he wipes the mirror, not so much to revisit his disappointing image but to glimpse Marjorie coming out of the shower. He splashes water on his face, cups his hands and drinks. As the curtain opens, he looks up, beyond his reflection and directly into Marjorie's eyes. She smiles and reaches for a towel. Without make-up, with her hair wet, without clothes from the Cosmopolitan Call Girl Collection, she looks even more beautiful. She wraps a towel around her head and, to Yates's right, wipes clean a patch of mirror for herself.

"I have aspirin."

"I need morphine, but it's a start."

"David called."

He shakes his head. Doesn't ring a bell.

"Your chaperone. He'll be by at ten to take you to the auditorium. The Mandela Room."

"Nelson or Winnie?"

"I told him your speech was brilliant."

He looks at his reflection. Pale, unshaven for forty-eight hours. Plump bags and charcoal rings beneath what were formerly the whites of his eyes. The cumulative effect is to obfuscate the fact that there's a beautiful, naked young woman beside him.

"Oh," she says, twisting the cap off the complimentary body lotion, "I almost forgot. Lauren called."

"Lauren?"

"We had a nice chat."

"You didn't wake me?"

"I tried. But you got testy. Which Lauren said is par for the course when you've been drinking."

"Did she leave a number?"

"No. She doesn't want you ringing her at all hours. I told her you had been ringing her phone for hours with your cellphone, which, by the way, died as the sun came up."

"Did she ask who you were?"

"No."

"Good."

"I told her."

"You told her."

"I told her that you were a gentleman. She's quite happy, you know."

"Did she sound concerned?"

"Concerned more along the lines of *I hope he doesn't do something stupid*. Otherwise you're wasting your energy trying to get her back. By the way, who is Amanda?"

He turns to face her. "Why?"

She smiles, clucks her tongue and rolls her eyes. "Never mind."

There's a knock on the door. Marjorie grabs a terry-cloth robe off the back of the bathroom door and says "Breakfast. You need it."

He nods. He tries to remember the speech he may or may not have written. Thinks of trying to reread it, or rewrite it, but there's no way. He doesn't remember the words, but he remembers feeling that this isn't at all what they wanted from him, and that it's the best thing he's written in a long time.

Marjorie brings her coffee into the bathroom. Yates sits in his underwear on the bed, closes his eyes and tries to ground himself, but it's like trying to ground yourself on a cloud in a dream. This is how it's been since he opened the message on the plane, but now he realizes that it's been like this for much longer. He tries to pinpoint the exact moment when it happened. When he changed from believer to cynic. When he abandoned his convictions for this. But of course there was no one moment. There was only a gradual tarnishing of the self, a long series of delusional compromises that could only be rationalized away for so long.

He opens his eyes to Sky News on mute and watches a demonstration in Jakarta. Skeleton masks and American flags. Back to the anchor, who has a graphic of the space station over his right shoulder that says DEADLY ORBIT. This is the vehicle on which a group of wealthy adventure tourists, in part because of Yates's unabashed endorsement, have booked cabins in the first civilian space hotel; an enterprise about which he knew little more than the fact that he'd be well compensated if, as a renowned futurist, in a covertly unofficial capacity, he sanctioned it as a good thing, on the cusp of an exciting new trend. "Space is the next Everest" was his officially agreed-upon quote. He watches but can't bring himself to activate the volume.

This is the how-to guide for all self-proclaimed futurists of limited ability who want to commit career suicide. This is what to say and who you say it to. This is the elevator you get off, wet-haired, holding hands with a wet-haired young prostitute in front of your peers. This is how you kiss her on the lips and tell her to take care, to stay in touch, that she saved you. This is the podium at which you stand, bloodshot eyes, raspy voice, enough of last night's minibar menagerie on your breath to raise the eyebrow of even the self-absorbed, recently made genius who introduces you. This is how you say good morning to the smiling assassins waiting for you to fail. And these are the glasses you put on to see the stunned faces of the offended spectators as you read the incendiary words, which will put an end to all of it, because in another irony that was never lost on Lauren, Blevins, Faith B. Popcorn or his father, the Futurist is near-sighted.

Google Response # 3,469

J.P. Yates, Futurist
Futureworld Conference. Johannesburg. Text of Keynote Speech. Popular futurist asks off bandwagon he helped create. Social Sciences > Futurism > people > **Yates, J.P...**
www.dreamkiller.net/revolt/yates/snake-oil - 14k - Cached - Similar pages

YATES:

I realized this morning over breakfast with a prostitute with whom I did not have sex who is a better human being than all of us that I've spent a good portion of my life seeking the approval of people I can't stand. Including myself.

The truth is, I know nothing. Understand nothing.

I try. I am not lazy. But the more I try to understand something the more intertwined and complex it seems. The more I realize I am out of the proverbial loop. The literal loop. The existential loop. The more I think of things the more I question whether anyone is properly looped. In fact, I challenge the very existence of the loop, proverbial, literal or metaphorical. So this is a fundamental problem, being out of a loop that I don't even believe in.

Most books or movies or creation myths have a hero who knows all there is to know about at least one thing. And they use that gift to overcome an obvious and blatantly evil adversary. They have insider knowledge. Special gifts. Ingenious ways of getting to the core of things. The answer. The solution. The truth. They know what's right and wrong. They know what's next. And they know what to do about it.

I don't.

I don't understand the present, let alone the fucking future.

Yet we claim to understand. Pretend to. Some actually believe it, that they do know. You know the people. The ones who talk about things with such cocksure passion that you think, Shit, maybe they do know, maybe they really do. *They speak in absolutes. Blacks and whites. They speak with soothing partisan simplicity. They speak with their hands and use PowerPoint like a sword. They quote people you ought to know more about. They work on a privileged higher plane and posit their views with a condescending subterranean confidence, convincing you not to worry, that forces are at work on other levels, levels that simple folks like you cannot even begin to fathom, so it's best not to worry your little head about it, and to trust them, the experts, that this is the way it is. And the way it will be.*

People get rich and powerful operating this way, perpetuating the myth of the über-*level, the exclusive loop. Dispensing their wisdom and opinions and edicts to the masses. Breaking down the conflicting moral, political and economic issues of 6.5 billion people into a binary proposition. Yes or no. War or peace. Good or bad. With us or against us. Ginger or Mary Ann.*

Presidents work on this level. And dictators. Talk-show hosts. Professional wrestlers. Actresses on the steps of the Capitol. Conservatives. Liberals. CEOs. Madison Avenue. Wall Street. Sesame Street.

They're all in the loop. All working on another level.

I'm not.

I don't believe in the sacred loop or the secret level.

In fact, I think the more people claim to absolutely know, the more clueless and insecure they absolutely are. Of course, I can't be sure of this.

Which brings me to us. And to me. Who do we think we are? Who did I think I was?

How can I call myself a futurist when I missed the most cataclysmic event of our time? How can I predict tomorrow when the world is on fire today?

How did I see reality TV coming but miss this?

And let's be honest: we all did.

We make all these pronouncements, but none of us ever goes back to check on their accuracy. Shit, if the people in this room were right just one per cent of the time, we'd all be telecommuting from Tahiti, eating dinner in pill form and having literal sex with our virtual selves. You talk shit long enough, sooner or later you may actually be right and, if by some fluke that is the case, watch out, because any successful prediction is always followed by the cannibalistic scramble for credit – the blood grab to brand an original thought as your own.

We all want to be the first to be there to identify a "click moment", but we live in a world that may never click again.

We're great at telling people the future they need to buy into instead of the present they ought to be making the most of.

And what's hilarious is that we all believe it. That we are geniuses. That we are all responsible for and deserving of our wealth. More deserving of the privileged life than, say, a teacher or a mason. A cleric or a hot-dog vendor. Despite the fact that 99 per cent of us did not create our good fortune. The markets did. Or luck. Or heredity.

I believed it.

But not any more.

You see, we may be able to identify cool, but we can never invent it. Cool is never manufactured. You never try to be cool. It happens.

Same goes for goodness. And truth.

And the only truth I know... is that I know nothing. And even though you may dress the part – the Missoni scarves, the yellow jumpsuits, the tiny glasses, the all-whites, the all-blacks, the Nehrus, the sandals, the magic glasses, the glittering gadgets – none of you know anything, either. Sorry about that.

We are not innovators. We're fucking abominations.

To paraphrase someone smarter than me, but who still knows nothing, the philosophical task of our age is for each of us to decide what it means to be a successful human being.

I don't know the answer to that, but I would like to find out.

In the mean time, I know absolutely zilch.

I am the founding father of the Coalition of the Clueless.

Emerging Threats and Opportunities

He once fired a man on Take Your Daughter to Work Day. He once spent the night at a Wellness conference holding a bingeing MacArthur Fellow's puking head over a toilet. He once wrote the introduction to a book he never read: *Beehive Management: How life in the honeycomb translates to winning in the workplace.* A recent lecture circuit saw him speak on successive days to a leading pesticide manufacturer and the Organic Farmers of America, and receive standing ovations from both.

Yates doesn't remember if he was simply booed off stage or physically removed from the premises. He does remember that two people clapped, an Irish journalist and a security guard, but they were immediately suppressed by the glares of those who were fairly sure that they had been offended.

This is what Blevins said: "Nice job, fuckface."

This is what the aide to the Johannesburg Minister of Business Development said: "You have disappointed many people who are now determined to make your remaining minutes in our country as difficult as possible."

This is what Faith B. Popcorn said: "Speak for yourself, asshole."

This is what Marjorie said: "The truth is better than sex, yes?"

This is what he said: "No."

This is what the reporter from *Pravda* said: "Do you hold yourself personally accountable for the lives of the dying civilian cosmonauts?"

This is what Yates said: "Yes."

And this is what Amanda Glowers says as she takes him by the arm and steers him into an anteroom: "That was one of the most spectacular suicides I have ever seen."

"Thank you."

"There are some people I want you to meet."

"Where, in the backseat of a car, with me in a black hood on a lonely Johannesburg road?"

She hands him a plastic key card. "They're in my room. 416."

"Aren't you coming?"

"I don't want to. And they don't want me to. Separation of this and that."

"Government?"

She smiles, shrugs. "You tell me."

He doesn't knock. Just swipes himself in. In the elevator he imagined they'd be sitting at attention at a table facing the door, expecting him. Perhaps a clenched-fist type in the shadows, coming forth to give him a perfunctory gun check. But instead the door quietly opens onto two middle-aged white men lying on a queen-sized bed. One is asleep. The other is fumbling with the clicker to turn off the muted pornographic movie he's been watching.

"I can come back. I mean, I don't want to ruin the dramatic conclusion or anything."

The clicker guy stands up, makes some kind of martial show of powering the TV down. Clicker as nunchaku. Clicker as six-shooter. "You could have fucking knocked."

Yates holds up his swipe key. "Didn't need to."

The other guy opens his eyes, rubs his face. He looks first at the blank TV then vapidly at Yates.

"I'm Yates."

Clicker man nods. "I'm Johnson." He smiles and nods to his partner. "And so is he."

"Lovely. Are you twins, or is the surname a mandatory requirement for entrance into the club?"

"Hilarious," says upright Johnson. "Listen, Glowers thinks you were made for this. I think you're wired all wrong. But you clearly have a gift. What you just did this morning. The Coalition of the Clueless. The philosophical task of our age. Good stuff."

"It's called a reckless disregard for one's livelihood. The gist of the speech is that my so-called gift is a sham."

Upright Johnson waves him off. Prone Johnson lights a cigarette.

"What agency are you guys with?"

"None. We work for a company that is loosely affiliated with the military, a bit more snugly affiliated with the party in power. When he's not sleeping, Johnson here sometimes works for a consortium called the Centre for Emerging Threats and Opportunities. Would you like a scotch?"

Yates looks at a bottle of Glenfiddich on the table. "Sure. I mean no. What am I thinking? Definitely no. May I leave now?"

"Any time. But I haven't given you our pitch. And since you're fairly well professionally neutered for the foreseeable future, I thought you'd give us some consideration."

"Go ahead. Seduce me."

"We want you to tell us what you think of the world."

"Right now? In one hundred words or less? Book-length? Or small enough to fit on a bumper sticker?"

"We want you to do what you always do, but with a more sociological, geopolitical bent. We want you to travel to the corners of the planet, occasionally on assignment, and tell us what you think about what they think."

"They?"

"The citizens of the world."

"That's easy. They hate us. Every shade of hate. Shit, there are already libraries filled with books about that."

"But the degree and variety of hate changes by the hour. By the longitudinal click. And you are right about the hate and the surface politics. But we're more interested in an assessment of the vibe, the emotional intangibles. The fads, the waves, what you people call the memes. What is the global preoccupation? What ideological truths are being crammed into the minds of unsuspecting children?"

"Didn't you guys already try this a long time ago? The Terrorism Futures Market. What are the odds on the next attack, bloody insurrection, assassination, violent coup, subtle regime change?"

"Space Disaster?"

"Funny."

"The Futures Market – which, for the record, we had nothing to do with – was poorly conceived. Should never have been released or even leaked for public consumption, which rendered it susceptible to the manipulation of the would-be perpetrators themselves. This is much more about the gathering of emotional intelligence for probabilistic risk assessment. You know how insurance companies calculate to mitigate? We calculate to prevent."

The other Johnson clears his throat. "And to enact. In certain situations, we might ask you to give a well-placed sound bite on behalf of our interests."

"Why me? Why not a numbers-cruncher? Why not a policy guy? Why not go to the appropriate wonk? Or to the inhabitants of some corporately funded, ill-intentioned think tank?"

"Because they're not intuitive. They're binary. Rational. Just like you said today. Black-white. Yes-no. We use them, but wonks and numbers-crunchers can't read the tea leaves."

"Neither can I. In fact I don't even know what a wonk is."

"Intuition is integral to understanding the probability of catastrophe. Insurance companies can assess the likelihood of earthquake, hurricane, nuclear-plant failure. How many drunken sixteen-year-old boys will crash their parents' SUVs into an oak tree on prom night? For that, it is entirely possible to ballpark a number. But not when one is calculating to interfere with the course of human events. We can use advanced game-theory techniques to emulate human decisions, geopolitical trends, to model the malicious intent of a potential adversary. But you can only play and calculate so much re the human psyche. Re the group psyche."

"And re me? You want me to..."

Johnson pulls an index card out of his pocket and clears his throat. "Go wherever you want. You will have golden credit and a golden ticket. Go wherever you want and watch the world and listen to its voices. Take its temperature. Its resting and agitated pulse. Listen to its sins and chronicle its beauty. All the while imagining the absolute worst. The most abject combinations of the tragic and the horrible. The unforeseen. The unthought of. Big and small. Go anywhere on earth. Consider the reality. Hope for the best, imagine the worst and come up with a tone of voice. A way to speak to these people. On behalf of these people. Or do something more dramatic. Discover a theme, an emerging pattern. An unstoppable wave in the ripple stages. It's quite heroic, actually. Being able to forecast and perhaps prevent the unspeakable."

"That's nice. Did you write it?"

The other Johnson nods his head. "He worked all morning on it."

"Well, it does sound... interesting. But I can't. I have no proclivity for this. I'm not global. I'm not worldly or political. I haven't even voted in the last three presidential elections. I'm a fake."

Prone Johnson stirs, taps his head. "But you have this."

"Plus I'm a coward. If you think I'm going to the so-called hot spots you're crazy. The Gazas. The Indonesias. The euro-Disneys."

"We understand. In the rare instance that we actually ask you to go to a specific location, your safety will not be compromised in the least. Whatever you are comfortable with. All that we ask is that you do what you've always done and tell us the parts you never dared to tell others."

"Maybe you didn't notice, but I just renounced all of this. I saw the light. I'm going to turn my life around."

Both Johnsons are standing now. One hands the other an envelope. "We're not stopping you. But it might be easier to turn it around with this." He holds out the envelope. "Everything you need is in here. The credit cards. The email addresses. There is one number to call for all of your travel needs. Hotels, cars, flights. Just tell them the credit-card number. If you decide not to play, we will terminate the cards in twenty-four hours. The cash is yours either way. If you decide to continue, a matching sum will be transferred to your Citibank account – which clearly can use a little help – every seven days."

"I have a lot of stock options."

"We know. And we're not impressed."

"How will we stay in contact?"

"Check your email. All we expect in return is some kind of regular update. A log, or diary. Bullet points of things you find interesting. Once a week or so. Do we have a deal?"

Yates stares at the outstretched hand. In twenty-four hours he's gone from run-of-the-mill sell-out, to self-destructive moralist, to what? The ultimate sell-out? A shadow patriot? A job? He doesn't know. He had wanted to walk away from it with dignity. No, that's not true. He had wanted to destroy himself, perhaps with dignity, but implosion was the primary goal. And now this, an option that is utterly devoid of dignity and likely to lead to the darkest of all possible worlds. Which is precisely what the jilted, drunken, morally confused Yates finds so compelling. Why not? Why the hell not?

"Can I travel with an assistant?"

They look at each other, shrug. "Sure."

He takes the envelope, shakes the hand.

The other Johnson unlocks the door and stands behind it as he opens it. "Of course none of this ever happened."

"Not even the porno movie?"

He orders a room-service steak and a bottle of Cape Town Merlot. He kicks off his shoes, counts the money. Ten thousand American. Ten thousand a week to do what? To travel, think disastrous thoughts? To jot down the recipe for hate in twenty-eight languages. He pockets the money, calls the boutique in the lobby, and, after a brief exchange, arranges to have a 140-year-old African tribal mask sent to Lauren. The saleswoman tries to tell him where it's from (the Congo) and what it does (wards off evil spirits) but he's only interested in how old it is. "Sign it *To Lauren, from everywhere but the future,*" he says, then gives the woman the number of his new credit card. *Show that to your history teacher.*

"Excuse me?"

"Nothing. That will be all." He hangs up and thinks. Maybe next he'll send her the Magna Carta. The Bayeux Tapestry. The Shroud of Turin. A Neanderthal femur.

The room phone rings. He waits, thinking of all the people to whom he doesn't want to speak. He watches it ring and then picks up the message. It was Marjorie. He calls the number that she left.

"Marjorie."

"Yates."

"I have something to tell you."

"Me too," she says.

"I wanted to thank you for helping me last night. This morning. Whatever. I haven't had much of that lately."

"You're welcome, but..."

"Do you have a passport?"

Marjorie thinks for a moment. "Yes. But not with me."

"Listen. Someone has offered me a job. It will involve some travel. A lot of travel. I'd like you to come with me. Be my assistant."

"When?"

"As soon as possible. I don't think I have a lot of friends here right now, and unless I'm mistaken, it's not much of a paradise for you."

"That's what I wanted to talk to you about."

"Tell me when you get here. How long will it take for you to be ready?"

"I don't know. I have to see."

"I can't tell you exactly what it's going to entail. In fact it's all pretty strange, but it's a chance for you to get out. To get away from the CBD thugs."

"It's not that easy. You see..."

He looks at his watch. "I'll wait until six. If you need more time, call and I'll try to wait."

"Okay."

"Okay."

"Be careful, Yates."

He hangs up and indulges his email compulsion. Nothing from Lauren, but there is one that's marked as high-priority, from someone with the screen name N-I-81. He double-clicks it open and sees the following:

From the human flock nine will be sent away,
Separated from control and advice
Their fate will be sealed on departure
K-Th-L make an error; the dead banished

The link to the accompanying URL connects him to a live feed from the space hotel. Prior to take-off some unknown network must have secured TV rights from the cash-strapped Russian programme, and now they own this ratings bonanza: the ultimate reality TV. Someone in a flight suit fiddles with a control. In the background a body floats by and offers a gravity-free wave. The title on the screen says: *LAST GASP?* He bookmarks the site and closes his eyes.

Ten minutes later the doorbell rings. He gets up, smoothes the bedspread and wonders where he'll have them place the food cart. The latch is less than halfway turned when the door presses in on him. He's rocked back against the wall of the narrow alcove. An arm reaches around and grabs him by the throat. He opens his mouth to shout or scream, but is punched in the jaw before he can muster the first sibilant hiss of *stop* or *shit* or *sorry*. The punch knocks him onto the bed. Someone closes the door. Someone turns on the TV and cranks the volume. The news, the space station. He's lifted off the bed and punched again, and as he's falling he thinks he hears his own incriminating sound bite on the TV. One of the men mumbles something to the other in a language that Yates does not understand, but Yates decides – for future renditions of the story – that it is Zulu. He stays down, staring at the claw foot of the armoire.

A pair of Nike running shoes walk towards him, and the right shoe draws back and kicks him. Yates makes a big show of registering its devastating impact, but in truth it misses his ribs and he'd already clenched his abs, and who thinks he can rough up a guy with a lightweight, soft-toed running shoe anyway?

"Up," one of them says in what Yates will call Zulu-tinged English. Yates gets to his knees and pauses. He imagines they've come because of the Johnsons, for the ten thousand in his pocket. Hand it over and that'll be the end of it. He lifts one hand as if to say, *Give me a second, I'm a lot more cooperative, a lot less dangerous than you think,* but he is kicked again. This time by a boot. He's launched backwards into the armoire and, as he falls, his left cheekbone rakes against the mini-key sticking out of the minibar door.

Then they are gone.

He lies on the carpet for a while, listening to the too loud news, blood tracing down the side of his face. He opens the minibar and reaches for a cold bottle to hold against the cut. Blindly feeling around for the coldest, he knocks down a half dozen bottles on the lower shelf. They tumble out around him. Flat on his back, he presses a half-litre of Korbel Brut against his cheek.

Thirty minutes later there's a knock on the unlocked door. "Room service." It's the same waiter who had brought Yates's breakfast into the bottle-strewn room this morning. He wheels the cart over to the side of the bed. While holding out the bill for Yates to sign, he takes in the scene. Yates sits up, signs and bumps up the tip with $20 American.

"Will that be all, sir?"

"Yes."

"Are you all right, sir?"

Yates nods. Asks, "Why are you smiling?"

"I was just thinking, sir, that the gentleman sure does enjoy his minibar amenities."

He wakes up on the floor. For a moment he thinks maybe it is morning and he hasn't yet given his speech, hasn't yet been wooed by Johnson and Johnson in Amanda's room. But when he sees that the liquor bottles surrounding him are full, not empty, and that his head throbs from the blows of a human in addition to the continuing alcohol-inflamed vascular pyrotechnics, he realizes for the second time in twenty-four hours that he has no such luck. His bad dreams are continuous and real. He wonders who turned off the television. Wonders if the steak is still warm. The part of him that's looking for meaning in his life hopes that his beating came at the hands of some foreign intelligence operatives, but the part of him that knows better is certain that it was a couple of street toughs working on behalf of the betrayed members of the Johannesburg Central Business District, and that he should have expected as much. He checks his messages for any word from Marjorie, but the mailbox is empty. He thinks of calling Johnson and Johnson, but they are probably long gone – and what would he tell them, anyway? *Mayday-mayday! Agent down!* He calls Blevins's room.

"Can you come to my room? It's Yates."

"I'm kind of busy."

"I've been beaten up. Nothing life-threatening but..."

"That's too bad, Yates. Not unexpected, but too bad."

"Look, Blevins. There's a girl I'm looking for. She was in my room last night..."

"I wish I could help you reconnect with your hooker friend but I'm kind of opposed to that kind of exploitation. Plus, you know I tried to help yesterday, last night. Last year, for Christ's sake. Before it was too late. Before you went and sold out on both sides of the moral table and screwed up a good thing for both of us. Yesterday, even after you abandoned me at the airport and forced me to get shaken down for a $200 taxi, I had to suck up to you because yesterday you mattered. Yesterday you at least represented the occasional paycheck and a chance to redeem yourself and make a difference. But today, you're nothing. I'm sure you'll forgive me if I'm a little... unsympathetic."

When he calls David the chaperone's 24/7 number, it rings and rings.

He looks around the room and thinks that this could be anywhere, this suite with the secretary and the armoire and the two-line phone and the Spectravision remote. He considers the sanitary cardboard caps on the water glasses, two layered sets of curtains with the plastic pull rods and the stainless-steel plate-warmer with the small hole in the middle over his uneaten steak, and thinks this could be São Paulo or Tokyo or an Appleton, Wisconsin Courtyard by Marriott. It's all the same, and now he feels that all of it, from the stationery in the top drawer to the dry-cleaning valet bags to the extra pillows in the closet is conspiring to suck every last molecule out of his pointless, rootless, time-zone-neutral, pampered life.

In the bathroom he touches the cut on his temple, dabs at the brown crusted blood with a white washcloth, revealing a one-inch gash that probably could have used stitches. He thinks of this morning, standing in front of the same mirror, with Marjorie coming out of the shower and sidling up to the other sink beside him. He looks from his reflection over to her sink where, on the marble countertop, he sees her hairbrush. He picks it up and puts it in his suitcase so he can give it to her later.

Ilulissat

He once took batting practice with the New York Mets, pretending not to notice the eight-year-old boy with leukaemia from the Make-A-Wish Foundation whom the PR Director let him cut in front of because he had to catch a plane. He once sat in on the drums with Wilco. He once brokered a venture-capital deal for a technology he didn't understand between friends he no longer has while playing Ultimate Frisbee.

He could have gone to France, to sample its specific brand of resentment in addition to its spectacular food and wine. He could have gone to Egypt or Indonesia. The Gaza Strip or the Golan Heights. Moscow, Mexico City, Morocco. Bali, Berlin, Buenos Aires. He could have gone almost anywhere and found plenty of people willing to wax apoplectic about their many forms of hatred for all things American.

But he decided on Greenland.

What better place to start your World Bad Karma tour than a country with a total of fifty-six thousand inhabitants, where eighty-five per cent of the land is covered by an ice sheet, a place where, he's been told, they do not have a word for stress. So if someone were to ask him, *How are you today?* Yates thinks, an accurately translated answer could be a problem.

* * *

From Johannesburg he flies overnight to Paris, then Copenhagen. From Copenhagen he flies direct on Greenlandair (*45 years of experience in Arctic and Remote Area Operations*) to Kangerlussuaq, where a helicopter takes him to Ilulissat and his friend Campbell. Other than the changeovers and customs checks, Yates sleeps through most of it. Somewhere over Morocco he awakes sweating and terrified, half inside some ghastly dream, wondering if there is a correlation between altitude and loneliness; wondering, if the FAA were to discover a black box inside the wreckage of Yates, what it would say.

Marjorie never called. Amanda Glowers never called. Lauren never called. The only person that answered his call was the Johnsons' magic travel agent, and she wasn't interested in anything but arrival and departure dates.

The chopper pulses up the coast, its shadow tracing a rough outline of the shore. Sunlight glints like shattered safety glass in the dark chop, flashing with a blinding force off walls of ice in the cluttered fjords. The pilot points down at something in the water, perhaps a fishing boat or a whale, but Yates can't see anything, can't hear anything. The other passenger, a disturbingly chatty Dutch tulip salesman, had put on the two-way audio headsets before take-off, but Yates had declined. He prefers the whir of rotors to thickly accented queries about the wounds on his face, to *What brings you to this neck of the permafrost?* He glances down as the copter bends towards land. Granite blocks of an abandoned Viking farmstead stand alone on a granite outcrop. A herd of caribou making their way across an ice field to God knows where. Staring at a trail of icebergs floating in a jagged line from an unseen glacier, he thinks not of Lauren, but of Marjorie. Why hadn't she called? If her story was true, he had provided her with a perfect way out. Yet, even though she had hesitated on the phone about having a passport, about him, she did sound like she wanted to come. That's what troubles him.

Otherwise it would just be another clean break. Another appellation of female rejection, just on a whole new continent. Maybe, he thinks, he could get himself dumped seven different ways on seven different continents; that would be some kind of record, if not the basis for a Hugh Grant vehicle. In the car, on the way to the airport, Yates had given David, who had shown up unannounced in his room to escort him out of South Africa, $500 to promise to try to find Marjorie and deliver an envelope containing a thank-you note, his cell number and email address, his address in Greenland and another $1,000. He did this in part because he cares, in part to alleviate the guilt that is overwhelming him. But it hasn't alleviated anything.

When he looks up, Yates catches the tulip salesman staring at the minibar gash on his cheek. Maybe he ought to answer with absolute truth the inevitable question of how it happened, just to check out the response. On the other hand, he realizes that if he would have allowed their conversation to play out a bit longer back at the helipad in Kangerlussuaq, he could have asked a few generic sociopolitical questions and checked Holland off his global things-to-do list for the boys in Emerging Threats and Opportunities. *Better yet,* Yates thinks. *Why not fake it? Why not fabricate an in-depth conversation with this Mr – insert interesting Dutch name here – the tulip magnate and email it to Johnson and Johnson?* He closes his eyes and composes in his mind the report he'll submit once he settles in.

Interviewed a Mr Van Blah Blah, of Rotterdam. A grower and international distributor of high-end tulips. On holiday in Greenland to photograph what he calls the never-ending ballet of the ice. Claims to love Americans but resents America. Most of his tulips are exported to America, through New York. Although he loves Americans, he's not a big fan of American Jews. Or fat American tourists in sneakers and baseball caps. When America is victimized by terror he cries on its behalf, but sometimes, before the tears have dried, he finds himself not so much sympathetic with the terrorists as understanding their motives, their anger. Ironically, terrorism in the US is apparently good for the tulip biz. He is outraged over American domination of the cultural and economic landscape. Says globalization will be the downfall of us all. He loves American television, particularly The Simpsons, CSI Duluth *and the reality show* It's Your Funeral! *But he has a big problem with McDonald's (except the fries), the city of Cleveland and the pop star Celine Dion. When I explained that Ms Dion was not American, he waved me off, with what I interpreted as a dismissive gesture. He blames America for many of the world's problems, calls us the quintessential bully, yet wants us to invade certain countries to right a number of "non-Jewish humanitarian wrongs". He says America would be a truly great place if the English hadn't gone and wrecked New Netherland back in the day. He says that Americans have no understanding of the Dutch beyond wooden shoes, dykes, tulips and the fact that Amsterdam is a hell of a party town. When it was pointed out that as a tulip magnate he was reinforcing the stereotypes, he gave me the same dismissive wave as earlier. It should be noted that he was not wearing wooden shoes, but throwback Nike Air Jordans. For what it's worth, this year's tulip crop was especially plentiful and US sales should reach all-time highs.*

Yates reopens his eyes to ink-blue waters filled with icebergs freshly carved from Sermeq Kujalleq, the world's most productive glacier, some thirty-one miles inland.

Every summer Ilulissat Kangerlua, a fjord two miles south of Ilulissat, hosts the world's largest concentration of icebergs outside of Antarctica. Some twenty million tons of ice break off each day, commencing an otherworldly voyage to the sea. In the distance he sees the first hint of civilization, the colourfully painted houses on green meadows overlooking Disko Bay. But the ice and the culture and the colourful houses are not the reason why he's come to Illulissat. Somewhere in the cluster of homes, most likely in the largest, lives the real reason that he has spent an entire day travelling for: Campbell, the son-of-a-bitch who got him started in all this.

They had met in their freshman year at USC, and for two semesters had shared an off-campus apartment. Then Campbell, in the tradition of Bill Gates, dropped out and started not one, but seven dot-coms before dot-com was part of the vernacular. He made money on all of them, but one made him obscenely rich. Finally, after spending a year on the cover of every business magazine in the world, Campbell did the second-most brilliant thing of his young life. He sold everything at exactly the right time, at insane valuations, then sat back and watched the Internet bubble burst, and hundreds of his NASDAQ super-rich (on paper) compatriots were super-rich no more. The first thing Campbell did in his new life was to buy a sports franchise, an NFL expansion team. But he always hated sports, and the emotional rewards did not outweigh the emotional investment. He eventually sold the team at an enormous profit, although finances had nothing to do with his decision to sell. Then he went on the lecture circuit. Got an honorary degree and gave a raucous commencement speech at USC, the college from which he had once famously dropped out. He learnt to play a passable acoustic guitar. He financed and participated in a successful summit of K2. But it did not satisfy him. Nothing satisfied him.

Then late one rainy night last year in a hotel room in Vancouver he saw a documentary on the icebergs of Greenland. He sat transfixed for two hours. When it was over, he called an assistant to find a DVD of the programme and have it overnighted to him. Then he got in touch with the documentary's producer and director and peppered them with questions. Next he called someone with real-estate contacts in Greenland. All the while, just to make sure the fascination held, he watched all he could of a streaming Internet video feed of a Greenland iceberg cam that ran live twenty-four hours a day. To Campbell it was better than porn. Within three months he had the biggest house in Ilulissat and had severed all ties to the digital world, the National Football League, the alpine-climbing community and the boards of no less than a dozen multinational corporations.

The thing about Campbell is that he never forgot Yates. Never forgot that Yates had listened to all of his ideas when he was an overweight geek on academic probation who smoked bong hits at breakfast. Yates was always there to tell him when he was crazy, when he was lazy, when he was delusional. And Yates was there to tell him when an idea was worth dropping out for and risking everything for. Which is exactly what Campbell did.

Along the way Campbell remembered his old roommate, and several times offered Yates high-paying, nonessential jobs in his companies, with titles like Director of What's Yet to Come, or Corporate Shaman. Yates declined. But still it was Campbell who had recommended Yates to the CEO of the hottest think tank in Silicon Valley. Yates was good at his job, but having unlimited access to Campbell and his fellow masters of the emerging digital universe quickly catapulted him to great. To a bona-fide commodity. Through brains, luck and cultural osmosis, Yates was suddenly living on the verge of everything. In short order, he was promoted three times, frequently quoted, and finally given free rein to do his own independently branded thing with the discreet backing of the corporation.

For a while, it was everything he thought he'd ever want.

On the helipad, Yates waves goodbye to the pilot and decides to shake hands with the Dutchman who's soon to be the unknowing subject of a high-priority, confidential, totally fabricated government email. Welcome to the international intelligence community, Mr Van Blah Blah.

Campbell is parked outside in a $150,000 Swedish-concept SUV. He's grown a massive black-and-grey beard since Yates last saw him, and he looks some fifty to seventy-five pounds heavier. Yates throws his bag into the back seat and climbs into the vehicle.

"Christ, you've put on a few kilos." Campbell shakes his hand.

"Well, you know, they don't have a word for stress here."

"I guess that fact must have eluded the five thousand men who committed suicide here last year." Yates shivers. "On the other hand, I bet they have about a million words for boring. A billion for freezing goddamn cold."

"This is midnight-sun time, bro. Downright balmy. High tourist season. As evidenced by two passengers on the chopper instead of none. What happened to your face?"

Yates looks out his window. In the fjord two fishing boats are heading out to sea, or back from it – he can't tell. "I got my ass kicked. At first I thought by a member of a foreign intelligence organization, but then it became apparent they were just thugs sent by a Johannesburg business interest I had pissed off."

"The speech?"

Yates stares at Campbell. Even in Ilulissat, they know.

"It's all over the Internet."

"It was a nice career while it lasted."

"You kidding? You've become something of a legend. The first to speak the heretofore-unspoken universal truth that none of us know anything. It's brilliant. You've diffused any issue about your credibility by denouncing it yourself. I imagine you'll be hotter than ever."

"Right now," Yates says, waving at the ice-cluttered water. "I need to chill."

As the truck winds along the paved main road, then onto a thawed mud two-track and finally onto little more than a path that leads to the bedrock of Campbell's compound, Yates tells him about everything, from the break-up with Lauren to the soccer riot, from Marjorie to Amanda Glowers to his speech and finally, in vague terms, his job offer from the Johnsons and his subsequent room-service thrashing.

Standing outside the truck in front of Campbell's massive, red-painted, steel-framed home overlooking the fjord, Yates turns to his friend and one-time mentor. "So you haven't heard from Lauren either?"

"Me? Nothing. The richer I got, the more she hated me." As Campbell walks around the truck, Yates just now notices that he is wearing a flowing, ankle-length, violet cotton tunic.

"Is that native attire? I mean is this what they all wear here in the summer?"

Campbell laughs and shakes his head. "I saw it on some show out of Thailand on the dish. I had some made up to wear when I go to town, just to freak the locals out."

Yates follows him inside. It is spare and modern and huge. The wall facing the fjord is made of thick tempered glass from floor to ceiling. On a table near the big-screen TV are two pairs of the largest binoculars Yates has ever seen, and on a tripod on the outside deck is a planetarium-quality telescope. Yates picks up a pair of binoculars and tries to focus on a berg in the channel, but the optics are so clear and the lenses so powerful they shake with the slightest breath or movement. "Keep looking. When one breaks free and drops into the fjord, it's beyond sublime."

"So you still like this? The appeal is still there?"

Campbell nods yes. "More than ever. Sometimes I forget to eat. It has a kind of narcotic effect on me."

Yates looks out at the fjord, then back at Campbell in his purple robe, Campbell with whom he once did beer funnels, had an ecstasy scare and played intramural basketball. "Do you realize how bizarre you look and sound? How 'bad James Bond villain' freaky this all is?"

Campbell smiles. "Absolutely," he answers, feigning something between Dr No and Dr Evil. "Welcome to my lair." Campbell clicks on the plasma monitor, which hangs from the ceiling and pivots to the cues of Campbell's remote. He flicks past content from around the planet and settles on the only show taking place off it, the one everyone is watching. Yates wonders if Campbell knows, if he'd ever mentioned to him about his endorsement of the civilian space hotel.

Campbell waves him off before he gets started. "I know. I know. In the last twenty-four hours I've heard your sound bite a million times in twenty-four languages. But don't you see, you were right. Space *is* the next Everest. Shit, people die on Everest every year. Do you know that the cosmetics heiress, the Sandy Pittman type of the expedition, cursed you out on global satellite this morning? She's one of the main reasons this is huge TV. I think half the planet wants to see her make-up fail her on her way to a slow, tortuous death, broadcast without commercial interruption."

"What's happening to them now? Do they know what went wrong?"

"The first mistake was travelling on a Soyuz spacecraft. Something happened soon after take-off from the Balkonur Cosmodrome in Kazakhstan. Actually, that was the second mistake. The first mistake was setting foot in Kazakhstan to begin with. There was some kind of guidance failure, which led to a docking collision with the station. Later, both oxygen generators failed. The collision knocked its energy-gathering panels away from the sun. Presently they're using an oxygen-generating candle, which won't last much longer. One option was an emergency rescue visit by an automated Russian space ferry. But that's got its hood up in the garage back in Kazakhstan."

"What a disaster."

"We need disaster to validate our existence. What's interesting is that yesterday an earthquake in Malaysia left more than a thousand dead. A train derailment outside New Delhi: 423 dead. Barely mentioned anywhere. A blurb on page thirty-eight of the national section of the *New York Times*. A hiccup on the BBC. But this: we're glued to our TVs because a handful of insanely rich people had run out of ways to find joy on earth and had to look elsewhere." Campbell clicks through several dozen channels, most of which carry the live feed. "What language do you want? Chinese? Polish? Al Jazeera? The network puppets in the States? I've been watching it on this station out of Turkey that just runs the video feed accompanied by classical music. Wagner. Tchaikovsky. Vivaldi..." He changes to it. Bach's *Trauerfeier* funeral cantata accompanies fixed-camera footage of the pilot calmly staring at a control panel. A pair of legs float past in the background, seemingly intent on staying out of frame. "Some of them can't keep their face away from the camera; others avoid it completely. I know this sounds perverse, but there is nothing more beautiful than the orbit of a dead spacecraft."

"Not even the 'narcotic effect' of the ice?"

"Don't make me cry, Yates. I mean, imagine being there. The silence, other than the grinding and popping of the thermal stress of the hull's expansion and contraction in relation to the sun. No pumps, fans, thrusters. The sporadic clicking of an instrument. Watching the earth drifting silently past, in portions, because they're too close to see the whole planet through the portal. Soon the ventilators won't be able to remove their CO_2."

"How long do they have, professor?"

"Without help from the troubleshooters in Russia and Houston, forty-eight hours."

"Isn't there a way to get to them in time?"

"Not with a shuttle. But I know people in military aerospace who say that we have a manned stealth spacecraft already in orbit that could help them. But, for security reasons, no one knows about it, so they don't want to use it unless we have to, because then everyone will know about it."

"So the question is whether rescuing a bunch of millionaires, a couple of scientists and an over-the-hill cosmonaut is worth compromising our national security."

"I imagine that's the conversation of the moment in DC and Houston. If there is such a spacecraft."

Yates walks to the window and looks at the sky.

"It will be the largest man-made object to enter our atmosphere. Most of it will burn up, but some thirty tons or so will shatter into thousands of fragments. Should it come to that. The next question is whether they will have already died before re-entry. Which is especially creepy. Like the crew in the first *Planet of the Apes* movie."

"Except Heston." Yates shades his eyes with his left hand, shakes his head. Campbell comes up alongside him.

"It's so low they say that if you look out your window at such and such a time you'll see it. Of course, you need darkness for that, something we'll have none of for a while."

"What time is it now?"

"One-thirty a.m. June twenty-one. This will be a day without darkness, a day with every shade of light. Are you hungry?"

"I should sleep." Yates puts his hand in his pocket and removes a scrap of paper. He'd written down the email from N-I-81. He hands it to Campbell, who reads it aloud:

From the human flock nine will be sent away
Separated from control and advice
Their fate will be sealed on departure
K-Th-L make an error; the dead banished

"God. Not this shit again."

"What?" Yates asks.

"Nostradamus. N-I-81, I imagine, denotes Nostradamus's first of 10 centuries, quatrain 81. Somebody's fucking with you. If you have enough time on your hands you can back Nostradamus's prophecies into the outcome of a high-school field-hockey game and make it seem spookily coincidental."

"Why me?"

"People covet the shaman. Then they despise him. They hear your name. They blame you. Or see you as a tool to spread the word to blame someone else. They always drag Nostradamus out of the closet for tragedies. Hitler. Nine-eleven. Drought. Famine. Typhoon. They used this same quatrain after the Challenger. The Columbia. At least this time the number nine is accurate."

"Again, I'm not so concerned about the prophetic accuracy as I am about the *Why me?* part."

"Because you're in the public domain. You're a bloody futurist. There is a direct correlation between psychotic stalkers and the amount of Google responses your name generates. Once more than sixteen syllables of your voice, or twenty-four frames of your image enter the digital broadcast universe you can be certain that at least one sociopath with an agenda is taking notes. TiVo-ing it."

"Is my bedroom dark?'

"As dark as you want it to be."

In his room he leaves the shades open and watches the ice, looking not for ballet or sublime, narcotic effect, but for something to happen, for something to disrupt the static panorama. There are no clouds coursing across the blue night sky. And there is no action in the bay; no boats, no whales, no spectacular calving of bergs from the great ice sheet. And the ice that has already calved moves so slowly that he cannot notice. But, while the sight is not particularly transfixing, Yates has to admit that it is relaxing, and soon, despite the late-night sunshine and the manic footsteps of his once brilliant friend and mentor in the outer rooms, sleep drops on him like a weight. Like an iceberg. Like the wrath of his colleagues, the fist of a Johannesburg thug, the faulty instrument panel of a doomed spacecraft. Like the future.

Magga

The screams of a hysterical woman, the sounds of household objects being deliberately destroyed, awaken him. For a while Yates lays still, trying to interpret the diatribe, some of which is in Inuit and some of which – "fuckhead", "ass-licker", "would-be fondler of altar boys" – is in English. Clearly an ex or soon-to-be ex of Campbell's, apparently a local. He closes his eyes and tries to guess what is being smashed. A ceramic coffee mug against a fieldstone fireplace. A crystal wine glass on the mahogany floor. Then another. A framed picture, perhaps the one of Campbell on the cover of *Forbes*, shatters on what can only be the tumbled marble backsplash in the kitchen. Then a series of thuds, either stones or her fists, pummelling Campbell's fleshy chest. *There are more effective ways to make your point*, Yates thinks, *than breaking the quotidian possessions of a multi-billionaire.*

He once stood in the White House Rose Garden flanked by Siegfried and Roy, Stephen Hawking and the NCAA women's volleyball champs from USC. In the late Eighties he came back from a trip to Kobe claiming that he had seen the future, and its name was karaoke. He once reset the nanosecond hand on the city of Antwerp's Millennium Clock. He is currently an honorary board member for a start-up company that has built selling out – its stock and its principles – into its two-year plan.

He washes his face in the bathroom, then sets up his laptop at a desk overlooking the fjord. He is hoping for one email, but finds many. Four hundred and sixty-eight, to be exact. A quick sampling indicates that most if not all pertain to the Johannesburg speech, and that most if not all are favourable. One correspondent writes that she has already started an unofficial Coalition of the Clueless website that has had 4,200 hits and 322 registered members in the last twenty-four hours. He scrolls, looking for familiar handles, bylines, names. His lecture agent wants to know where he is; Amanda Glowers wants him to call at his earliest convenience; and the Jo'burg CBD committee, apologizing for their rudeness, now thank him for choosing their city as the stage for giving such a paradigm-shifting (and publicity-garnering) speech, and inform him that, as a bonus, they have doubled his appearance fee, which has already been wired to his US account.

He scrolls down, past interview requests from the press, past congratulations from politicians of various nations and ideologies, from business leaders, an imprisoned CEO, from the former lead singer of a formerly popular boy band. From Noam Chomsky, who says *Hey*. Even Faith B. Popcorn grudgingly sends kudos for "shaking the status-quo tree by its very roots".

He has already become so used to the screaming and destruction outside his door that he only notices when it stops. Campbell and his woman friend have apparently reached the stage of their conflict where Campbell emits simpering, barely audible attempts at reconciliation and she scornfully laughs and counters with some Greenlandic epithets punctuated by cross-cultural gems like "prostate-milker", "goat-felcher" and "hollow-testicled he-bitch". Yates opens no less than ten five-figure offers for speaking engagements at events ranging from the usual corporate suspects to the MTV Video Music Awards, the NRA Celebrity Small Game Safari and Costume Ball, and a Friars Club roast of a one-time governor who recently resigned to pursue a lifelong dream of becoming a stand-up comic. Four hundred emails down he sees the name Marjorie. When he opens it, he sees that the note is not from Marjorie, but David the chaperone. David writes that he has been trying to find Marjorie, but no one has seen her at the hotel, the CBD offices or at the flat she shares with two other girls. He cannot be sure, but he fears that something has happened to her. In the mean time, David offers to return Marjorie's unopened envelope if Yates would be so kind as to provide a forwarding address.

Yates writes back:

Thanks for the note and the disappointing update regarding Marjorie. I am in Greenland, not particularly because it is Greenland, but because it isn't a lot of other places. Please hold on to the envelope, and please continue to look for Marjorie, whose safety I now feel responsible for. She mentioned an aunt in, I think, Sandton? I will compensate you accordingly; consider the contents of the envelope as a security deposit and please keep me posted.

Below David's email there's a message from Blevins, suggesting that Yates use his new-found popularity responsibly, and that he consider the forty-eight page attachment titled "Redemption". Below that, one last message of note, from Johnson and Johnson, saying:

Greenland? You're kidding, right?

In the kitchen, Campbell and his girlfriend-assassin sit at the table blowing into steaming mugs of some kind of fish soup. Her hair is a black tangle of knots. Her blotched face is covered with thick white fuzz. When she parts her lips, there is a dark gap where her lower incisors once were. "Good morning," Yates offers, but neither of them looks up.

"Afternoon," Campbell finally answers. "Twelve-thirty. Yates, this is Magga."

Yates starts towards her, ready to shake hands, hug, air-kiss. Whatever it takes. But Magga will have none of it. She shakes her head and waves him off. When she stands, Yates finds that not only is Magga dirty and ugly, she is more than six feet tall, layered with fat and smelling like fish and smoke – not to be confused with smoked fish. Yates freezes, then feints back towards his room. "I'll leave you two alone."

"No," says Magga as she slowly tips her bowl of fish soup onto the counter. "Do not bother. I was just leaving... leaving this impotent humper of fetid blubber." Yates backs up further, watches her pick up her Kate Spade handbag, a sack of dead fish and her pistol, a Glock nine-millimetre. He wonders if she realizes what it makes her if her boyfriend is an impotent humper of fetid blubber, wonders what aspect of this foul, nasty beast Campbell possibly finds appealing.

Campbell stares out at the fjord as the front door closes. Soon the diesel roar of an engine breaks the silence. Yates looks out of the window just in time to see Campbell's lover pull away in what looks like some kind of surplus, street-modified armoured war vehicle. When he looks back, he sees that Campbell's eyes are wet with tears.

"You just missed one," Campbell says, pointing a thumb over his shoulder towards the ice sheet. "Veins cracking in a pattern never to be replicated, a widening crevasse, walls the size of skyscrapers splintering, for a moment it gets lost in a white powder cloud of crushed ice. Then, after the splash, the water heaves and calms and the ice dust settles and this mountain sits shining in the water like it's been there for ever. Spectacular."

"I must have blinked." Yates looks away from Campbell and the ice.

"Want a mug of suassat?"

Yates looks at the puddle on the table, then back at Campbell.

"Seal-meat stew. Illegal in the US. Kind of like herring but... fishier."

"Don't you have any Cocoa Puffs?'

"Caribou? Musk ox?"

"Raisin Bran?"

"Pussy."

"Impotent humper of fetid blubber."

Campbell rises and walks to a computer on a kitchen counter next to the microwave. There are computers all over the house, already on, ready to humour his latest whim, to provide the revelatory spark that he believes will change everything all over again.

"I'm sorry I walked in on you two."

Campbell shrugs. "She's an artist. I'm a reformed megalomaniac. That's what we do. What we did. Crazy sex and crazy fights. I knew we were in trouble when I found myself fantasizing about the next fight while we were having sex. I have to be careful though. Her old man runs the Greenlandic Mafia."

"Is that how she got the latest-model-year version of a Bradley Fighting Vehicle?"

"Don't ask."

Yates stares at Campbell. He tries to process this latest flurry of information, but it's too much. "What is going on, Campbell? What are you doing here, with her?"

"I'm looking for the inspiration for the next seminal event in my life."

"And you think ice and a mobbed-up Amazon fish lady will provide that?"

"But for anything to qualify as seminal, the idea has to be more exciting and ultimately more successful – more culturally transformative – than anything that preceded it."

"Nothing like setting reasonable goals." Yates rolls out a clump of paper towels, starts mopping up the spilt suassat. "Don't you think that's a bit much? Don't you think this is just a tad unorthodox? It makes for good copy, but for real? It's insane, Campbell."

"Absolutely. But I need to know if I can do it again. If I can find something new that consumes me and fulfills me. Because anything less has been completely unsatisfying. Stultifying. I tried the rich-guy thing. The sports franchises. I've courted the press, created an eccentric mythological self and a mythological history. Christ, in one interview I said I only eat provolone and Twizzler sandwiches, and they ran with it. I've worked out until I look like a professional athlete, but I'll never be a professional athlete. I gave *Great-Gatsby*esque parties. But I hate rich people, I hate Hollywood and I hate parties. I dabbled in monogamy, but how can I ever tell if she's sincere, if I'm sincere? Plus, how can I possibly have a kid when I have this much money? How can he or she not be criminally fucked up?"

"I don't know. Unconditional love? A sound moral example?"

"Do you know what I was doing every day back in the States? A typical day? I'd wake up and say, *What am I gonna do today?* I'd say, *How about some ice cream, Campbell?* So I'd get dressed and go to the Ice Creame Shoppe with two 'p's and an 'e'. I'd consider the 118 different flavours. The fat-free and sugar-free. The frozen yogurts and the sorbets. I'd deliberate over the whole waffle-or-sugar-cone conundrum. Then I'd place my order, watch it come together, and then I'd pay, leaving an extravagant tip. Then I'd go outside, take an inventory of my cone, close my eyes and try to picture it. Then I would eat it. And then what? I'd think about it, trying to recall the exact taste and feel, the combinations of flavours. I'd compare it to past ice-cream experiences, from Little League post-victory cones at the A&W to making tequila sundaes in Mustique with two Hawaiian Tropic girls. Then I'd make mental notes for future excursions and congratulate or scold myself for my decision. And then what? And then what? And now what? Do you see, Yatesy? My grand plan to get rich never included a section on how to *be* rich."

Yatesy? Yates sits and stares out at the ice. Nothing moves. "What about altruism?"

"What?"

"Philanthropy. Giving back."

"Oh, shit. I've given back tens of millions. Some of these guys, these billionaires, make me sick. They think that, now that they're rich, they can satisfy their egos, alleviate their guilt, by thinking their accidental windfall somehow meant they were geniuses, cosmically ordained and therefore eminently more qualified to solve the world's problems. AIDS. Loose nukes. Illiteracy. They're delusional enough to think that they matter more than others in a larger sense. They think, *Now that I've made billions on a search engine that can locate highly specialized sub-genres of kiddy porn at thrice the speed of light, I'm going to teach the world to read*. When in truth they're rewriting history to say that their original business models – the ones that made them obscenely rich – were not driven by greed and hubris, but by some larger calling to transform the world."

"Can I use that?"

"What?"

"What you just said. It's brilliant and true and, I'm sure you know, all about you, too. I'd like to paraphrase a bit and give it to these think-tank dudes. I won't use your name. I'll say you're Japanese, or South Korean."

Campbell doesn't answer. "What they all really want is to know what the rest of the world is about to need. To know that is to be eternally rich."

"But you did know that. For a while you knew it better than anyone. It's impossible to sustain that for a month, let alone a life."

"What's weird is that our parents, my parents, sacrificed so much and worked so hard doing what they didn't love so we could get an education and do what we love. Now that I think of it, it was almost evil, giving us that kind of freedom, mandating that we try to identify something we love."

"You'd prefer it if you'd have taken over the plumbing business? The bubble-wrap empire? Gotten a job as assistant manager of the meat counter at the Grand Union?"

Campbell opens the freezer and pulls out a smoking-cold bottle of vodka. He tilts it towards Yates. When Yates waves him off, Campbell opens the top and takes a swig. For a while they stare at the ice. The more Yates looks, the more he is certain that it will never break apart, that the great mass has been there since time began and there it will remain, global warming be damned. The more Yates looks at it, the more he hates the bloody ice.

"What it becomes," Campbell continues, still answering unasked questions, "is a kind of addiction. For a while I believed it was an addiction to ideas, that the original idea was the only real form of currency left. But I was wrong. It's an addiction to wealth. Not to wealth because of its buying power, but the bragging power. How you stand in relation to others. I want to have more than so-and-so. My brother. My neighbour. My college roommate. The guy in the next cubicle. In the next seat over on the pork-bellies exchange. Then I'll be satisfied.

But then, someone else comes along to top you and then they are all that you think about." He takes another swig of vodka and is silent for several minutes. "Just for one moment," he finally says, "I would like to have the most. Just for one tiny moment."

"Do you really believe that? That it is the most self-absorbed, patently evil piece of bullshit I've ever heard. Because just the fact that you are sick enough to obsess over and covet that one moment makes it clear that it would never be enough. I can't believe that you actually want pity from me because of your so-called plight. Jesus, Campbell, I came here thinking I was fucked up, looking for guidance. A little support."

Campbell drinks again.

"Somebody said," Yates continues, "I read it somewhere the other day – I don't think it was me – they said find something more important than you are and dedicate your life to it."

"Christ. Don't patronize me, Yates," Campbell says. "That's like that other pop-psych pabulum: find something that you love and do it. That was the theory. But what if you can't find something you love? What if you don't know what you love? Should you maybe find something you hate and dedicate your life to avoiding it? Then find something else you hate, or at least don't like, and dedicate your life to not doing that, too? Until maybe you accidentally stumble upon something you can at least tolerate, or it finds you, something with three weeks' vacation, medical and a pension, and you go from there, settling for considerably less than love. Which is what ninety-nine per cent of the western world does. Is that what we should do?" Campbell asks. Then he raises the volume of the Turkish TV coverage of the space disaster to a level so high that a reply is not an option.

Kausuitsup Una

Just because he told Campbell that he didn't want to drink with him, it didn't necessarily mean that he didn't want to drink at all. In town, away from Campbell, who went into his bedroom to take a nap after tossing Yates the keys to the Swedish-concept SUV, the Futurist feels like he absolutely needs a drink – not with, but because of Campbell. The bar at the Hotel Kausuitsup Una, or Polar Night, is fairly crowded for any time, let alone a bright, sunny afternoon. At the tables and at the bar everyone is smoking, and somehow everyone looks simultaneously friendly and like they wouldn't mind killing him in an arctic heartbeat if events turn for the worse. Yates leans on the bar and contemplates the vodka selection, because what else does one drink in the great white north or wherever this is? He wonders if his choice should be driven by the aesthetic of the label, the idiosyncratic typeface, the hip factor of the brand's glossy magazine ads, the distinctive shape and colour of the bottle, the linguistic melody of the name, or where in the pantheon of cool the spirit's nation of origin now ranks. Then he looks around and sees that no one in Kausuitsup Una seems to be particularly obsessed with the currency of cool, or drinking vodka, or paying him the slightest attention. So he turns and points the bartender in the direction of the bourbon, the Maker's Mark.

To his left, a young white man with a flimsy beard drinking a bottle of Tuborg and a shot of a syrupy, anise-flavoured liquor turns to face him. "American?"

"Yup."

"Me too. Sort of. I'm an expat."

"Expat. Couldn't you find a better place than this? This is hardly Hemingway's Paris. Prague in the early '90s."

"Actually I'm in the Peace Corps."

Yates sips his bourbon. "Didn't know they had it here."

"They don't. I'm kind of AWOL."

"AWOL from the Peace Corps? Does this mean that you're running from peace, desperately seeking war, or just outraged by their lack of a political agenda?"

"No. It just means I'm impulsive. It wasn't for me."

"So is Ilulissat some kind of safe haven for you and others like you? Those AWOL from the Peace Corps? Deserters from the Salvation Army? Tell me, what is the punishment for desertion from the Peace Corps? A series of diphtheria shots? More peace?"

"I did the backpacking thing across Europe. Thailand. I came here because I didn't know where to go next. And because of the ice."

"Of course. The ice. So, how were you treated in your travels?"

"It's weird. I kind of joined the Peace Corps because I wanted to somehow compensate for the injustices America was imposing on the world. I was ashamed of being American. Everywhere I went I got an earful about globalization, Israel, unlawful military intervention – all the things I complained about in college in Oregon, but these foreigners, they never let me get a word in. Even if I agreed with them they'd shake their heads and say I was agreeing in the wrong way, in a typically American way. After a while I got sick of it, and once or twice I even found myself in the totally unfamiliar position of sticking up for my country. In a bar in Barcelona I smashed a guy in the mouth who said we're all rapists and criminals. Which is totally wrong, because I'm like a total pacifist. So I'm kind of ideologically homeless. Morally conflicted. And horny. All this anti-Americanism makes it nearly impossible for a guy to get laid."

They both drink. Yates looks around. With his eyes now adjusted to the interior darkness, he thinks he sees the tulip salesman from the helicopter chatting it up in a corner with a woman who can only be Campbell's ex, Magga. After a few silent moments the young man, apparently feeling that he's revealed enough of himself to move the relationship to the next level, extends his hand to Yates. "By the way, my name's Jeremy."

Yates reluctantly lets go of his bourbon and shakes the boy's hand. "Call me Campbell," he says.

"Cool. See that big chick, Campbell," says Jeremy, glancing towards Magga. "She's the first woman I've been with in more than a month."

"Lovely."

Now Jeremy looks across the bar in a way that Yates can only categorize as longingly. "She's totally amazing."

"Pardon?"

"She an amazing woman. Strong and smart and beautiful. A painter. Her name is Magga." Jeremy raises his shot glass and shouts over the noise of the jukebox, "To Magga!"

Magga and the tulip salesman cease talking and squint through the smoke to see across the bar. Magga whispers something to the tulip man, grabs her drink, a flute of champagne, and saunters over to Yates and Jeremy.

"Well, well," she says to Yates. "If it isn't the Oracle at Delphi."

Yates starts to get up, to clear out, to avoid every one of the dozen potential conflicts Magga represents, but she puts her large hand on his shoulder. "Please," Magga says. "Stay."

Yates shrugs and sits back down. Tongue-tied, lovestruck, considerably drunk, Jeremy just stares. Yates watches Magga sip her champagne, lick residual drops off her moustache and wipe her mouth with the sleeve of her filthy green parka. "So, how long are you staying?"

Yates looks behind the bar for a clock. Though he's not sure exactly when he will leave, he's currently thinking in terms of minutes rather than days. "Not sure. Not sure when the next chopper leaves for Kangerlussuaq."

Jeremy interrupts. "Magga. Hi Magga. It's me. Jeremy. Don't you remember my name from, um, like last night?" Magga just stares at the boy. Maybe she does. Maybe she doesn't. "Yeah," Jeremy continues, "well, this is, um, Magga. And this is Mr, um, Campbell."

This brings a smile to Magga's face. Yates figures twelve teeth total beneath that brief grin, though one could have been a piece of rogue fish cartilage. She extends her hand. "Pleased, Mr Campbell."

Jeremy reaches into his pocket, says, "More champagne, Magga?"

Magga looks at him as if he is a piece of bad herring, as if he has less value here in Greenland than a half-moon sliver of man-made ice. "Sure," she says. "Just be a good lad and have it sent over to me from your new stool across the bar. I'd like to have a word with Mr Campbell."

Eager even to be humiliated, as long as it will please the great Magga, Jeremy quickly gathers his things and makes for the other side of the bar. Magga grins and looks at Yates.

"Just because I'm using Campbell's name doesn't mean you can start throwing stuff at me, taunting me with your spectacularly strung-together expletives."

"You should be so fortunate."

The bartender backs them up with champagne and bourbon. Yates toasts puppy-dog Jeremy, but Jeremy will not be rewarded with a treat from his true master, who doesn't even acknowledge the receipt of his gift.

"Are you concerned for your friend?"

"Sure," answers Yates. "But not because you're sleeping with half the country. He's clearly having some kind of major, prolonged mid-life crisis."

"Do you think he would settle for a minor one?"

Yates smiles. "He's been a good friend for a long time."

"He needs someone like me to ground him."

"So do you know the tulip man?"

"Who?"

Yates lifts his chin towards the opposite corner. "Him. The tulip man. He was on my helicopter."

Magga rolls her eyes. Shakes her head. "He is not a seller of tulips."

"Really?"

"And he knows more about you than you might think."

Yates reaches for his drink. Tries to act like he doesn't care. He wants to ask a dozen questions, but decides not to bite.

"So how's the futurist business?"

"Bleak. Sales are way off."

"I heard about Johannesburg. And your girlfriend. Her mating with the history teacher was a nice – what is the word? – humiliating touch."

"I thought you'd appreciate that."

"Are you still heartbroken?"

"Crestfallen, I think, is more accurate. Heartbroken? Humiliated? Not really. Taken down a notch, yeah."

"Perhaps you needed that, to be taken down a notch. Just like your friend."

"There's a difference between egotistical and delusional. Campbell's got issues that can't easily be solved by therapy or yoga."

"Or bourbon."

"Or a sadomasochistic, Greenlandic fling." Yates looks at his drink, lifts it in a toast to Magga.

"What do you think of the ice?"

He rolls his eyes. "The ice is beautiful. Stunning. I'm sure if I ever actually see a piece calve into the fjord I'll weep like a child and swear never to leave this sacred place."

"I'm talking about the ice in your whisky glass."

Yates considers the cubes, then looks at Magga. "Did you slip a date-rape drug in there or something?"

"No. I just thought you'd be interested to know that the ice cubes in your glass, they are thirty thousand years old."

"No shit," Yates sticks his finger in his glass, swirls the ice around. Then he tips back the glass, catches a small cube in his teeth and crushes it. "Did you see it? Did you see the ice calve? Wasn't it sublime?"

Magga laughs, lifts her champagne flute and empties it in one swig.

"So what is it like, being a Greenlander?"

"Why do you care?"

"I don't, really. I'm just being polite."

"First of all, I'm from here but not really from here. I was born in Ilulissat, but as a child I was found to be a superior student, so the government took me away and sent me to special schools in Denmark. Then to university, while others stayed behind. But in Denmark I was not Danish, and when I came back to Greenland I found that, because of my education and the special treatment I received, I was not considered a true Greenlander here."

"So why did you come back? Why not find some place altogether new, like Antarctica?"

"Because here is where I feel most at home. Not so much now, when it is all light. But during the deep cold of Kausuitsup Una, the polar night this bar is named after. When there is only darkness is when I make my most powerful art. So now tell me about your job."

Yates takes a breath. "Today? It's to divine the global preoccupation, see why people feel the way they do."

"That's easy. The global preoccupation is *What horrible thing is going to happen next?* What, not why. I don't think anybody, especially your... audience... I don't think they give a fuck about why people feel anything. "

"Pardon?"

"They don't want to know why. They want to know what and when and where. They want to find out who feels this way and what they are going to do – not why – and then kill them. People like that want to know everything but the why."

Yates looks into his empty glass. "Is that wrong, to want to know that?"

"I'm not judging what is wrong. I'm explaining what is. Campbell talks about you a lot, you know."

Across the bar, the man formerly known as the tulip salesman rises and goes to the men's room. Yates gestures towards him. "So what's the story with the tulip-salesman impersonator?"

"I don't know. He just knew who you are."

"Did he tell you?"

"Mmm-hmm."

"Is he following me?"

She shrugs. "I'm just speculating. My family, we know lots of people."

"I forgot. The Greenlandic Mafia. But why would he follow me?"

"You obviously have become a person of interest lately. Quoted in the news. A controversial speech. Strange doings in Johannesburg, followed by a trip to, of all places, Greenland, and a sleepover with one of the world's richest, most eccentric men. Such bizarre behaviour has apparently attracted someone's attention."

"But I know nothing. I'm bogus."

"The more you say that, the more they believe the opposite. Now are you done with your questions?"

Yates waves to the bartender, points at his glass and Magga's, but she shakes her head. "I have to go," she says. "But first I have a question for you."

Yates shrugs.

"Do you want to come to my place and have sex?"

Yates sits upright, almost knocks over his empty glass. He looks across the bar at Jeremy, who's staring at them, and at the tulip man, who is back from the bathroom and lighting a pipe. He takes a breath and tries to look into Magga's eyes. "If I were to say yes..." he finally answers, "if Campbell ever found out, he'd be devastated."

Magga rises, zips up her parka. "That's what I thought you'd say." Then she says something under her breath that Yates partially translates into *impotent humper of fetid blubber*, which brings a satisfied smile to his face.

After Magga leaves, Jeremy jogs out after her. Soon after, the tulip man leaves. Yates savours his drink and stares around the bar. He considers the mounted fish and the ancient tackle that adorns the walls, before settling on a framed poem behind the bar.

> Were I laid on Greenland's Coast
> And in my arms embraced my lass;
> Warm amidst eternal frost
> Too soon the half year's night would pass.
> – *John Gay*

When the bartender brings Yates his final bourbon, Yates points into his glass. "Do you know," he asks, "how I could go about shipping a cooler of this stuff, this thirty-thousand-year-old ice, to a girl I know back in the States?"

Milano

He once gave a rousing motivational talk at the base of a spouting atrium fountain before the West Coast sales force for an erectile-dysfunction pharmaceutical maker. He once delivered a commencement address at a prestigious liberal arts college in southern Vermont that concluded with his professional assurances that the future could not be more promising for this special group, this class of June 2001. He once unknowingly slept with a corporate spy who out of frustration came clean the next morning about her idea-stealing intentions and called him an empty intellectual vessel, a complete waste of her sinister time.

He's been to Milan before, but he never really paid attention. But now, shuffling off the jetway at his arrival gate, he's already noticing. Airport as fashion show. Airport as design centre. As armed camp. Fellini film. Airport as white-collar hotel. Airport dressed in Armani and Prada, black silk and desert camouflage. Chinese travellers in white surgical masks. A *gelateria* next to a biometric security device that recognizes body features, facial contours. Men with guns. Guards with wands. German shepherds on short leashes. Fabulously accessorized businesswomen. Only the Americans seem to be wearing trainers. On the escalator to street level he contemplates the relationship between the degree of global anxiety and the acceptable size of carry-ons, but he cannot make an anecdote-worthy connection.

He hails a taxi, having declined an event chaperone this time round via email, and heads towards his hotel, towards his next gig, Futurshow Milan. At first they had cancelled him. Then, when they saw that his PR value had skyrocketed, they came after him offering more money and lots of perks. But he declined, via email from Greenland, saying he had no speech, had nothing new to say. They replied with an even larger monetary offer and the request that he just read the Johannesburg speech again, because that's all anybody wants to talk about anyway. For a while, he continued to baulk, but then he realized he had to get away from Campbell.

In the taxi, once again hung-over and helicopter- and jet-lagged from the "never to be repeated by himself, or for that matter anyone else" Illulissat-Kangerlussuaq-Copenhagen-Milan journey, he tells the driver in unintelligible Italian the address of his hotel. Then, again in Italian, he asks the driver how he's doing. But unlike the obliging chaperones and limo drivers he's grown accustomed to, this driver shrugs and spits something solid out of his open window. This leaves Yates with no choice but to look out of his own open window and consider on his own terms the outskirts of the city founded by Celts, conquered by Romans, sacked by Barbarians, reborn in the Renaissance, claimed by Napoleon, bombed into oblivion in WWII and reinvented by the fashionistas and financialistas at the end of the twentieth century. The Futurist looks at Milan, Italy's most modern city, but all he can think of is ice, the harsh wisdom of a giant Inuit woman, and the feeling that something horrible is going to happen, the end product of a bizarre chain of disparate events, all inexplicably connected to himself and all, ultimately, his fault.

* * *

Yesterday, after drinking at the bar at the Hotel Kausuitsup Una, he had returned to Campbell's compound and found his host alone and drunk and crying in front of the big-screen TV, watching the Turkish feed from the space hotel. For a long time Yates said nothing, just sat on the couch opposite Campbell. The camera showed an empty cockpit seat, with no peripheral movement. In the right-hand corner of the screen there was a digital clock running backwards from a little more than thirty-nine hours. Finally, when he saw that Campbell's sniffling and snorting were, if anything, getting louder, Yates asked him what was wrong. "I thought you thought these people were fools," Yates said. "You told me earlier that they should have known there were inherent risks in space travel."

Campbell nodded, drank more vodka from the bottle and tried to compose himself. "I was supposed to be on it."

"What?"

"I read an article about it, saw your quote, and enquired. I went through several weeks of tests. Put up a non-refundable $500,000 deposit, but midway through the training programme they gave me the boot." He patted his chest. "An arrhythmia. I tried to pay them off, but this is where the Russian authorities chose to have morals. They gave my bunk to the cosmetics heiress."

Yates let this soak in for a moment and decided to try the tough-love route. "You know what, Campbell? I don't think you're crying because you escaped death. I think that you're sitting here wishing that that was you up there, dying spectacularly rather than living ridiculously."

Campbell began to cry harder. Yates got up and went to his room to pack. With vodka bottle in hand, Campbell followed. "Where you goin'?"

"I don't know. I'm supposed to do a conference in Milan. I was going to blow it off. But now I don't know what to do."

"We hardly spoke."

"I know. Maybe this is a bad time for both of us." So much for tough love.

"Maybe next month you can come back. My treat."

Yates shook his head. "With all due respect to you, Magga and the ice, I don't think I could take it. To tell you the truth, you should get away from here for a while. See some asphalt. Some gridlock. Strip malls. Smog. And maybe a woman that doesn't take such extreme pleasure in humiliating you."

"You saw Magga?"

Yates nodded.

"Did she say anything about me?"

Yates shoved his dirty clothes into his leather duffel. Standing at the desk before closing his laptop, he glanced at his messages and saw an urgent email from N-II-30. He clicked on it.

"Shit."

"What?"

"Apparently I've become pen pals with Nostradamus."

Campbell wiped his nose with his sleeve and leant forwards to read the text.

From one prophet to another,
Congratulations on your continued success.
– N-II-30

"Cool."

"Cool?"

"This message. What you do. You think it's bullshit, but it affects people."

"Crazy people."

"And the not-so-crazy."

"Affecting them is pretty much the same as misleading them."

Campbell put down the bottle and looked back at the email. "You serve more of a purpose than you realize, dude. The world is based on futurism. On speculation. On finding clues in the chatter: *Will there be a war? Is it gonna rain tomorrow? What will happen if he's elected? Should democracy be applied like a tourniquet or a suppository? How will the chairman of the Fed's predilection for velour sweatsuits affect the markets? Should I bet the over or the under if the wind's blowing in off the lake at Wrigley Field?* And this, the prevailing mantra of mankind since that horrible moment in time when we were cursed with the ability to wonder: *Is there anything redeeming to look forward to tomorrow? Anything worth living for the day after?*"

"Yeah, but the only problem is that there is absolutely no reason to believe any of it. I'm too inept to be scientific. Too lazy to be original or deep. I don't have visions. Shit, I barely use reason. I go on hunches. I steal the thoughts of others and twist them for my own purposes. There's no cool in that."

"But what matters is that you think about this stuff, especially in the world we live in right now. When things are good, they all want you to tell them how they can get in on it, how they can get rich, ride in the barrel of the bliss wave. But when things are fucked, they want you to tell them how to save the world. Or avert catastrophe. Or get over it. What you do matters more than anything I ever did. Even the plagiarism matters, and the less well-intentioned stuff you slipped into over the years, because even that was compiled and edited and filtered through the soul of a good person."

Yates grabs the bottle of vodka from him and takes a drink. "You're a good person too, Campbell."

"What you did in Johannesburg might be the best

thing anyone could possibly tell anyone right now: that it's okay not to know the answers to the questions that this fucking world insists upon posing every second of every day. It's okay not to know what you want, where you want to go, who you want to become. It is okay to wonder. To ask. It is normal not to know. We all felt it before, Yates, but we felt like we were the only ones who ever felt that way. What's not okay is to stop wondering, right?"

"But the unthinkable continues to happen."

"We know that. But at least you give context to the unthinkable." Campbell walked over to an ancient PacMan video arcade game and pushed start. Despite his Internet wizardry, he still considers PacMan the ultimate digital experience.

Yates smiled. "I'm sorry I can't stay longer."

"I'm sorry I've become so fucked up."

After a moment, Yates glanced out of the window. "Holy shit."

"What?"

He pointed out at the fjord, where the ice meets the bay, and he widened his eyes.

"What?"

"It was beautiful, Campbell."

The hotel in Milan is everything he used to want in a hotel but never really took the time to appreciate. Now it just seems silly and ostentatious. Red satin swings on twenty-foot cables in the lobby. Hybrid model-bellboys dressed in the requisite black Mao jackets. Eclectic house music that makes him feel simultaneously exhilarated and ancient. Half of him wants to dance. The other half wants to commit suicide. His room key, which comes wrapped in soft, red rose petals, unlocks a cherry-wood door that opens upon the height of style – which to Yates means fifteen minutes of not being able to figure out how the bathroom sink works or where, exactly, the clothes closet is.

He ignores the flashing phone lights, doesn't bother to check out the plasma-screen TV or his own private gym. He showers quickly and, in a nod to Milano fashion, chooses a black Gap T-shirt to accompany his loose-fit jeans, saving the navy blue for the gym. He's about to go outside for a walk when the phone rings. He stares at it for four rings, until the message picks up, but it immediately begins to ring again.

"Yates."

"Mr Yates," begins the voice on the other end, in Italian-accented English. "I am with the gentlemen with whom you engaged in conversation the other day in the hotel at Johannesburg, please."

"Who?"

"Mr and Mr Johnson, please."

"I'm not... Oh. I met quite a few people in Johannesburg. And a name like, what – Johnson..."

"Please, Mr Yates. It is awesomely important that we meet. I must briefly talk to you please."

"I was just going for a walk."

"Perfect, please. If you might, Mr Yates, let me buy you a drink. At the Caffé Fiera in the Galleria Vittorio Emanuele, at perhaps five o'clock, please."

Yates checks his watch: two hours from now. He'll probably be needing a drink by then anyway. "Fine. What is your name?"

"My name is Mr Mabus. I will introduce myself at the café. I can recognize you from your press."

Yates writes *MABUS Caffé Fiera 5p* on a piece of hotel stationery and puts it in his pocket. In the lobby he asks the concierge for a walking map of the area and directions to Caffé Fiera, as well as to a church he had read about on the jet. Outside, from almost every corner he can see the absurdly majestic façade of Milan's great Duomo, one of the largest Gothic structures on earth. But he chooses not to go that way. Instead he heads towards Via Ruffini and the Church of Santa Maria delle Grazie. When he gets there he tries to open its main door, but it is closed. As he turns to leave, he hears the click of a security latch and stops. An old woman in black has just opened the door. She pauses and considers Yates, who motions towards the inside of the church and says, "*Per favore*?"

"American?"

He stops, wonders about her politics. Wonders if *Canadian* will get him inside while *American* will send him packing. Wonders if he could pass as a Kiwi, or a Brit. "Yes." He nods, bows, finally makes a choice. "New York."

While Cedar Rapids or Tallahassee may have been disastrous, this brings a smile to the old woman's face. She opens the door and waves him inside. He blesses himself with holy water and looks around the dark church. He starts towards the altar, but she shakes her head, motions him down a hall towards an adjoining refectory, where an overweight guard rises off his stool and puts his hand on his holstered pistol. The old woman says something to the guard in Italian, and for a moment the two exchange pleasantries while Yates stands, thinking of hockey and fur trappers and mounted policemen. He looks up when he hears the woman say the words *American – New York*. The guard stares hard at him, drumming his fingers on the handle of his pistol. After a moment, the guard finally nods, steps away. "*Due minuti*," he says.

"*Grazie*," Yates whispers, and steps forwards, through a space-age metal detector and into the ancient refectory, where he finds himself completely alone with Leonardo da Vinci's *Last Supper*. He had always thought that a work this famous would surely be in a major museum, the Met, the Louvre, the Uffizi. But here it is, just as the article had promised, the only work of Leonardo's that one can visit *in situ*, on the wall of a centuries-old monastic dining hall looking, frankly, like crap. Yates had decided to come here for inspiration, for a peek into the soul of an authentic visionary genius, but he feels nothing. Yet, while the painting fails to inspire him, the quarters in which it was created begins to cast a spell. He imagines Leonardo standing on rough-hewn scaffold planks, on and off for nearly three years, applying his "silent poetry" to the wall, while monks and noblemen and craftsmen no doubt stopped to watch. He wonders if the onlookers knew what or whom they were in the presence of, and if Leonardo took a long time completing the painting just to piss them off.

"You like?" the guard asks, in English.

Yates answers slowly. "I was thinking of what it must have been like then, in this room, before it deteriorated. I wonder what the monks thought when they ate here afterwards, in front of something so beautiful."

"Perhaps they think," the guard begins, gesturing towards the faded Christ, "*Better him than me*, eh?"

"Why did it take so many years?"

"He finished very very fast. But he could not find a Judas. No model. All the apostles he found on the streets of Milan. But not for Judas. He looked one year to find someone who looked bad enough to be Judas. Some people say he used the face of his benefactor, to make him angry."

Yates smiles. The painting is growing on him.

"Do you think it is beautiful?"

The guard considers the scene from left to right, studying each apostle and Jesus before settling on Yates. "I think it is beautiful, because without it I have no job."

Before he leaves, Yates bends to tie his shoe, picks up a loose piece of crumbled Renaissance mortar, and puts it in his pocket.

* * *

On via Molino delle Armi he walks into Shalimar, the bar of the moment eight hem-lengths ago, and orders a Peroni. Two tremendous golden fibreglass hands support the high ceiling, and a vaporous green light illuminates the white walls and furniture, flashing off the small chrome tiles embedded in the resin floor. Pretty people with severe features sip primary-coloured drinks from long thin glasses. Playing Leonardo, Yates looks at them, searching for a possible Jesus, a possible Paul, a possible John. Drinking his second Peroni, he finds it hard to believe that Leonardo had such a hard time finding someone to portray Judas, because in this dark and beautiful cave he sees the face of betrayal in everyone. When the waitress asks if he'd like a third beer, he checks his watch: 4.45. He's already regretting this Mabus meeting. In fact he's thinking of calling off the whole thing with the Johnsons. He doesn't need the money that badly, and that kind of work, however dark and intriguing and potentially nihilistic it might be, just doesn't seem worth it any more. It's much easier to drink and aimlessly wander the planet constantly repeating the same initially well-intentioned speech. Nevertheless, he tells the waitress, *No, thank you,* and settles his tab. He'll hear what Mabus has to say, have a drink, then he'll go back to the hotel and end this thing with the Johnsons.

Caffé Fiera is in a glass-enclosed nineteenth-century Galleria of shops, cafés and restaurants just down the street from his hotel. Intentionally touristy, but in an "old world meets new fashion" kind of way. At 5 p.m. it is filled with shoppers and guidebook-toting travellers. Yates is told that there are no available tables at the café, but when he mentions Mabus's name, a quick check of the reservation list lands him a prime spot overlooking the *piazza*.

He switches from Peroni to Campari-and-soda, then sits back and continues to cast for his own version of *Last Supper.* At 5.05 his cellphone rings. It is Mabus, profusely apologizing and promising that he will arrive at precisely 5.10. Yates doesn't care, doesn't even think twice about how Mabus got his mobile number. He's feeling good, three drinks into a Milano happy hour, with no responsibilities until tomorrow. Looking about a block down the Galleria in the direction of his hotel, he notices a small gathering of people, mostly young adults. They are chanting something, but he can't make out the words. He sips his Campari-and-soda and watches the crowd multiply, nearly a hundred strong now, and he can make out the word *America* in their chant, which doesn't have a particularly celebratory tone. Yates checks his watch again: 5.09. Just enough time to order another drink before his company arrives. He motions to the waiter, who nods. He gives the demonstrators another quick look. In his spontaneous casting session he still needs a Jesus and Thomas. *But wait,* he thinks. *Of course.* I *should be Thomas. Who better than me, staring sceptically at the miracle right in front of my eyes?* That just leaves Jesus.

At exactly 5.10, a pretty young woman on a moss-green Vespa slowly drives past Yates. He notices her because the Vespa is the only vehicle in the pedestrian-only Galleria, and because she seemingly goes out of her way to look at him with her wide, expressionless eyes before moving on towards the gathered demonstrators. Just as she reaches them, she explodes. Windows shatter, bodies are hurled backwards. The waiter drops Yates's second Campari-and-soda onto his lap. For several stretched-out moments there is only silence, and then there is only screaming. Yates stands and begins to jog towards the destruction, which is the opposite of what everyone else in the Galleria is doing. He stops at the place where he last saw the girl on the Vespa. Nothing remains but a blunt crater in the pavement and pieces of people who cared enough about something to shout it in the streets. To his left, a teenage boy with blood streaming down the left side of his face sits in a ring of shattered glass with his back against the wall of a *gelateria*. Yates kneels beside the boy and tries to ask if he's all right, but the boy is either in shock or doesn't understand English. First the Polizia arrive, then the ambulances. Yates tries to get the attention of the paramedics, but they move past him and towards the more severely injured. He gets up, grabs some paper napkins from a toppled holder and kneels back down. He starts to dab at the wounds on the boy's face. But the boy rages, jerks his head away.

"Please. No!" the boy says, crying now. Yates moves back from the boy and notices two things he hadn't seen before. A dagger-sized piece of glass sticking out of his left side and a bunched-up American flag in his left hand. "Go. Now, American!" the boy says, angrily waving his right hand, which is still clutching a cigarette lighter.

Yates steps away, looks for a paramedic and then back towards the café. For some reason he briefly thinks of Mabus, and if maybe he should check on him, but all the tables are empty. In his pocket his phone begins to vibrate, but he doesn't bother to look at it. As a paramedic passes by, running back towards his ambulance, Yates grabs his arm and points at the wounded boy, who looks almost disappointed to have been noticed, or to be helped by the likes of Yates.

A Horrible Undoing of People and Animals

He hasn't taken a bubble bath since he was six, but right now he feels like there's no way that he cannot take one. Once he figures out how the faucet and drain work, he dumps with trembling hands a large seashell full of lavender sudsing crystals into the deep white tub. Then he takes a San Pellegrino out of his mini-fridge, grabs the remote, tilts the bedroom TV towards the tub and opens the shutters, providing an unobstructed view of the news. He tries to convince himself that this feels good, sinking up to his neck in the hot sudsy water. The world may be full of evil, but it can't be that evil if a grown man can take stock of his life neck-deep in lavender-scented bubbles. He tries, but he can't stop thinking about all of the death that hasn't exactly been following him as much as it has been provoking him, performing for him, unfolding before him as if choreographed exclusively for his benefit.

There have been bombings to launch holy wars, to change elections, regimes, and the outcomes of soccer games. But why this bomb? Yates cannot imagine what the purpose of this bomb could have been. He thinks of the boy he tried to help and of the girl on the Vespa, and wonders what it must feel like to be willing to die to reclaim your individuality while others are equally willing to kill you to take it away. There's nothing about the explosion on the BBC or CNN, but a local Milano station is showing footage.

From what Yates can discern, the reporter is saying that three have died, with another twenty-two injured. He can make out the *gelateria* and its blasted-out windows, but he doesn't see the injured boy, or any trace of himself. He thinks that maybe his fear, or his lack of conviction one way or the other, made him invisible. He closes his eyes and lets his head slide under the water. As he comes up, he returns to watching the jittery video, the panicked faces and flashing lights, and he gets the sensation that he has no connection whatsoever to the scene on TV. But when he slides under once more and again comes up and opens his eyes, he feels the exact opposite. Feels that while maybe he's not responsible for what happened, he certainly has something to do with it. His cellphone rings, but there's no way he's going to answer. Instead he picks up the hotel phone on the tub wall and calls the concierge. He asks him for *risotto alla Milanese,* osso bucco and an English-language edition of the *Prophecies* of Nostradamus.

Back in the bedroom, in a black cotton robe, he gets onto the Internet and looks for more information on the bombing. Several accounts say that the gathering was a flash mob that had responded to a mass cellphone and Internet notification for a spontaneous anti-American demonstration at the Galleria, at exactly 5 p.m. Officials are wondering if the people who organized the combination social-phenomenon-political-rally are also the people who terrorized it. Or if a pro-American organization got wind of it and took matters into its own hands.

To his surprise, not one but two Nostradamus books arrive before the food. A biography and the abridged prophecies. He searches for the last email from the N-man and writes down the sign-off. N-II-30. He starts to skim through the prophecies, assuming that they are organized by quatrain, but instead he sees that in this edition they are categorized according to themes, like famine and Antichrists, nine-eleven, Hitler and the end of the world. N-II-30 is in the middle of the 'Once and Future Antichrist' section.

One who the infernal gods of Hannibal
Will cause to be reborn, terror to all mankind:
Never more horror nor worse of days
In the past than will come to the Romans through Babel.

The closest he can come to a link to this afternoon is the last line, about horror coming to the Romans. But Hannibal? Babel? He picks up his cellphone and calls Campbell in Greenland, who answers with a question.

"Bombs go off in your footsteps and you don't answer your phone?"

"Sorry. I was preoccupied. You okay?"

"Watching the space hotel, waiting for Magga."

"Magga's a slut."

"And?"

The exploding Vespa girl had caused Yates to forget about the space hotel. He picks up the remote and finds it on TV. In the empty cockpit an open paperback floats by. Yates tries to make out the title. "How come there's more hours remaining than last time I checked?"

"Apparently you missed this morning's episode. Somehow they were able to fire up a makeshift oxygen candle that bought them half a day of air, but it can't help keep them in orbit. Whether this means a more drawn-out death or a chance at redemption remains to be seen."

"I have a question about Nostradamus."

Campbell clears his throat, then recites:

"One who the infernal gods of Hannibal
Will cause to be reborn, terror to all mankind:
Never more horror nor worse of days
In the past than will come to the Romans through Babel."

"Are you messing with me?"

"You showed me the note with the call-out to this specific passage. Plus I saw the explosion, even though it was buried in the world news. One of dozens around the world. But I think the 'girl on the Vespa' angle elevated it from commonplace micro-terror to newsworthy, to lead-story sexy."

"It was anything but."

"You saw?"

"Front-row seat."

"Presumably you are fine."

Yates switches channels from the space tragedy to a broader variety of tragedies on the BBC. "It was horrible, Campbell. I tried to help a boy, but he wanted nothing to do with being helped by an American. And the girl who did it, she was beautiful, and I swear to God she looked right at me as she passed."

"You think it's related?"

Yates hadn't thought of this until now. "I don't know."

Campbell asks, "Have you heard from Nosty since the last message?"

"No."

"Anyone suspicious?"

"Lately everyone I talk to is suspicious." The doorbell rings. He opens the door and waves the waiter in, motions that he'll eat in front of the TV. "Some dude who knows my Johannesburg boys called," he continues. "We were gonna meet for a drink at a café in the Galleria, next to where the bomb went off, at the exact moment it went off. Of course, my sitting here saying it like this now..."

"Someone wanted you to see it."

"But the quatrain. It's so damned cryptic."

"It's close enough to make a point. What was the guy's name?"

"Begins with an M." Yates picks up his trousers and fishes the scrap out of the front pocket. "Mabus. M-A-B-U-S."

From Campbell, silence. Then, "Oh. Okay."

"Okay what?" Yates hears Campbell typing on a keyboard in the background.

"I've been looking into this a bit since you left."

"Got a lot on your plate these days, I see."

"Then maybe I won't tell you that Mabus is a name associated with Nostradamus's third Antichrist. Who, depending upon the interpretation, was supposed to arrive at specific apocalyptic moments ranging from five hundred years ago to five minutes from now."

"Accept my apologies."

"And here it says, depending upon whom you read and how much you want to believe, he was supposed to wage war on Israel or the West with all kinds of doomsday weapons."

"According to Nostradamus?"

"According to interpretations of Nostradamus."

"No mention of a pretty girl on a trendy motorbike as said form of doomsday weapon?"

"Nope."

"And in the quatrain in question, there's no mention of any Mabus?"

"Hold on a second." More keyboard clicking integrated with low-volume classical music in the background at Campbell's place, undoubtedly the Turkish coverage of the space station. "Okay. Same Century. Quatrain 62:

Mabus will soon die, then will come
A horrible undoing of people and animals..."

"Wonderful. Why does he have to drag the poor animal kingdom into this?"

"As for the latest note he sent you," Campbell continues, "I think he's alluding to an act of terror supported by Babel, i.e. Iraq or Syria. And the target – Romans – is Italy."

"But I don't get who Mabus is."

"Well, for Nostradamus's Mabus an etymological case can be made for everyone from Eminem to the new head of the PLO, from Spongebob Squarepants to the last five presidents of the United States. In recent years, this says they've tended to link him to Saddam, Osama, Kim Jong-il, Moby. Your Mabus, however, is more likely a small-time, run-of-the-mill psychopath having fun with you. Or a serious terrorist trying to get your attention as the prelude to something much worse yet to come."

"Since he's already killed in front of me, I'm kind of leaning towards the latter."

"Could be."

"Should I tell the Johnsons?"

"Who?"

"The guys from Johannesburg."

"Tell them to what end? If they can help you, sure. If they're going to get you in deeper, you may want to wait. Play this out a little. Do you even know who those guys really work for or what their true agenda is?"

"Not really. I have a feeling they're attached to the government in an under-the-radar kind of way. They clearly have a global network and some serious money supporting their interests. Whatever they are. Does this make any sense to you?"

"Not really."

"What about you? Have you thought about getting away from the ice and Magga for a while? Why not come here and hang out with me for a while, change the psychic scenery a bit?"

Yates listens for a reply, but Campbell's already gone.

The Future History of the World

He once began his week ringing the bell at the New York Stock Exchange and ended it giving a speech about the future of greed to a group of Philadelphia seminary students. He once was an advisor for hereswhatIdoMom.com, a company that made videos explaining people's nebulous jobs to their confused parents. He once was asked by the *New York Times* to write an op-ed piece on the death of literacy in America, and had his assistant – Blevins – ghostwrite it.

From what Yates can glean from these two books, the prophecies and the biography, Nostradamus's breakthrough moment came after he successfully foretold the death of King Henry II.

> *The Young Lion will overcome the older one*
> *On the field of combat in single battle:*
> *He will pierce his eyes through a golden cage,*
> *Two wounds made one, then he dies a cruel death.*

The king, apparently ignoring warnings from Nostradamus himself, had gone ahead and engaged in a jousting tournament, using a shield decorated with a lion. When his opponent's lance shattered, he was struck in the eye and temple, through the opening in his gilded visor. The King obliged the prophecy of a cruel death by suffering for ten days before succumbing. By this point in his life, Nostradamus had already completed most of his 1,000-quatrain *Future History of the World*, which laid out, in no particular order, his vision through to the year AD 3797. His wife and children had already died of the plague he had battled as a physician, and he was respected in many circles. But nailing this high-profile current event elevated his reputation as seer to another level. He now had street cred *and* court cred. And as Yates knows, once you get one big thing right, people tend to forget all the previous things you had got so very wrong. And sometimes the most devoted will even try to find ways to make your wrongs – past, present and future – seem right.

Inspired by the prose, the man, and now the Chianti, Yates decides to do some prophesizing of his own. According to this biography, before a nocturnal prophesizing session, Nostradamus would fast for three days, abstain from sex and wait for perfect meteorological conditions. He would bathe in consecrated water, don a simple robe and use a laurel branch as a wand. Then he'd sit hunched over a brass bowl filled with steaming water and infused with oils and, perhaps, narcotic herbs. With his wand he would touch the water and anoint his feet and the hem of his robe. Nostradamus once claimed that angels were at his side as he sat entranced in a "prophetic heat". Then at dawn he would write what he saw on consecrated paper with a pen made of the third feather of the right wing of a gosling. When he was done, he would toss the quatrains up in the air and gather them to be chronicled in the order in which they fell.

Yates decides to use his session as an opportunity to share a report with the Johnsons, or maybe as the basis of a future speech. Or perhaps it will simply impose some kind of shape and reason to the events he's been associated with over the last week. Or maybe it's just the drunken indulgence of a broken man. *Regardless,* he thinks, *like Nostradamus, I've abstained from sex for the three-day minimum and then some. And though the bathwater wasn't isn't necessarily consecrated, it did smell damn good. The plush terry-cloth hotel robe isn't exactly simple, but it's definitely comfortable enough to help induce a full-blown prophetic heat. In lieu of sniffing oils and narcotic herbs over a brass bowl, I'll make do with another large glass of wine. This TV remote is a worthy stand-in for a wand. And for a pen, not the third feather from a gosling's wing, unless I really want to test the abilities of the concierge, but a laptop keyboard.*

The Future History of the World
(addendum to the preface)

MILAN: Is there room for a futurist in a terrified, compromised, morally ambiguous world? A World in which everyone has the wherewithal to be a Strangelove? From a Sixth Avenue hot-dog vendor to a failed Bosnian poet to the person who just smiled at you in the canned-goods section of the Piggly Wiggly. And if by some chance there is a role for a futurist, what role should he play? The well-intentioned but consistently inaccurate predictor of a better tomorrow? Or the well-intentioned yet paranoid patron saint of many Doomsdays yet to come? Should he tell you to duct-tape your windows, have a plentiful supply of bottled water, flashlight batteries, potassium-iodide tablets, gas masks, germ masks and playing cards? Should he tell you how to avert disaster, or how to pretend it's not even on the ideological radar, to have as good a time as you can right up until the arrival of that first bright flash that will change everything? Should he tell you to regard every stranger as an apocalyptic evildoer out to hijack our Boeing 767s and our freedoms? Or as someone who has the potential to make your life less homogenous and more enriching? Tell me, what am I

> *supposed to do? What am I supposed to feel? What is the right moral thing for a human being to do in a world that makes less sense with each passing nanosecond? How does one go about performing an authentic, twenty-first-century act of heroism? By giving blood? Rocking the vote? Telling someone they're talking too loud on their cellphone? How about suggesting* Reading Lolita in Tehran *for your next book group? Tell me. Tell me, what wisdom or lesson can I possibly begin to share with the world about an afternoon's journey that began with the kindness of an old woman and ended with a front-row seat to a mass murder? How about,* Be careful out there. *Or,* This too shall pass. *Or this:* We're all gonna die. *Tell me. Operators are standing by.*

He sends it without rereading or editing it. To Johnson and Johnson as a field report. Then to Campbell as a brain dump. Then to N-II-30 as a taunt, an olive branch, an indulgence. Then to David the chaperone, and Blevins, the prick. Then, after he finishes the last of the Chianti, he sends it to the Unofficial Coalition of the Clueless website, because, in some primal way, he cares what they think.

Campbell via email, almost immediately:

> *This is what I was talking about in between sobs the other day. This is the stuff that matters, dispersed through the moral filter of a good and smart man. This is what you should be doing. What you should have been doing. I do hope that you didn't send this to the oxymorons in intelligence.*

Followed soon after by a response from the oxymorons themselves, via telephone.

"The amazing Yates, may I help you?"

"We're not paying you to ask questions."

"Even rhetorical?"

"In fact we should fine you every time you use a fucking question mark."

"I take it you prefer exclamation points. Preceded by outrageous and preferably false proclamations."

"How about a little insight."

"Okay. How's this? There exist in the city of Milan hundreds of teenage boys and girls whose displeasure with US policies runs deep enough for them to step away from their fabulous young lives and take to the streets."

"So you were there?"

"Close enough to see the look in her eyes."

"What else?"

"Well, one of these teens, a boy, felt so strongly about his convictions that, even after a bomb left him wounded and disoriented, he spurned the help of an American simply because he was American. The boy seemed more intent on burning an American flag than he was on surviving."

"See. This is good. Not the fucking philosophical crap."

"It is not good. Nothing that happened in that Galleria today was anywhere close to good."

"Why were you there? What are you doing in Milan?"

"And you give me shit about the questions."

"Do you think that they made it look like Americans terrorized an anti-American rally to present us in the most barbaric light?"

"What?"

"Who do you think did it?"

"I don't know. I was having a drink at a café. It's just around the corner from my hotel. I had just seen *Last Supper.*"

"I hear it looks like shit in real life. Do you think there will be more incidents like this today? Tomorrow? In other cities?"

"You're kidding, right?"

"Did you have any clue this was going to happen?"

"Yeah. The girl on the Vespa came to me in a dream." As he says this, he thinks about Mabus and Nostradamus and, remembering his conversation with Campbell, he decides not to mention them. "You guys really don't give a shit about what people think about us, do you? It's all about what's next, what's in it for us, right? "

"Perhaps we made a mistake with you."

"What's the most courageous thing you think a man or woman can do?"

"Easy. He overrides his fears and his ego by acting to preserve the liberties and freedoms of his country and family. His courage is greater than his fear. His actions are not fuelled by desire. They're fuelled by love."

"By this definition then, what that girl did today, was that courageous?"

"Are you drunk, Yates?"

"Doing what I'm doing, am I helping to preserve the freedoms of my country?"

"I think deep down you know the answer."

"And my country... do you work for it?'

For a moment Johnson says nothing. Then, "That's kind of complex."

"You know what? I don't want to do this any more. You can have your credit card back. Your money. This is too funky."

"Don't be silly. Now that we know you're there, we'd like you to sprinkle a couple of thoughts into your presentation at the conference. About democracy. Individual freedoms. Outsourcing."

"I'm done."

"Give it time."

"I have."

"Sober up. Then give it some more."

"That may take weeks. I want to know whom you

work for. What your goal is. And why you think I can help achieve it."

"Yates..."

"Johnson... Or is it Johnson?"

"If you know anything else about the blast today, you'd tell us. Right?"

"That's right. That's the thing. The headline. I continue to know absolutely nothing."

He hangs up and stares at the phone and waits for it to ring again, but it doesn't. An email-arrival tone breaks the silence of the room. It is from David the chaperone:

Got your note. May I call you?

Yates types *Yes,* then refills his wine glass. He answers his cellphone before it rings. "David. What's up?"

For a moment there is only silence on the other end. Then a woman clears her throat.

"Lauren?"

"Oh God. Still?"

"Marjorie? Are you all right? Where are you?"

"Not in Milan. Or Greenland. And no, I'm not all right."

"Did David find you?"

"I found him. He gave me your number."

"I waited for you."

"I know."

"Two guys knocked me around the hotel room. I waited, but after a while I just assumed you decided not to come, so I left."

"I know. I know."

"I figured you realized how crazy it seemed."

"You figured wrong. They visited me, too."

"The CBD guys?"

"Yes."

"They didn't want me to go anywhere near you. They asked me a lot of questions. Then, when they were about to let me go, the other men came."

"From the CBD?"

"No. Americans. Two men in bad suits. I overheard them. They said they had met you at the hotel. They said you were going to help them with the interests of the companies they represent. In Johannesburg and elsewhere. They told the Johannesburg Development people to leave you alone, obviously too late. But I wouldn't trust them either, Yates."

"What did they do to you?"

"The Americans? Nothing. I feigned ignorance. I told them that you had spent the night drinking with me and that, as hard as you tried, you were too drunk to fulfill your desires."

"That's what I get for being respectful."

"They asked me a lot of questions, but I acted like a tart. I told them all you wanted to do was talk about your ex and your speech. They kept me in a room somewhere in Soweto until, I imagine, you left the country. Then they told me they would kill me if I ever spoke to you again, or to anyone about their existence. Then they let me go."

"I don't want you to get hurt just because you know me. You don't have to speak with me again, you know."

"I know."

Yates waits to see if she will elaborate on this, but she leaves it at that. "Did you find your passport?"

"I did."

"I want you to come to me. If you want to, of course. I can't promise you how safe or how interesting it may be."

"It can't be worse that my current situation."

"I just have to figure out how to get you tickets without them finding out. And I have to figure out where we should go, where I'm going next."

"Okay."

"Marjorie?"

"Yes?"

"Do you have any idea who those other men, the Americans, work for?"

"They may be associated with a government, but from what they told the CBD people, they're primarily interested in money. In 'American interests'."

"Are you safe for now?"

She pauses. "Yes. For now."

"Can you call me tomorrow? Around noon? That will give me time to make some calls."

"Be careful, Yates."

For a while he sleeps and dreams about a more horrific version of his recent reality. Soccer riots, faltering spaceships, youth-killing bombs. He dreams of a world awash in innocent blood. With the lights on. The TV. The laptop. His robe. All on. The hotel phone, for some reason, is off the hook and pulsing. When he wakes up, he throws water on his face and calls room service to take away his trays. He looks for a clock near the bed, but can't see anything. To Yates, time in hotel rooms frequently loses context. In foreign hotel rooms, it also loses meaning. In hotels, TVs play looped content with no set start or stop times: the tourist show, the hotel-services channel, pay-per-view movies. Even the news from other countries seems taped, not just from another place but from another time, not always the past, but a future that he has seen before. At times, it becomes more than confusing, it becomes disorienting. Of course the alcohol, the stress, the jet lag and myriad atrocities experienced as witness and possibly as participant tend to enhance the effect.

He looks out of the window: it is either late-night dark or early-morning dark. Or dusk. He doesn't know and decides that he doesn't want to know. That will make things easier when he goes out to lose himself in it: an unchronicled moment in nebulous Milano darkness. But just when he thinks that he couldn't be more lost, his conscience finds him. And he knows that it's found him because he looked at the damned sky, which right now is the same as looking into the eyes of his father, eyes that watch but don't judge because they don't have to, because they have the uncanny ability to force you to judge yourself. Yates owes his father and his mother a call. Several calls. And the reason why he hasn't made them is no big psychological mystery. They'll know. Especially his father. Maybe not specifically about everything, but they will certainly have a general sense of what his life – and what their son – has become. And he can't deal with that now. Not with a whole world of denial waiting on the other side of the door to room 323. So he closes the curtain and makes a note to himself never to look at the sky again. Over by his desk he calls room service to clear his dishes and to mail a package for him, and they politely tell him that he called a few minutes ago and that someone is on the way. *Hotel-jà vu*. While he waits, he pulls on a new black T-shirt and checks his face in the mirror, not so much to see how he looks but to make sure that it is still him. He hears the elevator bell and opens the door before the waiter has a chance to knock. He smiles, waves the man in. These are the last people he can count on, the constants in his life: the limo drivers, the bellboys and chaperones. The personal assistants and maître d's. Always nice, polite, agreeable. Always willing to discuss the weather, the game, the local landmark; but thankfully never the disaster, the politics, the ethics; only in their inflection. Even though he had tipped when the meal arrived, he tips again lavishly, on paper, on the Johnsons' tab. Then he walks over to the desk and hands over to the man a sealed envelope, inside which is a marble-sized piece of six-hundred-year-old mortar. Inside the envelope is also a postcard:

Last Supper, by Leonardo da Vinci, at the Church of Santa Maria delle Grazie, Milan.

The envelope is addressed to Lauren. On the back of the card, the Futurist has written:

Greetings from the Renaissance. Wish you were here!

A Designer of Buttons

There's no way they'll let a guy like Yates, dressed like this, looking like this, at this hour (whatever it is), into Burlap Thong, the bar attached to the hotel. But they do once he tells them that he's a guest and, at their request, shows them the key to a suite no less.

The theme of the bar, apparently, is some kind of anti-fashion statement made by the fashionistas themselves. An inside joke that Yates isn't quite getting. Pretty people deliberately dressed ugly is his best guess. Some kind of mean splash of piss in the lazy eye of the rest of the world. Behold, lower life forms, even in polyester and work boots, white socks and comfortable khakis: guess what, we are still impossibly fucking beautiful.

Other than the beautiful part, Yates thinks he kind of fits in. He locates a gap in the mass of lithe bodies at the bar and orders a glass of bourbon. He toasts the woman next to him, a beautiful, auburn-haired model in grey overalls and a coal-miner's lantern hat who has painstakingly applied smudges of coal dust on her alpine cheekbones. Quickly deciding that Yates is nothing more than a wannabe ugly beautiful person, she gets up, coughs like she has a touch of the black lung and leaves. Yates grabs her seat and sets to work on his bourbon. He used to have a rule. Only drink when you're happy. When you're celebrating something. Or with a fun group of people. And never drink – especially alone – when things are going badly. When you're in the proverbial funk. He had always thought this a good rule, and often told it to others with what he now realizes was a kind of obnoxious, high-minded pride. Because, the thing is, until recently, things had never really been bad for Yates. He'd never been in a funk of any kind. Until recently he'd never been dumped by a woman. Never seen a soccer riot. A teen suicide bomber. Until last week he'd never got the shit kicked out of himself in a hotel room, never been stalked by a psychotic terrorist prophet; until right now he had never seen his job and his life quite the way he sees it now.

Stupid rule, he thinks, as he puts his lips to his glass. *Dreamt up by a stupid man.*

"You American?"

Yates looks up at a pretty boy in farmer's overalls. "I am. Are you a farmer?"

The pretty boy laughs. "I'm American, too. Though now I kind of live on the road. Modelling. Adventure travel."

Yates thinks of the space hotel. Wishes it had an extra bunk with a full-length mirror for this guy, who's apparently even too much of a jerk for the other models. Here comes the handshake.

"Chandler."

"First or last? Like the father of the crime novel or the drug addict on *Friends*?"

"Both. One word. They like that in the industry."

"Nice tattoo, Chandler." Yates motions to a mass of Asian characters that stretch from Chandler's right shoulder to the base of his sculpted biceps.

"Thanks. Got it in Thailand. Can I get you a drink? Good. I'll tell you a secret: when they were inking it, they told me it meant Warrior of Truth. Then someone in Cambodia saw it a few weeks later and told me that it meant Shit-brained Coward."

"The inimitable Thai humour. Your secret's safe with me, Chandler."

"Thanks. Cheers."

Yates drinks, looks around. Two female models dressed like petrol-station attendants are making out on the dance floor. An Adonis in a McDonald's uniform is pantomiming order-taking and burger-flipping, to the delight of a table full of faux computer geeks. "Tell me, Chandler. Do they hate you because you're beautiful, or American?"

Chandler laughs. Nothing seems to piss him off. "Unfortunately, I think neither. I think it's all about personality. A congenital defect of the attitude. I'm not nasty enough to be taken seriously. Or nice enough to be genuinely liked. I'm gay, but not flamboyantly so. In fact, I hate fashion. So I'm kind of an outcast. What is it that you do, Yates?"

"I'm a designer."

"Really?"

"Yeah. Yup."

"Should I know your work?"

"Only if you have a very particular accessorizing fetish. I'm a designer of... buttons."

"That is so cool."

"Everybody, this is Yates. He's a designer."

"Really? Awesome."

He's now at In Transit, an expat bar on Naviglio Pavese in the Ticinese Quarter, a neighbourhood of intersecting canals whose existence, according to an increasingly inebriated Chandler, is based on a sketch by Leonardo. Apparently the thing to drink at In Transit is Guinness or Budweiser or whisky. Anything that isn't trendy or Italian. At In Transit, the exotic is the everyman's drink of anywhere but here. Yates drinks whisky. Initially he'd asked for Maker's Mark. Then, to clarify, bourbon.

When that was met with a blank stare, he said whisky, and got this. Something brown and potent. Definitely not bourbon. Perhaps a badly blended rye.

"It's a living," answers the designer of buttons. Chandler is making a big show of introducing his very good friends, but Yates sees that the others at the table had only met Chandler the night before, and most don't remember his name. There are three Aussies, a Pole. And two, three, four Americans. All just back, according to Lydia, the Polish woman, from holiday in Afghanistan.

"And how was that?" Yates asks, pulling up a chair.

Four of them turn to Yates and say some version of *Wonderful*. The most animated on the subject is Deanne, a muscular, short-haired brunette from Branson, Missouri. "A stark, unforgiving land. Signs of devastation everywhere. Still incredibly hot."

"Temperature-hot or dangerous-hot?"

"Excitement-hot. Tribal unrest. Undetonated ordnance. Snipers." Deanne pours some of her Budweiser into her pint of Guinness and continues. "Which of course, is the main appeal."

"That your life might be in danger?"

"Absolutely."

Yates drinks. Continues to think on a back burner about bravery, heroism. He decides that the actions of this Deanne from Branson, Missouri and her group do not qualify as either brave or heroic. She is sort of cute, though.

"You wouldn't understand unless you experienced it."

"Let me guess: It's the possibility of death, the proximity of it, that makes you feel so alive."

Deanne nods assent until she realizes that, if Yates isn't outright mocking her, he's at least toying with her. "I said you wouldn't understand."

"I don't. But I didn't mean to offend."

She smiles. Decides to give him another chance. "It's

just that, at home in Branson, on this planet really, there's not much left that y'all can call 'exotic'. That can float my boat in an unexpected way. Every trip you take now to whatever corner of the world has been staked out. There are recommendations to eat this at this café. Order this dish. Use this map. Take this tour."

"Walk in these footsteps," Yates elaborates on her riff. "On top of these fingerprints. It's all GPS-coordinated, with trail markers in twenty-seven languages. Where else have you been? Or is Afghanistan the first trip of its kind for you?"

"Oh no. We've been to Bosnia. Haiti. Gaza."

"Iraq?"

"Spring break next year. There or Bas'ar."

"So for you to consider it, it has to be dangerous?"

"Yes. Because everything has been discovered. But when you add a bit of danger, even a discovered place can feel exciting and fresh. It makes me feel brave. And in my other life that's something I just don't feel any more."

"What do you do in your other life?"

"Pre-school."

Yates soaks this in. He considers Deanne's face. Tanned, smooth skin. Kind of chubby. Blue eyes that seem sad. Or maybe he wants them to seem sad, so maybe he can transform them, alleviate the sadness, get them to gleam the way they do when an RPG flies over the hood of her Land Rover. "Okay. You go to the world's most dangerous places. So what, other than the horror of couture shows and the creeping menace of second-hand smoke, are you doing in Milan, surrounded by B-level models and button-designers?"

"This was just a stopping-off point, a way station, before we head to Sudan. Ironically, though, the danger kind of followed us."

This, and only this, gets Yates to lower his whisky and, ultimately, his morals. He clears his throat, leans forwards and says with a troubled, world-weary voice that he's already ashamed of, "You mean the bombing?"

"Yes."

"Yeah. I saw it."

With this, Deanne sits up and pulls her chair closer to Yates. She leans towards him and her eyes no longer look sad. They look at Yates like he is suddenly not merely a designer of buttons but a danger zone unto himself, and they look hungry, if that's possible. "Do you have a girlfriend or wife?"

Yates thinks of Lauren. He realizes now that he's already got over her more than he's getting over the parts of himself that made her leave. Then he thinks of Marjorie. "No, he says. I don't."

Deanne wanted to know all about it. The café. The colour of the Vespa. The sound of the blast. The look in the girl's eyes. His proximity to the crater in feet. And everything about the bloodied, angry Italian boy. But she waited until they were back in his room in the middle of something too bizarre to be called sex to ask. They'd left the unpopular model and the jaded thrill-seekers at yet another bar – the name of which Yates cannot remember – without saying goodbye. And now she really wants to know everything, to experience it as if she were there in the Galleria. She's turning it into some kind of vicarious role play, foreplay, psychodrama and Yates is too tired to protest, too disoriented to care.

What colour were his eyes? His clothes? Uh-huh. Did you think he was going to die? That's it, button man. What did you do when you got there? Was the adrenalin pumping through you? Were you excited? Or afraid? Uh-hum. Mmm-hmm. Yes. Yeah. That's it. Tell me again.

When he loses track, or tries to direct her back to reality, she stops thrusting, squeezing, clawing. If he skimps on the concrete details of the terror, she shuts down, skimps on everything. So he has no choice but to give in, to run with it, to lie. *Of course I felt a rush. Tearing through my entire being. Every fibre, every nerve. Electric. This kinetic thrill, ramping up, heightened, sustained, absolutely devoid of fear.*

And then what? And then what?

I guess in a way it was just like the riot.

The what?

The soccer riot in Johannesburg...

Oh. My. God. That's it. That's the button, button man.

Many Questions, Four Aspirins and a Simple Misunderstanding

His first thought when he opens his eyes to two pistols trained on his face is, *Please, shoot me.* One of the pistol-pointing men says something in Italian to someone behind him. Another man steps forwards and looks at him. Yates blinks his eyes closed, then tries again. But it's still two men with guns, neither of whom seems willing to do him the favour of putting him out of his misery. He hears others in the background, presumably going through his things, but he's not about to try to look. Next he hears a woman crying from the area of his private gym. One more reason to want to be dead: Deanne from Branson. Now that he's involved her in a life-and-death thrill ride like this, he thinks, he'll never be able to get rid of her.

"Get up, Mr Yates." In formal, perfect English. From a man without a gun, in a very nice suit. Yates holds up his hands, signifying surrender, peace, guilt. He sits up. Blood drains from his head, leaving room only for pain. "We will need to take you with us. We have some questions."

They watch him stand with his hands still raised. One of the men with a gun picks Yates's jeans off the floor, sneers at their name-brand label and flips them to Yates. Then the wrinkled black T-shirt. Yates puts them on, combs his hair with his hand. If there's a mugshot, it won't be pretty. From the gym area he can hear Deanne talking fast and quietly. Hears her say, *Don't even know his first name. Button-designer. Bomber. Drunk.* On the other side of the room someone is packing up his computer, his cellphone, his briefcase.

They lead him unhandcuffed outside to the lift, down to the lobby and outside into the back of a red Fiat sedan with tan leather seats. One of the pistol-brandishers gets in beside him. The other gets in the driver's seat. After saying a few words to those who will be left behind, perhaps to search, perhaps to deal with Deanne, the man whom Yates assumes is the leader gets in the front passenger seat and lights a cigarillo. He turns on the CD player – Uncle Tupelo – and looks out of the window without so much as glancing back at Yates.

Two songs later they slow down in front of an ancient-looking tenement block. The driver pushes a code on a box on the visor, and two massive arched wooden doors automatically open upon a small courtyard and a circular driveway with a fountain in the middle. Maybe it's because he has a massive guilt- and alcohol-induced hangover, or maybe it's because he believes that he's done absolutely nothing wrong, or because, at this moment, he doesn't give a shit about anything any more – but Yates is more confused than afraid.

The apparent leader opens the door, says, "Please," and Yates climbs out.

"May I ask where I am?"

"A location we use for questioning."

"How about my Miranda Rights? My right to an attorney? Et cetera?"

The man smiles. "Mr Yates. Under the circumstances, you should be happy that you are alive. In fact, had you not been American, and such a recently visible one at that, you might have become the victim of some people who would not have been unhappy if you had tragically and mysteriously died in your sleep last night."

They lead him up a narrow stone stairway to a second-floor parlour. He's steered to a large distressed leather easy chair, into which he drops like an exhausted child. After a moment, he turns to one of the guards, points to his head and grimaces. "Aspirin, *per favore.*"

The guard looks at his boss, who nods. When the guard reaches the door, Yates calls, "Excuse me," then holds up four fingers. "*Per favore.*"

Finally the lead detective sits on a straight-backed wooden chair across from Yates. "I am Detective Marinaccio," he says. "Intelligence. I assume, Mr Yates, that you know why you are here."

Yates sighs. When he rolls his eyes he almost vomits, and then loses track of where he is. "The space hotel?" he hears himself say. "Which can hardly be blamed on me."

Marinaccio tilts his head, widens his eyes.

"I mean they paid me handsomely. The Russians. Their 'people'. To do what I do. Which, granted, is not always pretty. But Jesus..."

Marinaccio reaches inside his jacket, takes out a cigarillo and lights it.

"Why?" Yates continues, unprompted. "Was there an Italian citizen on board? I didn't think there was, but I wasn't really paying attention."

"I wasn't talking about the space hotel. Perhaps we'll get to that later."

"Then, Johannesburg?"

Marinaccio looks confused, then nods. "Yes, I've been made aware of Johannesburg. Is that in any way related to this?"

"The soccer riot? Or the missing prostitute – who technically is no longer missing. I just can't divulge her whereabouts."

Marinaccio coughs once. Then, unable to suppress it, he breaks into a fit of small half-chokes, half-coughs. From the guard who has just returned with Yates's aspirin, Marinaccio grabs the water glass, takes a sip, then passes it to Yates. As Yates washes down his four aspirins with the rest of the water, Marinaccio sits back down, seemingly recomposed. "I was actually referring to your speech in Johannesburg and how it relates to your more recent actions. We can get back to the riot and the missing woman later."

"And the space hotel? I feel strongly about that."

"Yes. But the speech?"

"Yes, the speech. You could say that the speech led to all of this. It opened the door to the other stuff. Faith B. Popcorn. Johnson and Johnson. Brand America. The madman who lives amongst the icebergs, and the hideous daughter of the head of the Greenlandic Mafia."

"Greenlandic Mafia?"

"I'm sure it doesn't hold a candle to your Cosa Nostra, if it exists at all. But either way she can't be trusted. Very promiscuous, despite her grotesque appearance. Just ask the Peace Corps deserter and the Tulip Man."

"Tulip Man? Is this an alias?"

Yates laughs. "Yeah. I gave it to him. It's all in my field report – which, to tell you the truth, is an absolute untruth. Totally made up to get them off my back. The covert government guys, not the Greenlanders."

Marinaccio rubs his eyes. "Okay. Can we refocus on your activity in Johannesburg? Did it play a link in your ultimately coming to Milan?"

"Well, at first I thought that would be my last gig. Between the space hotel and the soccer riot and the soon-to-be-missing prostitute and Lauren – my girlfriend of six years – dumping me, I'd just about had it. I wanted out. But it turned out to be the opposite. The Jo'burg gig made me even more in demand. Which led to this Milan assignment – which, I have to admit, I declined, but the more I resisted, the more money they threw at me."

"The more *who* threw?"

"To tell you the truth, I don't even know. I don't get involved in those things. I have a special agent who takes care of this type of assignment. It sounds cold but I always found it best if he just tells me where to go and the specific deliverables of the contract so I can just focus on doing my thing."

"And this 'thing' you do, Mr Yates. Does it not weigh on your conscience? Does it not weigh on you in any manner?"

Yates stares at the wall and thinks for a moment. Then his eyes widen, as if he's finally figured something out. "Of course it does. It disgusts me. Which is why I'm trying to get out. This isn't about what I did at the *Last Supper*, is it?"

"The *Last Supper*?"

"I know, even though it looks like crap, that it's a great work of art, but I don't think what I did can be categorized in any way as defacement."

"You defaced the *Last Supper*?"

"That's what I'm saying. No. I took a piece of mortar off the floor. Long story short, it's part of a private joke I've got going with my ex-girlfriend."

Marinaccio starts to speak, but catches himself. He stands and rubs his chin.

Yates decides to fill in the dead air. "So in answer to your question, Detective Marinaccio, it does weigh on me. All of it. Which is why I am trying to get out of it. Or at least only take on gigs I can live with morally. Ethically."

"So your Milan 'gig'... You can live with this? On all of those levels?"

Yates looks down at his hands. On the back of his left palm is the garish orange stamp of a club to which he doesn't remember going last night. But, just now, he does remember: Chandler dancing in an elevated cage, sewing fake buttons on his overalls, making kangaroo hops for the Aussies. Some kind of herbal absinthe shot. *Then* leaving with Deanne.

"Is something amusing, Mr Yates?"

"Sorry. Yes. To tell you the truth, this is one of the few assignments that I have no problem with... one that is in fact closest to my heart."

"Really."

"Absolutely. In fact, it's just a variation on what I did in Johannesburg. Just a few tweaks to make it that much more powerful and relevant for this specific target." With this, Marinaccio mashes his cigarillo out and steps towards Yates. He clenches his teeth and starts to raise his right fist, but stops himself.

Yates leans back, raises his hands. "Whoa, Detective. Have I done something to offend?"

"Offend? You repulse me. You... filth."

"*Filth* is a little rough. I know that what I do isn't for everyone, but let's face it, at the end of the day, as much as you and I may have some quibbles over it, there's a fair amount of people who truly enjoy the essence of what I do. In fact there's a fairly popular website devoted entirely to my recent work."

When Yates comes to he is still in the leather chair. His head still throbs, and in his mouth he can taste his own blood. It takes a moment to focus, to orient himself to the extent that he can. Across the room he recognizes the detective, ice on his right hand, glaring at him. The detective is being comforted by a new face, a female who puts her hand on Marinaccio's shoulder one more time before turning and heading over to address Yates.

"Mr Yates. I am Detective Spinetti." Yates flinches when Spinetti holds out her hand, then he slowly shakes it. "I assure you that you will not be harmed any more. We just want to know the truth."

"Which I've been telling. I would definitely like to make a phone call. To my lawyer. My embassy. My..." his voice trails off. Who? My ex-girlfriend? My crazy college friend in Ilulissat? My Johannesburg limo driver? He suddenly remembers that Marjorie was supposed to call him for his itinerary. Their itinerary.

"This is not possible right now," says Spinetti, who is thin and short and has dark sacks under dark eyes. "What we are interested in are your actions here in Milan. Your contacts. The places you've seen. We want you to take us step by step through your actions of yesterday, Mr Yates."

"Okay. Yesterday, I think, I travelled from Greenland to Milan. Checked into my hotel. Changed. Took a walk. Saw the *Last Supper*. Stopped at a bar, then a café in the Galleria. Caffé Fiero. Saw the bomb explode. Tried to help a wounded kid to no avail. Went back to the hotel. Took a bubble bath. Ate. Continued drinking. Read a little. Checked my emails. Passed out for I don't know how long. When I woke up I went to the hotel bar. Then other bars I don't remember so well. At some point I met the woman to whom I think you've been speaking in the other room. Nice girl. A little twisted sexually. Apparently she accompanied me to my suite. After that I'd rather not say what happened."

"Tell me more about the bombing. You were there when it happened?"

"Yes. I was at Caffé Fiera or Fiero, on my second Campari-and-soda. I forgot. Between the *Last Supper* and the café I had two Peronis at the other bar."

"Do you always drink so much, Mr Yates?'

"I usually only drink when I'm happy, but I've had a trying week. In fact, I think I'm still quite drunk right now."

"Tell me what you saw and did at the café."

"I drank. People watched. I pretended I was Leonardo looking for a Judas model for the *Last Supper*."

"Judas?"

"It was easier than you'd think."

"The bombing..."

"Yes. The girl on the Vespa. She drove right past me. Maybe I'm only imagining it this way now, but I swear she looked right at me, like we shared some secret knowledge."

"Did you?"

"I'll never know. Seconds later she exploded."

"You saw this?"

"Couldn't miss it. Right into the pack of demonstrators."

"Anti-American?"

"Yes."

"Did this bother you, their cause?"

"I kind of wondered why they felt how they did, but didn't have time to take it any further."

"Are you a patriotic man, Mr Yates?"

Yates stops to think and finally sees where Spinetti is going. Where Marinaccio was going. In his state, it has taken him a while finally to grasp that he is being questioned about the bombing, and only now does it occur to him that it might not be as a witness, but as a participant. "Yes, I am. But not enough to kill a bunch of idealistic teenagers exercising their freedom of speech. Look, I don't want to talk any more without a lawyer if you're trying to connect me to that."

"What did you do after the explosion?"

Yates pauses. Inhales and exhales. "I ran towards it."

"Really. Why, when most ran away?"

"I felt like I could help."

"Or assess the damage?"

"No. You could assess pretty well from the café. It was horrible." He opens his mouth to continue, then stops and folds his arms.

"Your woman friend back at the hotel says that you found the whole thing rather thrilling."

No response.

"She says that you told her last night that your skin tingled when the girl on the Vespa passed."

"Not true. I may have told her that, I'm ashamed to say, to kind of turn her on. But not true."

"And that you felt a 'mad adrenaline rush' when the girl went into that crowd and detonated."

"Yes and no. It's what she wanted to hear."

"The way she's been crying, this is hard to believe."

"Oh really. Do you know that she goes out of her way to find war zones? That rather than go to Disney World on spring break she goes to Terror World. Kabul. Chechnya. Any trail that has bloody footprints on it, she wants to blaze."

"Are you a designer of buttons, Mr Yates?"

He starts to laugh, then holds his head, shakes his head. Everything hurts. "No, I am not a designer of buttons."

"What do you do for a living, Mr Yates?"

"I give speeches, lectures."

"About what?"

"About what's next. In business, mostly. But also other topics. Recreation. Art. Politics. Relationships."

"Terror."

"Sure. It's an aspect of all of the above, one of the foremost, if not the galvanizing global preoccupation."

"Is it yours?"

"Contemplating it. Trying to understand its roots and how to avoid, prevent or learn from it – yes. Plotting or committing it – no."

Spinetti lights a cigarette. Offers one to Yates, who declines. "Are you Milanese *Polizia*? Or like the Italian FBI, or Interpol?"

She waves him off, exhales. It's a non-topic. "Tell me about Nostradamus, Mr Yates. Your obsession with him."

"I'm hardly obsessed."

"Do you feel a special kinship with him?"

"You mean, do I feel a delusional identification with him? No. Do I have a passing interest? Yes."

She hands him the two books he had in his room. "And to address this passing interest, you found it necessary to have two books on him delivered to your room less than an hour after taking part in a terrorist act?"

"Witnessing, Detective. Not participating in. I..." he stops, determined to talk no more.

"Tell me about Mabus."

Yates thinks. Mabus. The third Antichrist. His happy-hour date and the star of his emails. To Spinetti, he says nothing. Yates is a rock.

"How about N-II-30?"

Nothing.

"That's funny. It's highlighted in your email inbox. From N-II-30. Shall I read it again?"

He shakes his head, but she reads it anyway. "Nothing?"

"Nothing."

"But Mabus... no connection. What about this?" She hands him the crumpled scrap of hotel stationery that had been in his jeans. He reads it.

MABUS Caffé Fiera. 5p.

Yates slumps back in the chair, puts his hands behind his head.

"Who is Mabus, Mr Yates?"

"I don't know."

"Second century. Quatrain 62: *Mabus will soon die, then will come a horrible undoing of people and animals.*"

He shakes his head.

"Why is a message from him on your hotel phone?"

"If it is, I never got it."

"How about your cellphone?"

"We were going to meet for a drink at Caffé Fiera.

Someone I met in Johannesburg had given him my number. People are referred to me all the time."

"You were to meet at the exact place and moment that a bomb went off."

"He called me. And we never did meet."

"Killing three young people."

He glides his hands from the back of his head over his eyes. Spinetti motions to one of the other detectives. He steps forwards and hands her Yates's cellphone. She presses two buttons and hands it to Yates. On his LCD screen he sees the message ID from Mabus at the head of a video attachment. Before he presses Play, he looks around the room, already knowing what he will see. And for the most part, he's right: the girl on the Vespa looks at him as she rides through the frame. Just as Yates had followed her with his eyes, the video camera follows her slow, steady journey into the crowd, and death. But unlike the news footage that he'd seen today, which shook and spiralled and broke up as the cameraperson ran away, this footage stays locked on the epicentre of the blast, focused, solid, unflinching. It even does a slow zoom and then a widening pan of the carnage. At the end of the clip, Yates sees the one part that he had not imagined: his place in it. He sees himself near the crater, backing away, then turning to look back, presumably towards the boy outside the *gelateria*. Then he moves away quickly, with an expression on his face that can only be described as guilty. When he replays the entire clip, he slows down the beginning and sees himself sitting at the café before the Vespa passes, checking his watch, waiting for his next drink, thinking of Leonardo, Judas, Thomas and Mabus.

When it ends, he holds the phone out for anyone to take. Spinetti grabs it, hands it back to the other detective. "Are you a futurist, Mr Yates?"

"Yes."

A pause. "Are you a terrorist, Mr Yates?'

"No."

"OK. Then, one more thing: is there room for a futurist, Mr Yates, in a terrified, compromised, morally ambiguous world?"

"I don't know."

"A world in which everyone has the capacity to be a Strangelove?"

Pardon

He once helped a record label create a lifelike digital synthespian version of an immensely talented female R&B singer who was deemed too fat for mass-market consumption and whose subsequent debut CD went platinum. Once, a very rich man paid him to moderate a focus group in which twelve people handled and discussed at length the very rich person's personal belongings while the very rich person sat alone on the other side of a two-way mirror doing god knows what. He once took a meeting with the head of a production company interested in developing an adult cartoon superhero based on the continuing adventures of Yates, the Futurist.

They don't put him in a cell. Instead he is led to a tastefully decorated room with a plush leather lounge chair and a soft-cushioned, floral-patterned couch. Over the fireplace mantel is a large flat-screen plasma TV bordered by two very old vases. An old, double-hung window looks out onto the courtyard he'd been driven into, it seems, about a century ago. He takes off his shoes and stretches out on the couch. His headache has diminished somewhat, but it has been replaced by the stress of a potential life in prison and the pain of a stiffening, perhaps broken jaw.

After some time he is awakened by the soft tumbling of the door lock. There had been other noises, staccato conversations in Italian down the hall, the slamming of car doors in the courtyard, a distant siren that may have been real, may have been a dream. But only the door handle stirs him to open his eyes. He's already surmised that the next person through the door is going to interrogate him further, move him to a real cell that will be a shocking contrast to the antique elegance that surrounds him. Perhaps they're here to take him on a gallows walk for the international media – FUTURIST TERRORIZES THE PRESENT! Or maybe it will be someone to rescue him.

But Yates is wrong on all counts. Instead, through the door walks a middle-aged, overweight man in a stained orange Hilary Duff concert T-shirt, plaid boxer shorts and blue flip-flops. To Yates he gives barely a nod; it is the flat-screen that is the focus of his attention. He powers it up at the console and takes the remote back to the easy chair. "AC Milan," he says, pointing to the soccer game that has come on, more as a self-affirmation than as an explanation or a conversation-starter. Yates wonders if the man is a plant, a fellow terrorist, or somebody's down-on-his-luck cousin who rents the spare room down the hall. Or maybe he is a hallucination, a dream. But Yates has never had a dream that needed subtitles before, or one in which another man sits in an easy chair, scratching his balls and mumbling Italian epithets at an apparently ineffective midfielder. Finally he decides, after the man farts with great gusto and apparent pride, that this man is a plant, and that he is being subjected to an experimental form of torture. He closes his eyes and braces himself for the excruciating small talk that never comes.

When sleep returns and he does dream, it is first a simple vignette of Marjorie sleeping on his hotel bed. Then he sees the boy from the *gelateria* bleeding on the other side of the bed. Then he sees his dream self standing in the doorway watching them both, and he sees that his side is bleeding as well, that he is dying from the same wound as the boy.

This time it is Marinaccio who awakens him. He opens the door, then closes it and approaches the couch. The TV is off, and there is no sign of the grotesque soccer fan. On his right hand, Marinaccio now wears a thick ace bandage wrap that he tugs at as he stands over Yates. *Here we go,* Yates thinks. *The bad cop, back to finish off what he started.*

He sits up and holds up one hand. "Look, Detective. I can assure you. I swear, I had nothing to do with that bombing other than the fact that someone apparently wanted me to see it."

"Get up."

Yates stands, rolls the kinks out of his neck. "What happened earlier was a misunderstanding. Clearly I was still drunk. I'd be more than happy to sit down and tell you all I know about Mabus – which is little more than two phone calls and a couple of emails, which I'm sure you've already traced. And I want you to know that what I saw in the Galleria disturbs me greatly."

Marinaccio considers Yates for a moment, then turns and walks back to the door, where he stops with his back to Yates. He says, "You are free to go."

"Excuse me?"

"Please leave immediately. Your belongings will be in your hotel room." Yates tries to talk, but Marinaccio is already gone. Yates puts on his shoes and walks to the wide-open door. He steps into the hallway and listens for the others, but the building is silent. He finds a bathroom, urinates and bends over the sink to splash cold water on his face. The bottom of his right cheek is swollen, but not badly, and it is not yet visibly bruised.

As he steps out onto the street, he squints into the bright sunlight. He stops to gather himself, but he realizes that there is nothing to gather, nothing to do but walk and get oriented. And besides, when he stands still he has the sneaking suspicion that he is in the crosshairs of an assassin's rifle, so it's best to keep moving. What day it is or what time it is he cannot tell you. Only that it is daytime. A sunny day, probably morning, judging by the birds – in, presumably, Milan. A day in which, presumably, he is to give a speech before several hundred global-thought leaders about how little he or they actually know about anything.

Perhaps he should update it a bit so it will start with our hero being released from a phantom interrogation – not as a suspect but, as the police say, a person of interest – for a horrible crime he did not commit but to which, curiously, he was a witness. Perhaps it should follow him lock-jawed and penniless, strolling past the opening eyes of a city market where an old woman is stacking tomatoes on her stall. Where a bakery infuses the air with the smell of fresh bread and a hint of sweeter things inside. Perhaps he should mention how the businessmen sipping thimbles of espresso in a narrow coffee shop wedged between chic boutiques instantly regard him as an outsider, a stranger, a threat to their centuries-old ritual of place. Perhaps he could take a moment to articulate how he knows that they know that he does not belong, how he is certain that his presence at their slender chrome counter would fuck everything to hell. How he knows that they know that he is American.

Or maybe he should start the speech not discussing the specifics of place but rather the liberating emptiness he feels precisely because he is no longer of this or any place. Maybe he should describe the absolute bliss he now feels because he has no sense of time, no sense of urgency, no sense of family, or guilt, or fear. No love, no money, no plan, no real destination, no place to call home, no future. It's a wonderful thing, he should tell them, when no one knows who you are, or why you're here – including, to get a touch philosophical, a tad sentimental, yourself.

On the other hand, he thinks, rounding the corner of another unknown street, stomach grumbling, headache raging, this feeling isn't such a wonderful thing after all, but a terrifying, depressing, pathetic thing. It all depends how you look at it. As he stares down the length of the avenue, he can just make out the far-off spires of the Duomo, which he knows is fairly close to his hotel. So, no longer technically lost, and with a fixed point as a goal, he begins to walk with a purpose, and to dismiss all of his previous thoughts, all of that liberating emptiness bullshit. All of that terrified, depressing nonsense. Soon his head begins to clear, and he is now certain that this is indeed morning, and that this is definitely Milan. And, unless he lost a day in the cushy holding room, he certainly does have a speech to give this afternoon. He decides that it will be his last speech for a while. He'll speak, then he will absolutely go on hiatus. No, he'll call it, for anyone who cares, a sabbatical, which sounds a hell of a lot more well intentioned than a hiatus. You take a sabbatical to embark on a spiritual journey to the Himalayas, to seek enlightenment at the feet of the Dalai Lama, or finally to learn to play guitar. Bad sitcoms go on hiatus. People who watch the Game Show Network and don't bathe every day are on hiatus.

Yes, thinks Yates, his steps surer, his headache easing, the sniper paranoia all but gone, *I will give this speech – not the internal philosophical shit, but one that starts with the question about there being room for a futurist in a terrified, compromised, morally ambiguous world. Then I will seamlessly weave it in to a modified Jo'burg Coalition of the Clueless bit with a Milanese twist. Then I will tell Johnson and Johnson that I am through with them. Then I will call Marjorie and get on a plane and go on a well-deserved hiatus.*

I mean sabbatical.

Then, on via San Vittore, something churns in him again, and he is disgusted with himself. Again. At least with the self of the last twelve blocks. He is disgusted that he can be thinking heroic thoughts one day, one minute, and then, in the face of adversity, turn so weak so quickly. He is disgusted with his exceptionally acute instinct for avoidance and self-preservation. He is ashamed of how willing he is to bail out and run from crises: Lauren, Marjorie, the space station, the boy in the Galleria. From anything that requires him to step up, take action, to say no, to claim responsibility. And not to be such a pussy. Just ask Blevins. Or his father.

While several blocks ago he saw his situation as an excuse to cut his losses and run, he now sees it as a wake-up call. As an opportunity not to be such a jerk and perhaps do some good. To tell Johnson and Johnson to fuck off – yes, that's a constant. A must-do. But also, to get Marjorie out of Johannesburg, to let go of Lauren and admit that she was right, to apologize to Blevins, give his parents a call and maybe even a surprise visit, and then to use his talent to do some good in the world, to help people not by dispensing false hope, but enlightening truth.

He stops to catch his breath, to think this through, and because part of him fears that if he walks another two blocks he'll change his mind all over again. He puts his hands on his hips and looks around. He can no longer see any part of the Duomo, but he knows he is closer than he was. To his left, a young mother walking an infant in a Dolce & Gabbana pram meets his eye and does not glare or look away. She smiles, and the Futurist smiles back. He watches her cross the street and stop in front of what looks like a museum. He puts his hand over his eyes to block the sun and sees that it is not just any museum. The sight of his latest epiphany, perhaps his tenth in the last hour, is the Leonardo da Vinci Museum of Science and Technology. *Surely this is a sign*, he thinks. He didn't even know that Leonardo had ever gone to Milan, but he's been seeing his fingerprints everywhere. The fingerprints of mankind's most enlightened genius. Granted, Leonardo's fingers rarely finished what they started, but still... he was a man who challenged everything, never settled, always sought to break new ground and embraced the future. Yates starts back for the hotel, convinced that this was indeed a sign, this museum dedicated to that mind, that man, that spirit. This museum which, the Futurist doesn't happen to notice, is closed for renovation.

Back in his room, his phone, laptop and luggage sit exactly where he had left them the day before. He finds not one but three messages from Marjorie on the hotel phone. She has/had passport in hand, is/was excited to go, and is/was wondering where he is/was – and finally, she is/was worried about him. There is no call-back number, so all that he can do is email David and urge her to try him again. The revisions to the speech come easily. Substitute this for that. Lose the part about the prostitute. Insert the part about Leonardo and Judas. Keep most of the Coalition of the Clueless stuff, not because it's what they want to hear, but because even on a second and third reading, even after everything that has happened since then, he still believes it. In fact, he decides it's one of the only true things he's ever written for public consumption, the only thing that he can actually live with.

When he's done, he showers and dresses in his cream Prada speech suit with a black T-shirt underneath. He still has several hours before he's scheduled to appear at the convention centre. And curiously, besides Marjorie, no one has left any messages for him. None on the cell and none on the hotel phone and none waiting for him at the front desk, where the staff now regard him with a combination of fascination and fear. A check of his laptop reveals the same cultivated emptiness. No emails and not a trace of any of the old Mabus or Nostradamus entries. Surely they've been uploaded onto the systems of any number of government agencies, all trying to determine (if they haven't already) his mystery pen pal's whereabouts and identity. For a while, as he gathers his things to leave, he thinks about Mabus and Nostradamus. For a while he tries to make sense of his mystery liberators and his mystery captors. For a very short while he even thinks of Deanne from Branson, who at the end of the day got the perilous erotic international thrill ride of her dreams. He thinks of all this, but not for long, because he has no clue, not even a partial explanation for any of it. Because he hopes that if he stops thinking about them, they will go away and leave him alone.

Before he leaves, despite the fact that it's 7 a.m. Eastern Standard Time, he calls his parents' home in Pennsylvania. The machine picks up, and his mother's recorded voice says *Thanks for calling the Yateses.* Then his father's voice says, awkwardly, *Sorry we can't come to the phone just now, but if you leave a message...* Then mom brings it home... *we'd be delighted to call you back at our earliest convenience.* After the beep, which lasts a good five seconds, Yates says nothing. They had never had an answering machine before, and while its very existence has rattled him, it is the cheerily choreographed message that has rendered him flummoxed. They had to have planned it, he thinks. They probably even had a few rehearsals, a few dry runs with his mother giving his father his cue. He pictures his mother all excited about it and his father only doing it because it made her happy. He thinks of them checking it when they get back from running errands. From the hairdresser. The hardware store. The doctors. He imagines the sound of the phone ringing in the empty house and their digitally recorded voices echoing off the walls of the only home he ever had, and it makes him want to cry.

Back outside, under a pale blue Milanese sky, he gets into a taxi cab and hands the driver a scrap of paper with an address researched and handwritten by the concierge. Ospedale San Raffaele is not far away from the hotel, but he asks the driver to stop at an electronics store first. Inside, he finds a salesman who speaks passable English. From under a glass counter the man takes out an iPod music player. Yates nods, *yes*, then hands over Johnson and Johnson's credit card. In the back of the taxi, he connects the new iPod to his laptop with a firewire and shifts the entire contents of his music library – from Beethoven to Wilco to Johnny Cash and the Meat Puppets to Radiohead, João Gilberto, Loretta Lynn, *William Shatner Live* and his nephew Joey's garage band. Thousands of songs, hundreds of artists, each with some kind of personal connection, some kind of visceral relevance to Yates, revealing some aspect of his global, sentimental, badass, funky, classical, crude, manic, progressively nuanced soul. Copied for the pleasure of another. Kind of like sex, what the two small machines are engaged in. Digital sex. Cultural sex.

It's the only thing Yates could think of, to show him.

If the boy is startled by Yates's presence, he doesn't show it. He's laying flat on his bed, a tube at his side draining fluid from the wound to some hidden place beneath the bed. Playing on the wall-mounted TV is a twelve-year-old episode of a spy show starring Pamela Anderson going kung-fuey on a group of black-suited secret-agent dudes: America at its unapologetic, pre-breast-reduction best.

What Yates wants to do is pull up a chair beside the boy, a captive audience if there ever was one, and explain himself. What he wants to do is explain everything in his mind and in their world. To tell him that things are not that simple. Not that pure. That there are secret loopholes beneath every principle. Contradictions to every premise. He wants to tell him that it's all so unbelievably complicated, and that all we can do is try to sort it out, try to share what little we truly know with each other. But he knows that is not possible, knows that even if he could articulate it, in perfect Italian, the boy would not listen. So instead he hands the boy the box from the electronics store. The iPod. Designed in California. Assembled in China. Purchased in Italy. With components outsourced from who knows where. Filled with the music of Yates's terrified, compromised, morally ambiguous world. The boy considers the box and, recognizing the ubiquitous logo, opens it. The only sound in the room is the muffled action of machines feeding and draining his damaged body. When the boy sees that it is a music player, he looks at Yates. Sceptically, Yates thinks, then quizzically. Then the boy just looks at him without any hint of emotion. Finally Yates holds out his hands and the boy, constricted by an IV feed in his right wrist and the drain on his left side, hands the player back to Yates.

Because this is the way he saw it happening, the way he planned it and had hoped it would be, setting it up is easy. He fixes the earphones on the boy's head and powers the device up. When everything is in place, the boy nods. And, rather than selecting one specific, particularly poignant or appropriate song, artist, or theme for the boy to hear, to digest, to learn from, the Futurist selects *shuffle*, because whatever song comes up is a part of him, really.

Chandler is waiting near the lift doors at the end of the hall. They nod from a distance, then Yates, when he gets closer, speaks. "Here for a little cosmetic surgery?" He'd like to finish this thought with the man's name but Yates can't remember Chandler's name at all. In fact, he's surprised he even remembers his face.

"No. My only..." Chandler holds up his fingers as ironic quotation marks. "'operation' today was to get your ass away from Italian intelligence."

"Jesus. I thought you were a model."

"I am. A pretty good one, too. But I supplement it with spycraft."

"Like *Zoolander*."

"Never heard that one before."

"I'm sorry. But I don't remember your name."

Chandler turns the volume down. "That's probably for the best. I can't believe you left with that husky girl from Missouri."

"Muscular. Not husky. So who got me out? The Johnsons?"

They get on the lift. Chandler pushes 0. The doors start to close, catch, then open again. "Bloody hell." Chandler pushes 0 three more times, then another button twice.

"That's *Open Door*."

"Oh." Chandler steps back and it finally closes.

"So. The Johnsons?"

"They could have left you to hang there."

"But I didn't do anything."

"Maybe. But according to them, the Italians have enough to detain you indefinitely. Guilty or innocent, they have enough to brand your nice but slightly dated Prada suit there with a big scarlet letter T for terrorist for the rest of your professional life."

"Well, tell them thank you then, but I'm done with them. I'm taking a sabbatical starting tomorrow." The door opens to the lobby. Outside, near the entrance, someone steps out of the back seat of a car bleeding from the neck. "I told them as much yesterday."

Chandler reaches in his pocket for some lip balm, rolls it on. "You know, Yates. All they have to do it press *Rewind* and you're back where you're started, with Italian teenage blood on your hands."

Yates stretches up onto his toes to look for a taxi. "Listen, just tell them no. I can't do it. I'm not cut out for this shit. Obviously I'm unstable, a terribly high risk."

"Don't fuck with what you don't understand, Yates."

He stops looking for the taxi. "Okay. What do they want?"

"For now, relatively little. They want you to continue your correspondence with them. With Mabus. With Nostradamus. With the Pet Psychic, should he call. Give your speeches, continue your journey."

"That's it?"

"Again, for now. But I guarantee that there will be more. Probably a test at first, then something more substantial, I'm sure. They always do that. Did for me, anyway."

Yates tilts his head, looks at Chandler.

"You think anyone actually volunteers to do this shit?"

A taxi pulls up. Yates opens the door, then looks back at Chandler. "Jesus Christ. What if I refuse?"

"What if I say that Interpol, the CIA, the Milanese PD and a very fucking disturbing assortment of hit people, hit men and/or women, persons of hit, would be on your ass before you can say, 'I went to Milan and all I got was a roll in the sack with an ugly fat chick from Branson, Missouri'?"

Yates gets in the cab, says something to the driver, then opens the window. "You can't help me?"

Chandler rolls his spectacular blue eyes.

"Where should I go?"

"Give your speech. For now it's up to you. Just be ready for the call."

The Mamanuca Group

He once lay prone in a Speedo on a bed of Bimini palm fronds for a *GQ* fashion layout called "The Boys of Tomorrow". He once told a women's Bible group at a military installation in Huntsville, Alabama that the average American mother would drop a *nucular* weapon in a heartbeat if it would save one hair on her child's head, and received a standing ovation. Once, before a national gathering of the American Association of Retired People, he predicted, with no scientific support, that within ten years the life expectancy of the average American man would be "in the hundreds", and that "midlife crises will not arrive until you're in your late seventies – leading to a rush on cherry-red Porsches with prescription-lens windshields", and got a standing ovation from those who could stand.

Lately, on commercial flights like this one, while staring at the locked cockpit door from the first-class bulkhead seat, wiping in-flight germs from his hands with a complimentary hot towel while disease runs rampant on the other side of the curtain in economy, he thinks of a version of this scenario: two groups of terrorists of polar-opposite ideologies converge in the cockpit of the same hypothetical plane at the same moment. They all have the same type and amount of weapons. They are all not just willing to die a martyr's death, but absolutely intent on it, and all seem determined to do just that, to kill each other, until someone – the pilot on his last flight before retiring, the housewife who minored in psychology, the gay flight attendant who majored in international relations with a minor in cosmetology – points out that once the bloodshed starts it is likely that they all will die, and there is a fifty per cent chance that their martyrdom will be falsely attributed to their opponent's cause. Which would be a damned shame.

One version of Yates's fable has them all shrugging and, seeing the unresolvable nature of their conflict, returning to their seats to enjoy unlimited, freshly baked cookies and champagne courtesy of the folks in first class until they touch down in Topeka. Another version has the hijackers fighting over the radio handset to claim responsibility as the plane spirals out of control, finally crashing through the roof of a non-denominational church. There's another version too. He just can't remember it right now.

The flight attendant takes his soiled towel with a pair of tongs, as if it's riddled with anthrax, Ebola, or some disease that exists only because a spider monkey once had intimate relations with a chicken somewhere in China. He shuts off his reading light and reclines his seat until he is laying flat. He fluffs his pillow, closes his eyes and pulls down his sleep visor.

If you could take a trip anywhere on this planet, where would you go, if you knew that on the trip that was to follow you were going to die? Would you go to Paris for the food, the women, the cultural degradation? Or would you go back to reclaim your dignity and your ex-girlfriend in Southern California? To kick in the door on her and her teacher friend, not as the arrogant Futurist, but as a changed man, a man with a newfound respect for the past. For all tenses. But Yates hasn't changed, and he has no use for the past. Besides, the more he thinks of Lauren, the less he misses her. Only his ego does. So where, then? How about Poland, where – as Thomas Friedman of the *Times* recently told him – they actually like Americans, and where, for now, they equate them with freedom and liberty. Friedman called it a geopolitical spa. Sounds good. But Warsaw or Gdansk for your last hurrah, just because they're less likely to hate you? He could visit his parents, the house he grew up in, to make peace, get in touch with his roots, finally ask the questions he always wanted answered. But last time he visited his parents, though he did try somewhat, he experienced none of that. What he got was one uncomfortable moment after another. Helping his father unload lumber off the pickup truck. Driving at what they considered too fast, at thirty miles an hour in a fifty zone, en route to the early-bird at Sizzler. Hearing about the neighbours' children's children. Hooking up a DVD player for them that they didn't want and insisting that they did, that they just didn't know it yet. Thinking of it now, he realizes that it wasn't his parents who made him uncomfortable. He made himself uncomfortable. And only around his parents were the things that made him uncomfortable – mostly the person he had become – harder to ignore, deny and rationalize away. He will call them, he promises himself, and he will try not to be so defensive, so restless, but there's no way he can handle a trip there in this condition.

One more option is the path of redemption on a grand scale. He could go some place where people are truly suffering – cyclone, genocide, famine, war, revolution, take your choice – and help. He could, and maybe would, if he thought for a second that his ambiguous skills – *People of Darfur, Mr Yates is here to give the "What's hot in high-tech" speech that he just gave at Comdex in Vegas* – would make the slightest difference. Even still, he might, if he thought he was going to live a long, healthy life. But he is fairly certain that after this final trip, when they eventually find him, he is going to die.

Hence Fiji. Hence Déjà Vu, a decadent private island in the Mamanuca Group off the coast of Viti Levu.

Why? Because Yates does what he always does. He lets events play out on their own, lets all the options present themselves, then exercises his unparalleled ability to choose what is best for his own well-being. In this instance, rather than make a hard decision, he lets life present him with an easy one. And Fiji is a no-brainer. The chance to go to Fiji came about because he totally nailed the Milan speech this afternoon. He received an ovation when his name was announced, had to wait more than a minute until the chants of *CLUE-LESS! CLUE-LESS!* subsided. They loved the new opening, the "Is there room for a Futurist in a compromised world" bit. They loved the reprise of the Johannesburg speech so much that at times several dozen businessmen in the front rows, some with buttons that said *Coalition of the Clueless, Charter Member*, were reciting the words along with him. In particular, Parker Resnor, the Chairman of the British media empire HiRez, liked Yates's performance so much that he insisted that Yates get on the next plane to Fiji to repeat the whole thing to his top regional managers at an exclusive, highly confidential off-site. Resnor especially liked this new part, which Yates had entirely ad-libbed:

This is why people are so disappointed with the present. We talk so much about how wonderful tomorrow's going to be that, even if it's great, it can't help but be a let-down. Tomorrow is like a summer blockbuster for which the studio starts showing trailers the previous November. By the time it comes to your Cineplex you feel like you've already seen it. All the best lines and biggest explosions.

> *The most provocative coming-out-of-the-water bikini shot. You will already have seen the making-of feature and heard the actors on the press junket talking about what a privilege it was to work with so-and-so and how they all did their own stunts. By the time it comes, you have no desire to hand over $15 and actually sit through it in a cinema. What's happened is you've already experienced something that hasn't happened yet. In fact, when you think of it, the only real reason to go to the movies then isn't to see the feature, but to get a taste of the future, to see the trailer for the next big blockbuster, and to experience that before it happens. And this phenomenon isn't limited to the movies, it is the way we live today. And it is why I encourage you to ignore the hype of what's to come, and to get some popcorn and gummy bears during the previews, and to thoroughly enjoy the feature. In real time. Not in the black hole of expectation.*

Resnor told Yates afterwards that he particularly loved this part "Because it's fresh. It's deconstructionist. Against the grain of all the other motivational corporate bullshit out there". He loved it because he said Yates clearly doesn't give a shit what anyone thinks any more, and only then does real truth come to the surface. It didn't take Yates long to accept Resnor's invitation. The only contingencies are that no one is told he is doing the gig, he is to be paid in cash, and his accommodation is to be booked for him under an alias.

So, technically, he's running. An ideological fugitive. Upriver without authority. Technically he is on hiatus; the sabbatical will have to wait. At least for now. Before he left Milan this afternoon, to cover his tracks, to get a head start, he called the Johnson's travel agent and booked a first-class flight to Rio de Janeiro, departing from Milan in three days. Before he left he also called Campbell's cellphone using a prepaid store-bought phone. He briefly told Campbell about the interrogation, about the incriminating Mabus links, about Chandler (but not Deanne from Branson) and his surprising release from custody. He then gave Campbell the contact information for David the chaperone and urged him to explain what happened to Marjorie and have her get in touch with him as soon as she could.

So, Fiji. So Déjà Vu.

He sleeps most of the twenty-six-hour flight. At one point, somewhere over the North Pacific, en route to a stopover in Sydney, they serve a snack, an omelette, yoghurt and a plate of smoked salmon. It must be breakfast somewhere. He nods hello to the passenger in the seat next to him, a small, impeccably dressed black man around fifty years old whom Yates doesn't remember sitting next to at take-off.

"I envy your ability to sleep," the man says. "For me, nothing. I read until I'm too tired to read, but no sleep."

Yates says, "Sometimes I've tried to drink myself to sleep, but if that doesn't work I'm in trouble, because then I'm too drunk to read or work. Just a wide-awake drunk staring at the pictures in the in-flight magazine."

The man smiles.

"So," Yates continues, nodding towards the pen and paper, then at the flight attendant. Sure. A little breakfast champagne would be nice. "Are you a writer?"

"Yes. A novelist, actually."

"Wow. Going home?"

"Oh, no. I'm going to give a lecture in Sydney. I am from Somalia. Exiled."

Yates takes a bite of his omelette. Chases it with a gulp of Korbel. He had no idea how hungry he was. "Really? What type of novels? Thrillers?"

The man laughs. "No. No thrillers. Although one day I would like to have the liberty of trying to write one. But right now my primary theme is the dilemma of post-colonialism, the break-up of the nation state, factionalism, displacement, departure and return."

As Yates takes this in, as he tries to think up even a remotely intelligent follow-up relating to the break-up of the nation state, he swallows the champagne and slowly slips the paperback legal thriller he has twice tried to get into under his lap blanket. "Goodness," he finally says. "Fascinating."

The novelist, a Nobel finalist last year, waits to see if Yates has more to add, a request for the title of one of his award-winning books, or an enquiry about the plight of his nation, or perhaps an anecdote about his own profession. But no follow-up comes. Finally the displaced gentleman novelist asks Yates, "Do you mind if I enquire about what brings you to this part of the world?"

"Oh, sure. Absolutely. I'm a, uh. I am a salesman." Then Yates pulls his blanket up to his neck and makes a big show of yawning. "I sell buttons," he says, thus ending their conversation.

In Sydney he is met by a chaperone who takes him to a separate terminal, where he boards a private jet for the five-hour flight to Nadi Airport on Viti Levu in the Fiji Islands. From there another chaperone escorts him to a private helicopter pad for the fifteen-minute flight to Déjà Vu. In a blue-black dawn the helicopter rises out of the volcanic basin in which the airport lies, rises high above the surrounding cane fields, then heads west, over the budget hotels that straddle the airport, the thatch-roofed luxury villas along the shore, then across the lightening blue surface of Nadi Bay, towards the Pacific and the Mamanuca Group of reefs and the exclusive, sand-fringed islands. With each island they pass, the chaperone points and calls out its name and nothing more. Yakuilau, Daydream, Malolo, Malololailai.

To Yates, the names have a narcotic effect, each taking him further away from the life he is trying to escape. Wadigi. Qalito. Mociu. And finally, Déjà Vu.

Déjà Vu is not on any map. No true place really is, Resnor told Yates back in Milan, paraphrasing Melville. But Déjà Vu is hardly a true place. It is an invented paradise, a covertly manufactured Eden. It is a 474-acre private island, with a twenty-three bedroom great house, fifteen guest villas, three tennis courts, nine hot tubs, four infinity pools and a full-time staff of 135. Even the island's name is false. Resnor had rejected the native name of Navula as insufficiently magical and came up with the name Déjà Vu because, while the 180th meridian technically cuts through the centre of Fiji's 322 islands, the international date line was allowed to swing east so the entire group could share the same day. Resnor manipulated this longitudinal loophole into an anecdotal creation myth about the name of his island, where – he boasts with tedious frequency in front of guests and staff – it is entirely possible to live the same day twice. Dramatic pause. Especially the good ones.

Before Yates can retire to his villa, the Fijian chaperone first walks him to a sort of registration hut, where he is obliged to sign a series of non-disclosure forms as well as several disclaimers that prohibit him from ever suing Resnor, his publicly held company or any of the guests on the island. In effect, the forms state that you can never tell anyone that you were ever here, and should you experience anything that you might find offensive, harmful or physically or emotionally damaging, long- or short-term, then tough shit. You were here voluntarily, and you were warned. There's nothing you can do about it other than not sign the papers, and in that case get the fuck off my island.

When he's finally inside his guest cottage, he sits on the bed, eases himself back and closes his eyes. But he can't sleep. He's slept for twenty of the last twenty-three hours. So he checks out the room. Balinese fabrics on the bed. A large locally crafted tapa cloth with bright geometric patterns hangs on the far wall. Exotic shells on the teak dresser and nightstands. A long board for the eight-foot swells on the reef on the windward side of the island. And a TV. He's as far away from civilization as he's ever been, in his own hut on a private island, thousands of miles from CNN headquarters in Atlanta, yet Yates can't keep his hand off the remote. Can't help but wonder, *What's on? What's better anywhere else than what I'm experiencing here?* Which turns out to be a big mistake. Because the only thing on right now is the final minutes of life for the remaining two residents on the space hotel. The scroll bar on the bottom of the screen says DEATH IN THE COSMOS. Four people have already died, and two are still alive. Annalise Kinkaid, the cosmetics heiress, is on-screen, staring into the camera, saying the Lord's Prayer, with more grace and dignity than Yates had ever imagined she was capable of. When she is done, the American pilot Rusty Eberheardt slides into frame and says goodbye to his family, his wife and two daughters, and to the child he will never see, due next month. Then to the world he describes the patches of Earth spinning by his cabin window. In conclusion he says that heaven is not way out here, where this doomed spaceship floats; it is in every small inch of the blue-green soul of the planet Earth and the people who live there. When he is done, he drifts away from camera and it seems like the perfect time for them to die, having said their prayers and farewells, having spoken so eloquently and movingly. But they don't die. Annalise Kinkaid starts to sob off-camera, then she begins to scream. Then we hear the pilot, Rusty Eberheardt, tell her to please stop, that she's using up all the oxygen – and Annalise Kinkaid, she tells Rusty to go fuck himself. On live TV. Everywhere. Even Fiji. She tells him to do her a favour and use his last gasps to fix the fucking oxygen generator or else go ahead and die. "And don't think I'm going to strap you neatly into your seat with your hands peacefully folded like you did for the others," she tells him. "Because that's not my job."

A while later, after maybe fifteen minutes of silence, Annalise Kinkaid gets back in front of the camera. She has fixed her eponymous make-up and seems to have calmed down. The pilot is dead, she says, and after the earlier exchange one can only picture his gravity-free face smashed against the trash receptacle, the toilet, the armpit of another corpse. Then Annalise Kinkaid unfolds a piece of paper and begins to read her last will and testament. Her estranged daughter, Chloe Moonstone Kinkaid, is to get everything, with one stipulation: she is to spend whatever it takes to have her attorneys sue with every ounce of their being the following corporations and individuals for ever letting her get onto this fucking deathtrap: the Russian Space Programme, the makers of the Soyuz spacecraft, Morton Thiokol, Chuck Yeager, Tom Wolfe, the editors of *InStyle* magazine, the Boeing company, the Discovery Channel, Sirius Satellite Radio, the makers of Tang, and the shareholders and subsidiaries of Space Hotels Unlimited, including its employees, advertising agencies and every last one of their despicable, misleading spokespeople.

Including Yates. The Futurist.

He presses *Mute*, gets up and walks to the far side of the room. He figures this is as good a time as any to pop the complimentary chilled Dom Perignon that sits in a crystal bucket on top of his hand-carved desk. He tries to drink right out of the bottle, but it foams up in his mouth, runs down his chin. Reluctantly, he takes a fluted glass and pours a proper drink. Next he unpacks his laptop, plugs the AC cord into an outlet and wirelessly logs onto the web. On regular email, nothing unusual – more importantly, nothing from the Johnsons, who presumably think he is still in Milan, humbled, getting ready to fly to Rio. Then he checks the private Hotmail account that only Campbell and David know about. It is empty. He tries to check his cell for messages, but apparently there is no service on the island of Déjà Vu, despite the fact that its owner also owns a global telecommunications company.

A half-hour later on the muted TV they're doing a slide show of photographs of the deceased residents of the space hotel, with dates of birth and death titled beneath. He waits to see if Annalise Kinkaid's photograph comes up, and it does, right after the photograph of the pilot she spent her last breaths humiliating. He feels guilty. And remorseful. But what he feels most is embarrassment, for himself and for all of them. He clicks off the TV, finishes the glass of champagne and reaches for the bottle. He wonders if Campbell had meant it when he had said that he was supposed to be on that flight. Wonders what Campbell makes of all this now. Outside, all he can hear is the soft churn of the surf in the sandy cove below, and every twenty minutes or so the arrival of another helicopter from the big island. Occasionally, businessmen and Fijian valets pass his window en route to their villas and their rooms up in the great house.

He wants to go outside to take a walk, to clear his head, to get a taste of paradise. But he won't. Because even on a remote private island he feels trapped, not yet ready to mingle with the people he is being paid to entertain, people to whom he is sure he will be obliged to lie.

When his email alert sounds, he rushes to see who it's from, but it is only Blevins, sending his regrets about the Space Station. The words seem sincere, but Yates knows better. He can't help but twist the guilt knife into his heart one more time. *Not only are you immersed in the most trivial pursuits of a corrupt society, not only are you ignoring the real issues, you've actually managed to kill someone this time.* That's Yates's interpretation of "Just saw the news about the space hotel. Hope you're okay because I know this must be a difficult time for you".

Yates replies with an all-caps FUCK YOU, and is staring at the screen, waiting for Blevins's patronizing response, when he hears a knock on the door. He doesn't answer it. He stands frozen near the desk holding the half-empty bottle of Dom Perignon. He figures it is a valet who will know his place and go away, but then he hears the voice. Loud, British, privileged. Resnor, whose place is everywhere, and who isn't about to go away.

"Come on, Yates. I know you're in there. Put your clothes on and stop trying to divine the future. The present awaits."

He puts down the bottle and opens the door. There's Resnor, remarkably fit for a fifty-five-year-old man, lean and tanned, shirtless in orange floral board shorts and flip-flops.

"*Bula.*"

"Excuse me?"

"*Bula*. Welcome."

"*Bula* right back at you, Mr Resnor."

"Rez."

"Sure, Rez. I was just trying to get my thoughts together before my talk this afternoon."

"Rubbish." Resnor peeks around Yates to see the desk. "I see you're into the champagne already, a Fijian eye-opener, and I can't say I blame you."

"I'll be fine for later."

"I'm sure you will. They'll love what you have to say, because I'll tell them as much when I introduce you. Besides, they'll be in breakout sessions up until you speak, so they'll be happy to just kick back and listen."

"Great."

"Then it's off to dinner, which I insist you join me at, then a bit of a show I put together for them, for everyone, as a reward."

"What kind of show?"

"You signed the papers at reception, the legal crap?"

"The disclaimers. Yeah."

"Well, you'll see, then. Local customs and ceremonies, for starters. Then some corporate spectacle. Ever since those buggers from Tyco and the like wrecked it for the rest of us by getting caught with their bloody toga parties, you can't do a thing without fear of a lawsuit, a scandal. I remember when a juicy scandal was good for business, but now I have to fly them halfway around the world for a secret unofficial gathering and pay for it out of my own pocket just to have a bit of fun. A bit of camaraderie."

"Well, thanks for having me. I hope this goes well for you. Is there anything special you want me to mention in my talk?"

"Just your gratitude to me, the world's media magnate."

"Magnate? The press calls you a media mogul."

"Never say bloody mogul. Mogul comes from Mongol, which meant a Muslim ruler of India. A powerful person with autocratic powers which, technically, now that we're a publicly held company, isn't even true."

"I see. Rez the Magnate then."

"By definition a magnate is a great man, a noble man, in any field, especially in a large business. From the Latin *magnus*. Now, is there anything you need before we see you later this afternoon?"

"Actually, I'm having a bit of a problem with my cellphone."

"Not a problem. One will be brought to you immediately."

"Thanks. And Rez?"

"Yes?"

"I don't have any official forms or anything, but I wanted to remind you and your people that I'd prefer that they keep my appearance here entirely amongst ourselves."

"This have to do with your role in that space disaster? Bloody shame. Hiding out, then, eh, Yates?"

"I like to think of it more like a sabbatical."

Here they come, to the beat of supposedly tribal drums, three supposedly Fijian war canoes paddling through softening happy-hour light towards the shore of Déjà Vu. Yates sits cross-legged in the sand in a post-speech stupor drinking hard liquor out of a coconut shell with Resnor's top managers. All of them, except Yates, who's wearing khaki cargo shorts and a black T-shirt, are wearing the same matching blue-flowered tropical-style shirts and shorts. There's a fire in a pit on the beach. Women in tapa wraps dance a supposedly traditional dance at the water's edge, heralding the approaching craft. As the canoes get closer, Yates sees that the men on board have their faces painted with charcoal, and those not paddling are carrying war clubs and spears. When the lead canoe rides the mild surf onto the lip of the beach, its occupants give a great roar that is matched by an even greater roar from their corporate western audience. At the head of the lead canoe, in full-blown warrior regalia, is Resnor. He leaps off the right gunwale and does an improvised dance in the shallows that is met with more cheering and applause, not so much from the Fijians as from his paid employees, to whom this kind of spectacle, this kind of behaviour, is nothing new. To Yates it is, but it doesn't really surprise him. Nothing seems to any more. As he watches the others disembark from their canoes, male Fijian waiters walk politely through his group, taking great care to refill the many coconut shells with more of the unknown clear liquor, which Yates drinks as if born to it. Now they're in a long line, singing and waving their weapons. The men are in frangipani leis and skirts of frayed palm leaves. The women are fluttering brightly painted fans. Yates takes a gulp, and for a moment he gets the queasy feeling he always gets when rich westerners, when rich white males, exploit the cultural traditions of an economically challenged indigenous culture.

Resnor strut-dances his way up to where else but the head of the line, and leads them to a group of young Fijian men and women performing the *vakamalolo*, a sitting dance. The magnate-not-mogul does a great show of moving up and down the line, making threatening motions with his war club, which has *REZ* painted on the sweet spot in orange, punctuated by a neon-green lightning bolt, his company's logo. Finally he stops in front of a young, pretty Fijian girl with wide dark eyes and short, tightly curled black hair. He motions with the club for her to rise, and then turns her to face Yates's group with her back to the sea. They do an awkward dance for several minutes, with Resnor imposing a series of bizarre steps into the supposed ritual that the girl does her best to keep up with.

When Resnor stops, the music stops a beat later. He raises his club, lets out a primal scream and the group throws it right back at him, as if they've performed this bit a million times before. When the shouting subsides, Resnor motions with his club to the other warriors, who respond by raising their clubs and spears, and as the drums begin again, they close ranks upon Resnor and the young girl, who doesn't seem particularly thrilled with this aspect of the floor show. As they press closer, the drums beat more rapidly, more violently, and the singing of the others takes on a manic, bloodthirsty edge that is not unlike what Yates had heard at the soccer game in Johannesburg. He tilts back his coconut, closes his eyes and takes a long gulp. He hopes that when he opens his eyes this scene will be over, or that it will never have happened at all.

But it's happening all right, and it's hardly over.

From the centre of the group, Resnor's club rises high, pauses, then falls. When it rises again, it is joined by the clubs of the others, all poised to strike false blows on a make-believe virgin in the Déjà Vu twilight.

Soon the drumming and singing and fake bludgeoning reaches a crescendo, and finally the noise stops. The mock warriors peel back from their violent scrum and reveal the girl prone on the beach covered in what Yates hopes is fake blood. As a group of indigenous pallbearers carry the girl away, Resnor steps forwards towards his people, with something bloody in his hands. Something like an organ, like a human heart. Resnor holds it up to the group, the sky and the sea, and with great gusto takes a bite out of it.

"The sacrifice of a beautiful virgin," he hollers, for the first time using actual words, "to give thanks for a year of unprecedented growth, and to a year yet to come which, our Futurist Mr Yates assures us, will see us rise to unprecedented heights! Now let us celebrate and feast!"

With that, the drums and the singing begin again, this time in a less aggressive, more festive rhythm. From the palm-tree line at the back of the beach there emerge several dozen waiters, who light a string of torches surrounding a group of elaborately decorated tables. Then, to show everyone that this was just a show, that a young alleged virgin girl was not actually killed, the girl jogs out of the tree line to take a bow. Yates rises, clutching his coconut cup like it is a life raft, and looks for a way out. Perhaps he can feign a stroll along the beach and backtrack to his hut through a path in the side of the hill. Or perhaps he can just stride right past them all as they jostle for power seats at the tables. But now there's a hand on his shoulder, covered with fake blood. Resnor. "What did you think, Mr Yates?"

"Very impressive, Rez. Everything I ever could have wanted from my first human sacrifice, and then some."

"You're at my table. Come."

The food arrives in waves. Some local. Some native. Some flown in from the corners of the earth. Local skipjack, albacore tuna and chilled yellowfin sashimi. Kobe steak from Japan. Brazilian lobster tails. French Bordeaux. Jamaican Rum. But Yates can hardly bring himself to eat. The only thing that appeals to him is the bourbon from Kentucky, which he is now drinking out of a coconut.

After the salad and several rounds of appetizers, Resnor makes his way to his seat. "So where are you off to next?"

"I'm not sure. I'm hoping to take a bit of a break."

Resnor looks at the beach, the ocean, the feast with a hundred people serving them. "Yeah," he says. "I can see how all this could get so draining. Going to the world's most interesting places, giving a canned speech for an hour, then enduring the likes of this."

Yates doesn't have a response. In the centre of the dining area a group of men are laying heated stones on the flames of a wood fire for a fire-walking ceremony. At the next table, a Fijian woman is administering native face painting on a three-hundred-pound regional brand manager, and a man in a hybrid clown suit-ceremonial robe is making animal shapes out of balloons.

"Where will you go on your sabbatical?"

Yates smiles at the word. Rez gets it. "I don't know. Maybe I'll stay in this neighbourhood for a while. Surf. Fish. Go native."

"And when you're done with that? Will you go back to it? To Futurism?"

Yates drinks whisky out of his coconut, winces at the strange taste combination. "I really don't know, Rez. But for now I'm thinking no fucking way."

Like the dancers, singers and performers, the fire-walkers have been brought in for the night from the Sheraton Royal on Viti Levu. The leader tells the legend of Fijian fire-walking, how the gift was given to a warrior who had spared the life of a spirit-god long ago. How indulging in sex or coconuts is forbidden the night before a ceremony. The wood has been removed from the fire, and a carpet of stones glows white-hot behind the leader as he begins to sing and chant around the pit. Soon he is joined by four Fijian men who come out of the trees with the energy of professional football players taking the field before a play-off game. Yates sits back and watches as the leader picks up someone's dinner napkin and makes a show of laying it on the coals, where it bursts into flame. The men begin chanting a new song as they enter the pit and walk slowly and confidently on top of the glowing stones. Their faces are expressionless, almost tranquil. As the men step back onto the cool sand, Resnor walks up to the edge of the pit and applauds them, encouraging his people to applaud them as well. One employee, Resnor's Chief Technology Officer, is so moved by the ceremony and the six coconuts filled with over-proofed rum he's had in the last hour and a half that he feels compelled to run towards the pit. Before anyone can stop him – and it is debatable whether anyone has any desire to – he kicks off his Tevas and runs barefoot across the last patch of sand and onto the stones. When his left foot first comes down upon the stones, he shrieks so loudly and with such apparent cowardice that everyone begins to laugh, thinking this is fake as well, this is all part of the show. Then the man's momentum carries him forwards for another step. Because he has lifted his scalded left foot so quickly from the stones, he comes down harder than usual on his right. And because the musicians and singers have stopped performing and watch in stunned amazement – and not without a touch of amusement – it is possible to hear the flesh on the bottom of the Chief Technology Officer's soft feet sizzle on the five-hundred-degree surface. With this disastrous and excruciatingly painful second step, the man attempts to stop and turn around, to backtrack rather than cross the length of the pit, which would require four or five more steps. But he stops too quickly. And the combination of his momentum, state of inebriation and intense pain proves too much for his equilibrium. He loses his balance midway through an awkward pirouette, hops on his right foot for a moment, then hangs in the air long enough for someone to yell "Holy shit, Phil", before toppling arse-first onto the scalding stones. First the seat of his flowered shorts catch fire and then, as he shifts his weight from his arse, his shirt goes up. Quickly, but not so quickly that they could have stopped any of this, the fire-walkers turn into fire-runners and scramble back onto the stones to lift up the screaming man and throw him with a synchronized motion onto the sand, where he at least knows enough to roll and extinguish himself.

As the Déjà Vu medical staff puts the burnt man on a stretcher, Resnor turns on a wireless microphone and announces, as recorded steel drum music begins to play from speakers in the trees, that everything is going to be all right, that the party is just getting started and will continue, right after this short break. Taking advantage of the chaos, Yates gets up and walks down to the water.

The sky is a black darker than he's ever seen, and because it is so dark and there is no moon tonight, the stars pop hard-edged and brilliant against the black. Despite his self-imposed ban on stargazing, Yates can't help but look. Can't help but look at his father's sky, but this is the sky of another place entirely, the sky of Lupus the Wolf, of Columba the Dove, of the Chameleon and the Southern Cross. He walks further down the beach, away from the party torches and the lights of Resnor's great house. Next to an overturned sea kayak he stops and looks to the south, where the Milky Way sits on the horizon, vast and prominent and for the first time registering as a tangible thing to Yates rather than a concept. Within the Milky Way he finds two of its brightest stars, Beta and Alpha Centauri, the pointers that lead his eye up from the horizon and to the Southern Cross. It isn't particularly beautiful, Yates thinks. Nor is it the most prominent feature of the southern sky. But it is something that cannot be seen where he grew up, something his father could only have imagined. Looking at the Cross, and at the same time trying to remember how to get a bearing that will point him towards the South Pole, Yates knows that it does not take a psychologist to determine why, over the years, the more he has veered from the man his father wanted him to be, the more interested he has become in the stars which have always held such a fascination for a man whom he still cannot even begin to figure out. At the edge of the horizon, where the sea meets the cosmos, something catches his eye as it flashes briefly before sinking out of sight. Perhaps it was a shooting star, or the lights of a far-off ship. Or the space hotel, a 150-million-dollar funeral train moving at the speed of light.

When he gets back to the party, they seem to have got over the Chief Technology Officer's fire-dancing accident. In fact Yates can already see one of the other managers performing, to the amusement of a group of six others, a little hop-skip-pirouette routine followed by a fall onto make-believe hot stones. Just like their colleague had done, except for the scalding-rocks-and-first-degree-burn part.

He had intended to go directly back to his room, but he wants another coconut filled with bourbon to take with him. So he sits at the empty head table and watches the developing spectacle while waiting for someone to get his drink. The traditional Fijian drums and chants departed with the man on the stretcher, and now it's purely dance music, techno-house stuff that these mostly white, mostly older, mostly men would hate anywhere but here. But here there is a fireworks display being rolled out, and here there is a perpetually open bar, and here you can do whatever the fuck you want, because you're all sworn to secrecy. It takes a few tries for Yates to explain the concept of bourbon, let alone Maker's Mark, to the new waiter. Finally he sees the waiter who had served him earlier and points this waiter towards him, with the request that he "fill it right to the top of the damned coconut".

The lights flicker on and off. At first Yates thinks that this is happening in his head only, that this is the precursor to a blackout, the next stage of a mental breakdown. Then they flicker again and the music stops. He looks for the drink, but the waiters are still talking and looking his way. He waves, makes a praying gesture that is more serious than they think. Mid-song the music stops again. Off to the side of the entertainment circle, Resnor elbows one of his employees. *Pay attention. Wait till they get a load of this.* The music starts up again. A powerful bass line. A hip-hop rhythm. Yates knows the song but can't remember its name. From the tree line again, more entertainers. About a dozen people, a dozen women, in native leaf skirts and tapa cloths wrapped over their shoulders, around their torsos. Each is wearing a painted tribal mask. When they get to the centre of the circle, they begin to dance, and Yates can see these are not Fijian women, that these women are not part of any hotel floor show in this hemisphere.

He gets up to leave, but Resnor spots him and bears down on him just as the waiters arrive with his drink. "You can't leave now, mate. Things are just beginning to get interesting."

"It's all been interesting, Rez." Yates sips his bourbon, chews off a piece of coconut flesh. One of the dancers has removed her tapa cloth and now her leaf skirt. She is in a sparkling silver thong and is bursting out of a tiny matching bikini top. Yates turns to Resnor. "I didn't know they had such talented plastic surgeons in the Mamanucas."

Resnor smiles, laughs the hearty laugh of a magnate with absolute power and the disclaimers to prove it. "Mamanucas, indeed," he says, putting his arm around Yates's shoulders. He sings out to everyone, "Show us your Mamanucas!" Then to Yates, "Now come. Sit with me and have some kava with your ghastly bourbon."

"Some what?"

"Kava. It's a ceremonial drink. Non-alcoholic. Comes from the dried root of a kind of pepper plant. It will mellow you out, numb your lips a bit."

"Are the American strippers usually part of the kava ceremony, kind of like the vestal virgins of Rome, or is this a Rez original, your uniquely inspired contribution to the Fijian culture?"

"Actually, they're Aussie, these girls. Sydney's finest. And there is nothing vestal or virginal about them. Now sit down here alongside me." They sit on mats spread before a *tanoa,* a large tub more than three feet long carved from a single block of *vesi* wood. Inside the *tanoa*, the *waka* roots have been pounded into a mortar, put inside a cloth sack and mixed with water. "Clap once when the he offers you the cup, the *bilo*. Then take it in your hands and say '*bula*' just before it meets your lips.

Try to finish it, no matter how piss-poor it may taste, or you'll offend them."

"And the strippers, they don't offend them?"

"There are compromises that must be made any time two cultures intermingle, Yates. We make every effort to show proper respect for their ceremonies."

"And conversely," Yates responds, "they must make every effort to respect if not tolerate ours. Their culture is synonymous with the *meke* dance, we just happen to worship the lap dance."

Resnor considers this, then nods, as if he's heard a profound universal truth. "Exactly. Well put, Yates."

"I was wondering, what do your female employees make of all this?"

Resnor shrugs. "They know what goes on at these things. They're not obligated to attend, of course. Some, however, do make the absolute most of it." Resnor points across the fire pit, where one of the strippers has the head of Resnor's SVP of Marketing – a fifty-four-year-old mother of three – wedged between her substantial breasts.

Now all of the masked dancers are topless, swaying around the perimeter of the group, their backs to the fire at the core. They probe forwards and pull back, close enough to seduce but not yet close enough to make contact with their audience, or for their audience to make contact with them. "Now don't forget," Resnor reminds Yates. "Clap, say '*bula*', drink it all up, then clap three times and tip the cup to show you've had enough for now."

"What if I screw it up?"

"You don't want to know, Yates," Resnor says, with exaggerated menace. "You don't want to know." A man in a leaf skirt with a blackened face, his chest shining with coconut oil, approaches Resnor, who claps once and flawlessly performs the ritual. "Ahh." He wipes his mouth with the back of his hand. "Bloody nasty. But slightly addictive."

The man with the cup shifts over to Yates, who does exactly what he is supposed to do. But he doesn't tilt the cup when he is done. He holds it out, says "*bula*" again, and he drinks a second cup. After he claps the second cup away he raises his coconut and chases the Fijian kava with Kentucky bourbon. Still, the dirt taste lingers. After a few minutes he leans over and tells Resnor that he was right, the kava really is disgusting. But his voice is garbled, the words unformed.

"Thiff ftuff weewee iff difffufftingg."

"Say again?"

"Nefffer miiin."

"You're not making any sense, Yates."

An old 50 Cent song comes on and, on cue, the dancers remove their thongs, and move closer to the group. An Amazonian blonde has a sack full of erotic toys and is looking for a grounded electrical outlet. Seeing this, one of the Fijian waiters, an older man, begins to cry. He puts down his drink tray and tries to walk away, but two younger waiters put their hands on his shoulders and escort him into the shadows to talk their version of sense to him. Now a thin brunette with enormous fake breasts wearing only a painted mahogany devil mask approaches Resnor, who whispers something to her and points at Yates, who holds up his hands and makes the universal *Not me* sign. "*No* fanks," he says. Then he tries to say "I'm very numb", but it comes out sounding like *I'w bewy humb.*

This only brings the woman closer. She smiles, straight white caps beneath the dark mask. "I'll bet you're very hung, mate," she says, and proceeds to envelop her breasts around his kava-paralysed cheeks. She begins to swing her shoulders and thus her breasts, snapping Yates's head from side to side. Resnor is laughing so hard that he doesn't notice when Yates's shoulders begin to shake and his gut spasms and heaves. Doesn't notice until Yates bathes the woman's tanned, coconut-oil-slathered, $5,000 investment with a stew of bourbon, kava, albacore tuna and bile.

Déjà Vu, Part II

He once told the board of a pharmaceutical company being investigated by the Securities and Exchange Commission Plato's line that the rulers of the Republic may sometimes be required to tell noble lies for the good of its citizens. He once was conscripted by the inner circle of a failing presidential campaign to brainstorm ways to make their female candidate seem less detestable to rednecks without alienating her liberal base. He once spoke before the graduates of a Bible college in Virginia about the future of God, and one week later delivered the keynote address to the Adult Video Distributors Conference in Vegas about the future of porn, and received standing ovations at both.

She only hit him once. An open-handed punch on the side of the head. She missed him the second time, not because of his superior evasive skills, but because he fell so quickly onto his ceremonial mat after her first punch, and because he no longer had the soft vice of her breasts to hold him up.

How he got back to his hut, or how long he's been laying on his bed like this, he couldn't tell you. Not too long, he assumes, because it is still dark out, his tongue and lips are still numb from the kava, and he is still drunk. Drunk for the last time for a long time, he swears to himself. The TV is on, so he watches it. Still the space hotel. Now that its occupants are all dead, the fascination factor has increased exponentially, which Yates would never have figured. Something about dead people in a beautiful place, maybe. Or, as Campbell said, the phantom pops and groans the ship makes under thermal stress. Or the fact that every ninety minutes it completely circles the planet, always visible to the morbidly curious eyes of millions, a perpetual, celestial wake. Or not quite perpetual, because at some point soon the laws of physics will get the better of it and it will fall and burn.

At first he thinks that they have found him. But when he opens the email from the Johnsons he can see that they still think he is in Milan, preparing to fly to Rio today.

Yates:

We very much enjoyed your speech at Futurshow Milan. Nice additions to the Johannesburg original. Nice insights. Did you have them tucked away for a rainy day? Did you steal them? Or do you just work really well under pressure? Under the influence? Or under the beefy body of a kinky preschool teacher? (LOL! What were you thinking?) Anyhoo, before you depart for your sabbatical in the land of thongs, we have some questions about your upcoming assignment, which we will be briefing you on in the next few days. First, have you done any seminars or speeches or white papers on the Middle East? The Muslim world? (We have checked, of course, but there's the slim possibility we may have missed something.) How about anything on the topic of freedom and democracy? Anything (beyond what you were originally scheduled to talk about in Johannesburg) about free and open markets? The commercial viability of reinvented Old World capitals? And finally, do you speak Arabic? If so, which dialect and to what degree – i.e. conversational, fluent, or you can manage to place an order at a Ninth Ave Lebanese kebab shop? Please get back to us asap. Once again, it's a privilege to have you back on board for this upcoming adventure. There's a lot at stake, and much to be gained, for all of us.

Yours in futurism,

J&J

PS: don't hesitate to take pictures for us in Rio.

His first instinct is to fire right back, and he does, but he doesn't send it directly to them. Instead, hoping that it will make him less traceable, he sends it to his Hotmail address, then on to Campbell for forwarding to the Johnsons.

J&J:
Greetings from Milan, where I'm kind of bored, now that the suicide bombing and subsequent interrogations have apparently ceased. Unless you know something. I will get to the questions in your email, but first I would like you to answer some questions that I didn't get a chance to ask what's-his-name – the gay model, spy – that lately have been preoccupying me. Did you have anything to do with the soccer riot in Johannesburg? Was it done for my benefit? Did you have anything to do with the bombing in Milan? Was that done for my benefit? Ditto the space station? And what do you know about my pen pal Nostradamus? Is he a pseudonym for Johnson & Johnson? And who are you with? For what government, branch of government, political party, intelligence agency, multinational corporation or evil genius do you work? What's your agenda? Your goal? What's with all the Muslim stuff which, understandably, scares the absolute shit out of me? And finally, most importantly, why me?

Why not someone more capable? Someone who knows better? Someone who cares?

–Y

He pours a glass of mineral water, sits on the edge of the bed and sips, trying not to dribble it down his numbed lips and chin. There is a knock at the door. It is a young Fijian bellboy sent by Resnor. "Making sure the gentleman all right."

"The gentleman is doing better, thank you. In fact, as soon as the gentleman vomited on the stripper's breasts, he began to feel better. Physically, if not spiritually."

The bellboy smiles. "Can I get you anything, then, sir?"

"No, thank you. What is your name?'

"R.J."

"Actually, R.J., there is something. I'm going to be leaving here tomorrow, and I was wondering if you knew of somewhere nearby, some other island I might be able to discreetly visit for a while, perhaps a long while."

R.J. looks at the door, then down at his feet.

"Of course this would be between us. Mr Resnor doesn't have to know. In fact I'd prefer that he didn't know. Ideally, I would take the shuttle chopper to the airport at Viti Levu and move on to somewhere else from there."

"I see. I think about it, sir. I got to make some calls."

"Thank you. By the way, what did you make of all that tonight, R.J.? And please, say what you want. I'm not really with them."

Looking down, R.J. quietly answers. "I think it was unfortunate, sir."

"Yeah. And they wonder why people hate us."

R.J. looks up at Yates and thinks for a moment before deciding to speak. "That not necessarily true, sir. Assuming that we hate you. When I hear such thinking, I wonder why it always put that way. Why do we hate you?

The rich and the powerful? When the truth is so many of us are wondering the other side of that question. Why do you hate us? Because only someone who hates us could act like these people. And not just tonight, on that small bit of beach on this tiny island."

It's not long before he gets a response from the Johnsons, via Campbell and Hotmail.

Yates:
So many questions. So little we are at liberty to answer. First the easy ones. We had nothing to do with the soccer riot. Nor did we have anything to do with the space station, or with your being dumped by your girlfriend. In retrospect, this all proved rather serendipitous for us. We had been wanting to recruit you for some time. In retrospect, your state of mind as a direct result of the aforementioned combination of events may have worked in our favour. At least temporarily, since this same state of mind has proven also not to be without its risks. Now, regarding the events in Milan, the answer, if one can call it that, is much more complex. Was that carried out specifically for your benefit? Absolutely not, but it's nice to have such delusional thoughts now and then, isn't it? No, that activity was going to happen anyway. We were made aware of it, in what some officials like to call "the chatter". We knew of it but did not plan it, nor did we assist in it being carried out. Our contacts in Milan were already making specific plans to spin the event, should it happen, to our benefit. Did this include having Mabus placing you in an orchestra seat at the café? Yes. We were Mabus, leading you there, to get your attention, to create a series of links, just in case you chose to abandon us. You will probably be equally surprised to discover that while we were Mabus, we were not and are not Nostradamus. We just happened to have stumbled upon his missives in your inbox, and we ran with it. We used it for our own benefit. Because you had become

disrespectful of our agreement, we were forced to forward to you those video attachments – which we had hoped to keep for a rainy day – sooner than we had wanted. We simply wanted to intimidate you by making you aware of their existence, but then Nostradamus broke into your files, found the videos and changed the dynamic. He leaked them to Italian intelligence, which led to your unfortunate arrest. After some negotiations and assurances, we bailed you out, and then brought you back in to complete the original terms of our agreement. But what remains a mystery in all of this is who, exactly, is this Nostradamus character, and why he hates you so. If it didn't affect our interests, it would actually be quite entertaining. What else? You ask, Who are we with? What's our agenda? *Well, contrary to your opinion we are not "with" any administration in any official capacity other than when our corporate interests often intersect with whatever interest that administration might have. Sometimes this happens serendipitously, but sometimes these interests need to be nudged, nuanced and occasionally pushed so that they intersect with more frequency and transparency. It's nice to have the most powerful nation in the world working on behalf of your interests. But it should be made clear that we represent neither Liberals nor Conservatives. We represent the interests of an organization above all else, and these interests can quickly be modified to work with the idiosyncrasies and superficial goals of whatever party or faction is in power, just about anywhere. Finally, you ask,* Why me? *(It's always about you, isn't it, Yates). Well, we hate to knock your battered ego down another notch, but you're not such a big deal in all of this. You're just one of many contributing from one of many, many angles. Think of it as if you're a content provider, or a channel (and perhaps a false one) to share ideas, perspectives and items of interest that ultimately may have some value to the organization. Johnson and I, we're just drones, the proverbial middle managers, trying to make sense of it all for the boys in the metaphorical top-floor corner office. Now, the good news is that this is an organization that has outperformed every S&P 500, every best-bet mutual fund, every IPO there's ever been, and there's plenty of profit-sharing to be had by all of us. Including you, Yates. We like to think that we work for a very special special-interest group whose goal is to leverage ideology for profit. More on the Muslim stuff later. Enjoy Rio. And don't try to save this, because in about five seconds it will be as if it never happened.*

–JJ

Yates doesn't even bother trying to save it. A few seconds later, every word of the email disappears.

He begins to pack again. It is almost dawn. He's not scheduled to fly off the island until 9 a.m., but he can't get out of Déjà Vu quick enough. Even though it may not be on any map, even though it is many thousands of miles from anywhere, it is not remote enough for Yates. There is a soft tapping at his door. Probably R.J., he thinks. Hopefully with news about a new place to stay.

"Come in," he says. "Door's open." More tapping, even softer. "Jesus Christ." He walks across the hut and abruptly swings the door open. Marjorie.

"Howzit."

"My God."

"Indeed."

"The Johannesburg CBD must be really determined to pimp you out, sending you halfway around the world to me."

Marjorie doesn't laugh or smile. She is wearing jeans and a red tank top. Her hair is pulled back under a blue paisley bandanna and she is carrying a large backpack. Big difference from the outfit she was wearing in his room in Johannesburg. She looks the Futurist up and down and says, in an accent that makes even humiliation sound desirable, "Don't flatter yourself, Yates."

Newly-somethings

"Are you drunk?"
"No."
"Well, you're slurring."
"It's the kava."
"The what?"
"A Fijian ceremonial elixir. Calms the spirit."
"Distorts the mind."
"And numbs the tongue."
"I see."
"How did you find me?"
"David. The chaperone. And your friend in Iceland."
"Greenland."
"Right. But he's all about the ice."
"So David's legit?"
"Apparently. Who can know for sure? All that I know is that he paid me a visit after our missed connection – when you were supposed to call from Milan – and then he connected me with your friend, who arranged for me to come here. So here I am."
"*Bula*."
"Pardon?"
"*Bula*. Howzit. Welcome. To Fiji. To Déjà Vu."
"It's quite beautiful."
"It's quite frightening, actually. What I saw last night.

Anyway, we're leaving in a couple of hours for another island. That is, if it's okay with you."

"Fine," she points to her backpack. "I'm already packed."

"I have to warn you, with my current situation – which Campbell may or may not have clued you in to – I can't promise that it will be much of an upgrade from the situation you've left behind."

"Anything is better than the situation I left behind. Unless you're a pimp or a murderer."

"No. Just a suspected international terrorist. But I guess if this helps, if it saves you in any way from..."

Marjorie's stare cuts him off, frightens him a little. She looks around the room – the empty champagne bottle, the half-empty coconut, the muted TV, and the God-knows-what crusted on Yates's sandals by the door – and she says, "I wouldn't be so sure that I'm the one who needs saving, Yates."

"Okay. Fair enough."

"And just where is it we'll be going?"

"Another island in this group. Someone is arranging it. A valet who works here. Right now, no one knows I'm here except Campbell, some wildly hung-over executives and Resnor – the man who owns the island – and it's important it stays that way. I'll explain it all, to the extent that I can, later. Hopefully the place we'll be going will be even more remote than this."

"We'll need an alias, a story."

Yates scratches his chin. "Simple. We'll be a husband and wife. Blissful honeymooners."

"How about brother and sister."

"Lovers."

"Father and daughter."

"Star-crossed, long-lost lovers."

She shakes her head. "Old friends who have quit their tedious jobs to embark on a therapeutic world backpacking tour."

"Backpacking and sex."

"We're colleagues."

"No. We're newly-weds, but we have a very open sex life."

Marjorie frowns and looks around the room again. "Maybe not newly-weds," she says, "But definitely newly-somethings."

While Marjorie showers, Yates packs. R.J. knocks at the door with breakfast for Yates and his "lady friend" and information about his recommended destination. A small, recently shut-down surfer camp Resnor owns on an island off Namotu. R.J.'s cousin used to run the shuttle boat that took surfers out to the reef breaks, but now he's just a sort of caretaker, mostly making sure the place doesn't get overrun by freeloading backpackers until Resnor decides to sell it or give it another shot.

"Is it crowded?"

"No, sir. Just four thatched huts near the beach and a small dormitory. All empty. There's a small village where my cousin lives about fifteen minutes away by foot. He stops by to check on things couple of times a day. It's a one-hour boat ride from this place."

"Thank you, R.J."

"Not a problem, sir."

"How's old Resnor doing? Did he get the virginal blood off his hands yet? I imagine I'll have to stop up at the great house and say my goodbyes. Apologize for last night."

R.J. smiles. "I doubt Mr Rez remembers much from last night. Besides, he flew out at the end of the party. Very late. The chopper landed on the beach. I'm surprised you didn't hear it. He left with several of the performers from Australia."

"Lovely."

* * *

While he waits for Marjorie, who is half singing, half humming a reggae song in the bathroom, Yates picks at his omelette and watches television. He unmutes the sound, but it hardly matters. It's just a different kind of silence. At some point he closes his eyes, lulled by the thrum of the shower, Marjorie's half-singing and the black noise of outer space. He's happy that she's here, and pleased that she's safe. But he wonders why she's really come. Solely to escape? Because someone sent her? Or because, in addition to wanting to escape, she actually liked some aspect of him? The shower stops and Marjorie stops humming, and for a while it's just the interior noise of the spacecraft. Then he hears it. The faint clicking of a switch. The whirring of a fan. A series of synchronized beeps and then the churning of a pump. One at a time, the systems on the doomed space hotel come back to life, like something out of Ray Bradbury. Yates knows what it is before he opens his eyes, and for a few moments he decides to keep them closed, to listen to what Annalise Kinkaid and Captain Rusty and the rest of them had been praying for. Now the thrusters, which pivot the ship's energy-gathering panels back towards the sun, kick in. When Yates opens his eyes, the cockpit of the space hotel is filled with light, bright floodlights and on the instrument consoles dozens of smaller, flickering coloured lights, red and yellow, orange and green. Then the oxygen generator comes to life, and you can hear the whissssh-whisssssh-whissssh as it begins to churn out the fresh, breathable air that would have saved them, or at the very least put off death a while longer.

But of course, it's too late. They've all been dead for hours. For a moment Yates wonders if this was done on purpose, if someone in charge of the TV rights had paid off someone to manipulate the plot line – maybe do some sound design and digital paintboxing of the picture of the cabin down on earth – to add this final touch of irony to the tragedy. It's possible. But that seems too far-fetched a conspiracy even for Yates. The oxygen that would have saved them, that they had so desperately tried to coax from their environment, simply arrived on its own terms, clean and rich, but too late to save anyone. He looks at his belongings stacked by the door, then towards the bathroom, where Marjorie has begun to sing again, and he can't help but acknowledge the parallels.

Desperates' Rights

The funny thing is that none of this seems strange. Not being on a yellow-decked, white-hulled eighteen-foot wooden surfer shuttle boat with a sixty-five-horse outboard in the Mamanuca Group of the Fijian Islands. Not Jope, R.J.'s smiling, handsome nineteen-year-old cousin and the captain of said boat. And not being here with Marjorie, who is up on the foredeck in cargo shorts and a tank top, taking it all in. It doesn't feel strange. Doesn't feel special. It just feels like it is. He looks at Marjorie and wonders how it feels to her.

He's at sea, but there are islands everywhere, from small patches of uninhabitable mangrove to green mountain resort islands with white sand beaches. Depending on its depth, and the presence of reefs or channels or shallows, the water takes on myriad shades of blue, each unlike any Yates has ever seen. He had thought they would spend the trip catching up, with him explaining himself, giving Marjorie the blow-by-blow. But she just wants to hang out. Which is fine, because he had feared that she had come expecting some kind of plan from him. Some kind of vision. But clearly he has no plan beyond getting to this island and hoping it works out for a while. He looks back towards Déjà Vu, which he can no longer see, then ahead of him, but not very far. For a while he tries to focus on the patch of water just in front of the boat, seemingly calm and flat, but all new to him. Just a few minutes earlier, Jope had asked Yates what he did for a living, and Yates had told him that he used to be a futurist. It then had to be explained to Jope what exactly it was a futurist did. What a futurist believed. When Yates was done, Jope had responded by saying that in the Fijian language there is no past or future tense. Just the present.

"Is that just some crap you tell the tourists?"

Jope shakes his head, smiles. "Truth, man."

Staring at the sea now as Jope names the islands and reefs, the passages and breaks they are passing, Yates smiles, digging this existential tidbit, which he still doesn't believe. Just a few weeks ago, a few days ago, he would have committed it to memory for later use, true or false, to help reinforce some bogus point, to impress someone with a chequebook, to demonstrate worldliness.

Jope eases up on the throttle, and when the bow planes down flat he points to an island far off the starboard side. "That is Tavarua Island. Exclusive resort. Very private. And out there" – now he points straight ahead – "that's Cloudbreak, one of the great surfing spots in the world." Yates squints to see, but they are too far away to make out the swells. Before Yates can speak, Jope pushes the throttle down and the boat lurches forwards, towards Cloudbreak.

Soon they are close enough to see the swells rolling up over the reef and forming massive, clean, open wave faces and flawless barrels. Even from this distance, even though they can barely make out the forms of the surfers rushing down the faces, squatting and disappearing in the closing barrels, the swells look tremendous.

"How big?" Yates calls out as the boat slows again.

"Six to nine feet. Sometimes they're twelve and more, but now the trade winds make it hard to predict. See that blowback? That's the trades. When they blow steady, they flatten swells big-time."

"I used to surf in college," Yates says. "Nothing like this, but..."

"I wouldn't ride Cloudbreak unless you are expert. Very dangerous. Reef sharp like razors. This too," Jope explains, pointing back towards Tavarua. "Resort owners on that island claim to own rights to Cloudbreak. Say it's just for their guests; outsiders surf only if they say okay." Jope has hardly finished saying this when a surfer shuttle boat from Tavarua starts heading their way. "You see," Jope says, pushing the throttle down once again. "Already too close. But you do not worry. There are many more breaks, some more beautiful, more powerful, more difficult than Cloudbreak. Depends on the day, and which reef the swells choose to bless."

They turn away from Cloudbreak and Tavarua Island and head across the Malolo Passage towards a much smaller island, Namotu. As they get nearer, Yates stands to get a better look. The sea seems relatively flat and beautiful, but closer to the beach at Namotu it swells almost as high as at Cloudbreak, and its left breaks crash within fifty yards of the shore rather than in the open sea. "Namotu Island," Jope announces. "Home of Namotu Lefts. Good for trick-riding on small days and some serious shit on big days. If you like longboard, it's good for that, too."

Yates looks more closely at the island. He can make out three or four thatched huts near the shoreline and the hint of a dormitory back in the trees. Marjorie sits up, seemingly excited for the first time. "Is this where we'll be staying?"

Jope shakes his head. "Close, Missus. You are just around the corner, very close to Namotu. The island you are going to, no one lives there any more."

"What's its name?" she asks.

"Mr Resnor calls it Desperation Island, cos surfers call its breaks Desperates' Rights and Desperates' Lefts. But now that surf camp is closed up, and surfers stay elsewhere, it is without a name." Jope slows the boat and trims the engine as they negotiate the shallows over the reef. Soon they round a bend and an even smaller island comes into view. Mangrove comes right up to the water except for a small stamp of white sand at the far-right end. Jope points at the beach, which is less than half a mile away from Namotu, and says, "Home."

"I like Desperates better than Desperation," Marjorie says.

Yates smiles. "I'll be Desperates' Right, you can be Left."

Jope points the bow towards the beach, trims the engine more because of the shallows, and then shuts it down and lets the mild surf coax them onto the shore. Just off the beach he hops up onto the bow, grabs a line and leaps off the tip of the boat into the shallow water. As he pulls the boat onto the beach, Yates looks at the three abandoned huts, an equipment shack and something that must have been a tiki bar. "I guess we don't have to worry too much about getting our story straight," he says to Marjorie, "because there's no one here to tell it to."

Jope ties off the boat on a large piece of driftwood, then comes back to help with their bags. Yates hands over his leather duffel, but Marjorie already has her pack on her back. She jumps off the bow into the shallows and doesn't look back as she makes her way up the beach towards the huts. Humbled, Yates waves off Jope's offer of further assistance and eases himself over the starboard side. The water in the shallows is clear and warm. He looks at his feet, white like bones in the clouding sand, and imagines himself fossilized. Imagines some highly evolved human unearthing him aeons from now – perhaps giving him a name like Hiding Man, or Denial Man, or Puking Man. He imagines what conclusions they would draw about the life he must have led based upon his wardrobe and the contents of his luggage, his laptop, his stomach. He wonders if by that point in time they'll also be able to determine his exact state of mind just before beginning his career as a fossil. Desperation Man.

"Which one is ours?" Marjorie is peeking inside one of the huts.

"You pick," Jope answers. "Take a new one every night if it pleases you."

Yates walks up from the beach and joins them.

"You like it?" asks Jope.

He looks inside. The hut is clean and empty, its thatched roof in excellent condition. "I do."

Jope motions for them to follow him to the next hut. Inside there are two cots, each with fresh linen folded at the bottom. In the back corner there is a water basin on a mahogany pedestal, and three coolers are lined up against the far wall alongside a dozen gallon jugs of water. "I stock it with fresh water for a week, plus three or four days' worth of dry foods, eggs. Some chicken. Also, everywhere there are coconut and banana trees. Plus other fruits and vegetables. And of course plenty of fish in shallows and on reefs."

Marjorie walks inside, lowers her pack onto the floor at the end of the cot on the right and sits down. For a moment Jope and Yates wait for her to say something, but she just rolls her neck, lies back onto the cot and closes her eyes. Jope motions for Yates to follow him. Outside of a long narrow hut with no windows, they stop. "Former activity centre," Jope explains, then points to himself. "Former manager." He opens the door and waits a moment for their eyes to adjust to the darkness. The hut is filled with water-sports equipment. Longboards, shortboards, windsurfing rigs, kayak paddles, fishing rods and tackle, spear guns, snorkelling gear, paddling vests and rash vests and boots.

"Use what you like. Just put back when done. The windsurfing boards and kayaks are in the back, locked to a coconut tree. If you surf, use the rash vest and boots. Reefs can cut you bad."

"No wetsuit?"

"Water's like eighty degrees, man."

"Where's a good place for me to ease into it?"

Jope points down the beach to the left. "Walk about 150 yards. Around the corner you'll see a nice left break just off the beach. Three feet. Five feet. Sometimes better. Be careful. Even smaller breaks get big, and the rips can change quickly. Two tips: don't ever ride straight down the face. In Fiji, unless you're an expert, you ride straight down, the wave will pitch you over the top and onto the reef."

"And the second?"

Jope smiles. "When the wave does flip you over the top, fall flat. Flat like a pancake, so you don't get cut, then swim as hard as you can to the surface. You still gonna try it?"

Yates stares out at the unseeable break and nods.

"Good. If you want more, I'll come back with the boat and we try some shit that will blow you away."

Yates looks at the boards racked on the walls, then back down the beach. "Sounds good, Jope. Sounds good. So, there's no electricity anywhere on the island?"

"No. Had generators, but Resnor took them back to Déjà Vu when the camp went *pffft*. But you have a phone and my number." Jope starts to head back towards the boat, then thinks of something. He points at the equipment hut. "Almost forgot. Right there, where you're standing..."

"Yeah?"

"Wi-Fi hotspot. Resnor's idea."

* * *

Outside the open door to the hut he stops and looks in at Marjorie. She's stretched out on the cot on her stomach, asleep. The engine on the boat turns over. He watches Jope ease it away from the beach, spin it around in the shallows and head out towards the reef and Namotu Island. When he can no longer see the boat, Yates looks once more at Marjorie, then starts back towards the activity centre.

When he told Jope that he had surfed a bit in college he wasn't necessarily lying, but he was pushing it. By "a bit", he meant three times more than fifteen years ago: twice with Campbell, who was an excellent surfer, in mild swells in Santa Monica, and once at the pier in Huntington Beach on a disastrous date with a local girl, where the five-footers kicked his arse with such ease that she wanted no part of him by the time they made it back to beach. Nonetheless, whenever the topic had come up over the ensuing years, Yates had always told people, to the point that he had almost convinced himself, that he was indeed a surfer. Paddling slowly through the shallows on an eight-foot tapered flip nose, in a too-tight rash vest and just now remembering the boots Jope had told him to wear, he realizes what a lying ass he had been.

Near the shore the water is almost flat, but as he paddles towards the reef he can clearly see the left break, clean and consistent, untouched by wind. Beneath him the sun pierces the water and lights up the reef. Damselfish and fusiliers swirl and dart. He looks up, partly because he doesn't want to see anything bigger that might be lurking below, partly because he's approaching the end of the break and already – even though he knows these are no more than two- or three-footers – feels like he is making a mistake, that he is overmatched. But he continues to paddle. Up until now he had taken his time, conserved the energy in his creaky shoulders. But the surf forces him to paddle more aggressively. Because there is no wind and the break is so clean, and because he feels so absolutely alone, the waves sound like thunder as they cascade over the reef. With a final burst he paddles through a pause in the swells and is past the break and on the other side of the reef.

For the next ten minutes he bobs in the swells, watching the break, terrified. He wonders what possibly could have compelled him to come out here alone. If it was a death wish, which he thinks it must have been, he'd like to retract it. Then, while he's trying to figure out how to get back to shore without dying, he discovers that, seemingly without the cooperation of his mind, he's paddling hard towards the beach – and then his legs snap up and he's on his feet in an exaggerated squat, on the lip of a swell, on a Fijian reef break, albeit a small one, but still, here he is, squatting maybe too much and rushing straight down the face of the wave, maybe too fast and too straight. Definitely too straight, he's realizing, remembering Jope's first tip and trying now to correct, too hard, too late. He overcorrects and cuts sharply across the face and rides straight up and over the top. If he had been the expert surfer he had led people to believe all these years, this might have been the beginning of a really sick trick. But he's not. He's barely a novice, he's realizing, as the board flies out from under him straight up towards the perfect sun and he begins to plunge headfirst onto the reef, with complete disregard for Jope's second tip.

Although he does manage to get his hands up (down, actually) to break the fall, he prepares for the worst, the razor gash of the coral, the school of sharks waiting to feast on his white, cholesterol-rich blood – and even the sexy headline, which he had already conjured up while hanging out in the swells: FUTURIST DIES IN SURFING ACCIDENT IN FIJI. But as he somersaults through the white rumble, waiting for death to have its way with him, his flesh never touches coral. As he begins to straighten out his submerged body, he finally remembers and does something that he had been told. Jope's final tip. *Swim hard towards the surface*, which he does, like someone who never wants to surf again. Like someone who actually wants to get back to shore, to Marjorie, to his sabbatical, his exile. Like somebody who just may want to live.

He paddles into the shallows and catches his breath, then retrieves his board and floats face down staring at the break and the world beneath the surface and trying to think of nothing for almost an hour, until the wind picks up and the wave faces begin to fall apart mid-curl. He surfs for the next hour, catching some decent rides, still falling regularly, but with more control. His legs give out first, then his shoulders.

When he gets back to the beach, he sees Marjorie sitting in the sand in shorts and a bikini top.

"I didn't know you were a surfer."

He drops the board and sits down next to her. "I'm not," he says. "One ride was all it took to crush the 'I'm a surfer' fantasy. What's depressing is, over the years, I'd actually conned myself into thinking I could. In truth, it terrified me."

"That's good," Marjorie says. "A person who is terrified is a person who has not yet given up. A person who has at least one thing he doesn't want to lose." She stands and steps out of her shorts, revealing a matching bikini bottom.

"Like what?"

She shrugs and starts to walk towards the water. "You tell me." At the water's edge she looks back.

"Nice ass," he says. As she turns away and lowers

herself into the water, she raises her right middle finger at him, and for a while it is the only part of her above the surface.

It doesn't surprise him that she is a graceful swimmer. Probably a strong swimmer if she has to be. Without stopping, she does a steady, precise crawl out to the inner fringe of the reef. Where the waves wash out into the shallows, she stops and treads water, considering what's left of the wind-buffeted swells before heading back to shore. For some reason he feels awkward because he has waited for her, watched her the whole way out and back. *But what else should I do?* he thinks. *Where else should I go?*

"You swim really well. I thought you grew up on a farm."

She smiles, looks for a towel that isn't there. "We had relatives in Cape Town." she says. "We would holiday there several times a year, and when I was fourteen and fifteen my brother and I summered with my aunt and uncle and we surfed every day."

"I didn't know you had a brother."

She nods, brushes back her wet hair and loses what was left of the smile.

"Why don't you grab a board and catch a few waves?"

Marjorie shakes her head in a way that leads him to believe the subject is not open for discussion. "Ah," she cries. "I don't know. I'm not a surfer any more."

Rather than head back towards the camp and their hut they walk the other way. They stick to the strip of beach while it lasts, but soon the mangrove reaches right up to water's edge. Without stopping, they wade into the water and continue, stepping carefully through the shallows.

As they walk they point to things – palm trees, banana trees, reef fish, cloud shapes – but they withhold comment. It's as if they both feel that talking about the surrounding beauty will only diminish it. Halfway around the island they stop and sit on a piece of driftwood on a small sand beach. Looking west across a passage, far beyond the reef, they see another island, some kind of resort. There are high-rises off its beach and a crane juts far above its treetops, piecing together the next phase of another timeshare paradise. Because the view is less than pristine, less than perfect, Yates feels that it is okay finally to talk. He feels that he's not breaking any natural spell, because the crane and the towers across the passage already have.

He begins with the moment that he last saw her, exhilarated by his self-destructive rant, circled by angry people immediately after his speech, and he takes her right through to this moment. He tells her about Amanda Glowers and the Johnsons. The beating at the hands of the CBD. About Campbell and Magga, Nostradamus and Leonardo, Mabus and the Vespa girl, Chandler and Resnor, the Italian police and the Australian strippers. The only person he leaves out is Deanne from Branson, Missouri.

After he finishes, after he's clearly spelt out the mess that he has made of his life and why he thinks it is a good idea to become invisible on this tiny island, Marjorie doesn't say anything. She doesn't have any follow-up questions or suggestions. She doesn't have any immediate answers. Instead, she just stands and brushes crushed coral off the back of her thighs and without looking at Yates says, "And I thought my life was a mess."

They begin to walk again, choosing not to backtrack, but to continue their circumambulation of the island, even though they don't know the tides or the terrain or how far they have to go to get back to where they started. They proceed as if it's their only option. When he finished speaking and Marjorie had a chance to comment, he thought that she would at least begin to tell him some aspect of her story. Perhaps she'd explain why she never came back to his room with her passport that day. Or perhaps she would tell him more about her brother and what happened in Greylingstad and how she really ended up with the CBD. But more than anything he wants to know why a smart, attractive young woman would travel halfway around the world to join the likes of him. He wants to know what could have made his mess seem more appealing than hers.

Yates can sense that she realizes this, that he is curious about all of these things. But Marjorie doesn't say another word for the entire walk back to camp.

Desperates' Lefts

Not having an unwatched television flickering at the foot of his bed, or an open laptop and a two-line phone within arm's reach – making himself totally inaccessible to miscellaneous stalkers, clandestine operatives, mind-fuckers and ex-girlfriends – and not having at least a minor buzz going on for the first time in a long time, Yates finds it difficult to fall asleep, and almost as difficult to stay awake. So he floats in the slack tide of a psychological netherworld in which he's aware of every last problem, everything that could possibly be wrong or go wrong with his life, but he has nowhere near the focus or wherewithal even to try to consider solutions or ways to prevent problems from happening in the first place.

Outside, the late-day sun creeps like lava across the flattening surf. Inside the hut, its faint light flickers upon the reed walls like flame. He puts a pillow over his face, and only when he thinks of waves, only when he imagines himself riding a much larger break than the one he had tried to surf today, rushing across the face of a barrel so big that to fall would surely be to die, is he able to sleep.

The smell of food wakes him. Marjorie is outside the hut standing over a smoking fire pit. She is wearing a sulu wrap and is pulling giant strips of banana leaf off the fire. It is night, but a three-quarter moon provides enough light to see.

"How long was I asleep?"

"I don't know." The removal of the last of the banana leaves reveals two white fish fillets cooking on hot embers.

"Jope left this for us?"

She shakes her head. "I caught them off the reef, in the kayak. Jope told me how to do the fire this morning."

"What kind of fish?"

"Don't know." Marjorie takes a piece of white meat from the end of a fillet and holds it up. She's seasoned it with diced mango and banana. "I reckon it's not poisonous."

Back under the palm trees she has lit a torch next to a picnic table. She brings the fish on two plates and then comes back with a pot of rice, also seasoned with mango and banana. In the centre of the table is a giant white hibiscus in a Coke bottle vase. Yates digs in. He is starving.

"I could have caught more. Just didn't want to be out there in the dark. Tomorrow I'll plan better."

"This is plenty. This is delicious."

When they are done, he clears the table, takes the plates down to the water and washes them in a tide pool. He comes back with two bottles of drinking water and sits across from her. For a while he looks at the stars, tries to make the new sky familiar.

"Do you see it?" she asks.

"What's that?"

"The Southern Cross."

He looks at her, then back up. At first he doesn't see it, then it snaps into focus, clear and obvious. "Yeah," he says. "Now I do." He thinks about telling her about his father, his fascination with the stars, but he fears that would lead to talk of vocation and ethics and estrangement. Eventually, he hears himself say, "I love looking at the stars," and when he thinks about it, he decides that he means it.

She takes her water bottle and walks down to the edge of the beach. Yates stands and follows. He groans as he sits beside her.

"Sore?"

"Sunburnt. Sore. Old."

"Go back in tomorrow morning. It'll feel better in the water."

"Can I ask something?"

She nods.

"Why did you come here?"

She looks away from the water, stares at Yates for a moment. "First, you tell me why you asked me to come."

He knows that if he says it was to save her, to rescue her, even to help her, it will offend her – and even so, that would not be the entire truth. "I asked you to come," he says, "because you ordered me breakfast in Johannesburg. You could have left the next morning and let me wallow in it some more. But you did something no one asked you to do, for me. Not that I want you to do things for me, or that I especially enjoy someone doing things for me. It's just that you did it."

"Maybe I did it because I thought you would help me. Maybe I saw that you represented a chance for me to get out. Do you think that would be wrong of me?"

He considers this. Shakes his head. "If you really wanted to be helped, there were better options than me. You don't see many white knights bingeing on minibar nips. Prince Charming isn't usually neck-deep in a midlife crisis."

"Tell me about Lauren."

"Tell me about Greylingstad."

She stares at him, runs her upper teeth along her lower lip. "Not yet. You know I wouldn't have told you the little I did that night if I thought for a minute that I'd ever see you again."

"Then tell me why you came here. Why you would come anywhere that I am."

"Because you respected me. You were a gentleman. A drunk, self-absorbed, depressed gentleman. But respectful nonetheless. And, of course, because I had to leave. Maybe you helped quicken the process, but I had to. To get away from bad memories, and because it seemed like it was only getting worse."

"The least you could have done is lied."

"Hey?"

"You know, you could have told me something like you couldn't stop thinking of me since we met. Or that maybe you left because you might even love me."

No answer. He thinks he's got too flip again. Too something.

Out in the passage, he can make out the running lights of a boat headed towards the mainland. "You know, the last person who had ever got me breakfast, made it, ordered it, whatever, was my mother."

Marjorie looks at Yates. "Don't tell me that on top of everything else, you have Mommy issues."

"You do kind of look like her."

"Gross. So, Lauren."

"Yes."

"Did you love her?"

Yates thinks. "Our anniversary was September the eleventh."

"No way."

"Absolutely. It's too outrageous to invent."

"That year?"

"No. But still. Talk about a sign."

"How come you never married?"

"What's funny is we never talked about it. We just let everyone else talk about it. When you're together that long, it comes up a lot. I think we never discussed it because we didn't want to know. Aren't you going to ask about kids? That's the usual progression."

When Marjorie doesn't respond, he continues.

"My last birthday, she bought me golf clubs. Because I'd gone to the Masters with a client and had said I had a good time. We didn't know what we wanted from each other any more. Didn't know what to give. I got her skydiving lessons for Christmas last year and she started crying. She said she thought I was trying to kill her. Yet we never fought. Maybe some people are truly happy because they never fight. But we never fought, I think, because we were so *un*happy, and fighting would have amounted to admitting something we couldn't bring ourselves to do."

"What finally prompted her to do something? What made her leave you?"

"Someone who paid attention, I guess. Maybe someone who liked something that I hated, or the other way round. The anti-me. Anyway, I'm glad she did it, for both of us. Because, you know, I'm not such a total ass. I've thought about this. And I've realized that the reason I didn't give her all of my attention, all of my love, the reason we didn't have vicious fights and make crazy monkey love afterwards is because she wasn't the one. She wasn't the one to make me want to drop everything, travel less, work less, be less of a jerk and more into her. And I clearly wasn't the one for her."

"But you think you're capable of that kind of selflessness, where you'd drop everything for someone?"

"Like you?"

She decides to smile. "Hypothetically."

"I'd like to believe it. But if you love someone, you shouldn't be dropping anything that you love, right?

Because if they make you do that, then they really don't love you."

"There's no way to know until it happens."

Yates stands. Marjorie stays seated, tracing her forefinger in the sand. "What about you?" he asks. "Ever been in love?"

She rises, stretches and touches Yates's cheek with the back of her right hand. "If I told you now," she teases, "what would we talk about tomorrow?"

While she sleeps in the hut, he stays on the beach, listening but not seeing the waves breaking out on the reef. Every few minutes he can make out the silhouette of a fruit bat, large wings flapping in the moon glow, rising up from surface reflection, disappearing into the sky's black centre.

Later, when he goes inside, he sees her stretched out on her cot on top of the sheets. He wants to pull a blanket over her, but doing so would only make him feel better, because it is too hot for blankets or sheets tonight, and she is sleeping fine without them. Next to his cot he quietly picks up his laptop case, then heads back outside. He walks down the beach beyond the last hut to the equipment hut, Jope's one-time activity centre, the supposed Wi-Fi hotspot. Yates truly doubts this, and part of him hopes it isn't true, hopes that this part of Resnor's connectivity obsession is no longer active and they are truly isolated. But he pulls his computer out of the case and tries to boot up anyway.

It takes an extra minute, but he gets onto the Internet, gets at his email. He walks the open machine to a two-person tiki table, sits and scrolls through the messages, and there are hundreds. In an effort to save battery life, he skips the non-essentials, the spams, the fans, the press, the second-tier colleagues, his lecture agent.

From Campbell, a cryptic message two days old:

Greetings from Greenland. Stumbled upon that thing you were looking for when you were here. Even from afar, I have to admit I was tempted to keep it, but as you know, it wouldn't be fair, plus, it was clearly meant for you, and you do deserve it, and of course it really wasn't my decision anyway. Regardless I've arranged to have it shipped to your room in Rio. Please try not to lose it again, and let me know if it arrives intact.

– Campbell

PS: Magga sends her love.

From Blevins:

Thank you for your charming response to my well-intentioned offer. I take it that this is the end of our once rewarding, once promising, and recently disturbing professional relationship. I guess I now will have to watch from afar as you squander what's left of your formerly impressive talents and once unlimited opportunities. To be sure, it will hurt, but not as much as it did when I was an accomplice to it.

– B

There is a message from his father, who never contacts him on the phone, let alone via email. It's also two days old:

Son:
I tried your phone but no one answers. You should do something about that. The Gallaghers' son Phelam was kind enough to stop downloading pornography for a few minutes and type this for me on his computer. I know that you were just here, but I think you should try to come back again, before Christmas. I worry about your mother, she is lonely and your visits always seem to lift her spirits. Mine too, believe it or not. I just reshingled the roof with a nice

> *architectural-grade product. They wanted to give me the thirty-year shingle but I said no go. Give me the forty. So that's one less thing to worry about for the next four decades, at least.*
>
> – *Dad*

He scrolls to the top of the message and writes down Phelam Gallagher's email address. Something must be up for his father to contact him at all, let alone via the notorious Internet. Maybe it's his father's health. Or his mother's. Or maybe his father had seen all of this coming, this crisis of faith, of everything, and decided to reach out in this strange way. *Leave it to dad to use shingle talk to get me all choked up*. He decides that he will write back to his father and mother later, from his anonymous Hotmail account, as soon as he's done with the other messages. But what exactly will he tell them? That he's on a deserted island in Fiji with a South African hooker? That he's hiding from... what? Everyone and everything? Or tell them that he's in Rio, that their very important son is at a very important conference, and he'll call them as soon as he gets back into the States. This is what he'll do, he decides. And this is what they'll think they want to hear, that this child of theirs is still successful and worldly and important. It's great for bragging to the neighbours, and to an extent it validates their child-rearing skills, that they raised someone so important that the world is his office, that even his failures are newsworthy. But he's certain that they'll feel something different. They'll feel a kind of loneliness that only a parent can feel. A loneliness that can no longer be rationalized away by the knowledge that their far-from-home child is successful, doing the kinds of things they had always hoped he would do, because down deep he knows that they don't believe any of it, that they realize now that their very definition of success for their son had been so wrong.

There are two messages from the Johnsons:

Tried you in Rio but no answer at the hotel or on your cellphone. Are you avoiding us again, Yates? Or are you just on thong patrol? Curious, do you have an event scheduled in Rio, or are you on holiday? Either way, enjoy, because your presence is requested at the Destination Capitalization Conference in the newly democratized, or about-to-be-democratized, nation of Bas'ar. You are to leave one week from today, arriving a week before the actual conference. So you can have a chance to be "in-country" for a bit to get oriented, to get the proverbial feet wet, the lay of the land, the Kevlar fitted to work with the cut of your suit. More details to come, including backgrounder links, white papers, contacts, lodging, etc., etc. Please do call us soon.

Twelve hours later, the second message:

Hello... knock-knock. Anybody home? You're making us worried, Yates. Don't like that at all. Call. Write. Now. Seen any good Italian movies lately?

This last sentence is accompanied by a video attachment. He knows what it is before he opens it, but he opens it anyway. He watches the girl on the Vespa, watches her pass him at the café, watches her look his way, then he stops it, shuts it down, just before she reaches the crowd.

He writes back:

Gentlemen. Apologies for not getting back sooner. I have been on a bit of a bender. Thongs, mojitos, steak, etc. Not a lot of time spent in the old room, if you know what I mean. FYI, this is strictly a pleasure trip, and who can blame me for living it up a bit since you're sending me to what is perhaps the most God-awful, dangerous place on the planet? I will look at the background links when they arrive and will do my best to hone up before departing. The Destination Capitalization Conference. Just rolls off the tongue. I already have a good sense of what kind of shite you want me to shovel there, but of course I'll do my homework. In the mean time do me a favour and cut me a little slack. Peace out.

– Y

This, he first sends to Campbell's Hotmail account. As they'd previously agreed upon, Campbell will forward it on to the Johnsons from there.

Back in his regular email account for one last peek, he finds this, from N-IV-31:

The Moon in the middle of the night...
The young sage alone with his mind has seen it.
His disciples invite him to become immortal...
His body in the fire.

He shuts off the laptop and looks at the moon, sinking and barely visible now behind horizon clouds. It is almost dawn. The fruit bats are flying back to treetop havens as the birds of the day, terns and frigates, begin to stir. For a moment he is certain that Nostradamus knows where he is. The young sage, alone with the moon, waiting for the fire. Then he calms himself down, convinces himself that no one except Campbell knows where he is, and even Campbell doesn't know exactly where. He convinces himself that he is safe for now. For the time being. But what he can't or won't bring himself to do is to think beyond that, to any version of tomorrow.

Namotu Lefts

Is there symbolism in shingles? Was his father telling him, *I'm going to live for ever?* Or, *Even when I'm dead, I'll still have it together, I'll still be the one in control, doing things the right way, protecting your head, so don't mess it up, and don't go blaming me when it all goes to hell.* Yates wonders. As he opens his eyes, feeling hung-over despite (or because of) the fact that he hasn't had a drop of alcohol in two days, he wonders, and he reminds himself that he still owes the old man some kind of reply. He vows to figure out by the end of the day exactly what that will comprise.

When he goes outside, the sun is well up in the sky – near noon, he reckons. On the beach he sees Jope's boat up on the sand and tied off on the same piece of driftwood. Jope and Marjorie are at the picnic table when he joins them.

"*Bula,*" they say together, both smiling, and Yates says "*Bula* right back at ya. What's in the cup?"

"Tea," Marjorie says. "Ceylon. Jope brought us a bag and a propane stove." She holds out a cup for Yates. He smells it and sips.

"Delicious."

"And here," she says, "honey biscuits."

"You ready to step up and ride the left today?" Jope asks. "Swells are picking up."

Yates stretches his sore back, shakes his head. "I had an inside-the-barrel epiphany yesterday just before the reef almost carved me to pieces. I decided I want to live. Marjorie's the one who ought to ride."

Jope looks at her. "You surf, Miss Marjorie?"

She changes the subject. "I told Jope about dinner last night. He's been giving me more recipes. Today I want to do octopus. After lunch we're gonna go with spears out on the reef."

"Sit, brother," Jope says, and Yates obeys. "If you want to see something beautiful, I can take you to Namotu this afternoon. Right off the beach, it's a long, glassy left, perfect for the longboard and the break – they say on the two-way – is rising."

Yates looks at Marjorie. She's smiling. "Sure," he says. "I'd like to see it. But I'm done surfing. You gonna surf?"

Marjorie shakes her head. She takes another biscuit and stands up. "Jope said he can take us onto Namotu Island afterwards. He works at the camp there and he's invited us to have dinner with them tonight."

"Who's them?"

"The surfers he's taking care of."

"What about the octopus?"

"We can bring it, with some kava."

Yates looks into his mug of tea. He doesn't want to leave. Doesn't want to see anyone, even if they have no idea what his story is. And he definitely doesn't want to experiment with kava again. Then he looks at Marjorie and he can see that this is something she wants. He thinks about what it must be like for a woman of her age, from her background, in the exotic South Pacific for the first time, stuck alone on an island with the likes of him, and he is embarrassed for having hesitated. "Sounds good to me. On one condition."

"What's that, old man?"

"I'll stay for dinner, but first I want to see you surf."

* * *

It's just a ten-minute boat ride across Malolo Passage. Marjorie and Jope had spent the rest of the morning beachcombing and spear-fishing, and now, in a tub in the back of the boat, they have a decent-sized octopus that Jope had speared as well as a dozen Pacific baby lobsters plucked from lava tubes on the outer reef. While Jope drives, Marjorie stays at his side, listening to his descriptions of the surrounding waters and islands. Yates sits on the back rail, near the lobsters and the octopus, the bundled banana leaves and the jugs of fresh coconut juice that Marjorie and Jope had gathered for their dinner. It's a short ride, but to Yates it seems like the water changes every minute, from flat to choppy, shallows to deep blue-black channels and then to big rolling swells.

First the island comes into view and then, as the boat rises in a swell, he can make out the line of surfers just off shore. As they get close to the pack, Jope slows the boat and tells Marjorie to put on her gear, the vest and boots and the sunblock. After she straps the leash to her ankle, she looks at Jope for instructions.

"Tide is good. When it's too low, the current gets too strong to surf. And the wind is still down, so the break should stay clean. Bigger than what you saw yesterday morning," he says to Yates. "Over seven, looks like. But it breaks in deeper water, so don't worry none about slicing yourself up on the bottom. And if anyone gives you a hard time, because resort people are claiming rights to this break too, you tell 'em you're with Jope. Once we bring the boat in past the reef I'll get my board and join you. If you want to stop, if it gets too tough, just paddle in. There's a bar right on the beach."

"Which is where I'll be," says Yates.

Marjorie zips up her rash vest, looks at Yates.

"You don't have to go if you don't want to," he says.

"I know."

"I only said it because I thought you might like it. And that it might make you feel better."

"Uh-huh." Marjorie stands up on the back rail of the boat and jumps. Yates watches her paddle for a moment, long enough to see that she will prove to be a much better surfer than he could ever dream of. Part of him wants to jump in after her, but he realizes it would only slow her down. They watch her paddle over to the eight surfers in the line-up near the break. He expected them to give her attitude, but they're all friendly. Yates hears them shout "*Bula!*" even though they're all Americans and Australians, and he hears Marjorie shout "*Bula Bula!*" as she glides alongside them.

He watches as the others tell Marjorie about the break, how it's holding up, and how she shouldn't mind their mates back at the bar who are drinking Fiji Bitters and holding up mock scorecards after each set. Yates and Jope wait in the boat to see how some of the others attack the long right-to-left break, to see what they do with swells larger than anything Yates has ever seen. He's looking at the others, but Marjorie pounces first. Without a word she dips her head and begins to paddle, slicing through the round top of the swell and then rising up onto her board with such grace that it gives Yates joy just watching her, knowing that he knows her, sort of. From behind he sees her upright and perfectly balanced only for an instant before she drops the tip of the board and starts down the wave face. For a couple of seconds she disappears, then rises back up into view before dropping away again.

"Your lady's killin' it," an American college kid shouts to him. "She's fucking smokin'."

"She's not my lady," he says, but not loud enough for the kid to hear. When he looks back, Marjorie reappears on the crest of the wave, and for a second, as Jope's boat dips into a trough and Marjorie's wave peaks, it looks like the whole world is rising up beneath her.

On the beach he surprises himself by declining a Fiji Bitters, by declining any alcohol. He's content to sit on the sand and watch Marjorie through borrowed binoculars. He watches her laughing with the young strangers, watches her attack the waves with a growing intensity, a growing confidence and an obvious joy.

It is late afternoon and the wind, calm all day, rises slightly out of the west. "It's picking up," Jope says. "Getting bigger." Yates picks up the binoculars. He's been watching for more than two hours and now there are only two surfers left, Marjorie and an Aussie the guys on the beach are calling C-Mac. Two sets pass before Marjorie sees something that excites her. "Here we go," Yates sees her say, and she begins paddling up the back of a massive swell. Just as it starts to curl into a barrel, she pops up, but the thing with this wave is that it keeps rising, rising and curling more than the others. Marjorie flexes her knees and turns up the wave face, which forms clear and smooth as it curls over her. Yates watches her slash in and out of the teeth of the growing barrel. He watches it wrap over and around her, a wave so high that it blots out the setting sun. But then she reappears again, backlit by fire inside the tube. Then he sees her reach out to touch the back of the still-forming glass of the inner tube. But she doesn't. She brings her fingertips as close as she can, but she doesn't let them touch. It's as if, Yates thinks, touching it would bring it all down too soon, the most perfect thing he's ever seen. For a moment he loses her, and he gets up off the sand and looks to the others to see if they are also concerned, because for the first time it occurs to him that she could actually fall. But then she reappears, her silhouette crashing through the white foam mist into the light like a ghost through the wall of a dream.

There are only twelve of them at the camp, including Marjorie, Jope and Yates. Four women and eight men. Rather than surf, and perhaps because he was intimidated by Marjorie's skills, Jope ultimately decided to stay behind and prepare a fire and the hot stones for the *lovo*. At the tiki bar everyone is drinking Fiji Bitters, cans of Fosters lager and some kind of rum drink. Everyone except Yates. Despite feeling sore and flat-out old, he feels good, and he feels like drinking might jinx it, might make him think of something other than the waves and the laughter of Marjorie with the others, and the smell of coconut-milk-marinated octopus wrapped in banana leaves, smoking over hot stones.

As he listens to the surfers talk about music and books and waves he has never heard of, he feels even older. But rather than regret his age or envy their youth, he's happy just to listen to them, content to ride in the draught of their energy, to feed off the vibe of the living.

C-Mac is slicing yellow-fin sashimi on a flat stone and telling Marjorie how he saw the tuna chasing bait fish this morning and caught it in a skiff on the far side of the reef. He dips a piece in a chilli sauce he's prepared and holds it up for Marjorie. She leans forwards and he places it in her mouth. While she's chewing, C-Mac says something that Yates can't hear, and Marjorie does something Yates has never been able to get her to do. She laughs.

Even though he's the only Fijian of the group, Jope insists that they all drink some *yaqona* from the ground-up kava root. When his turn comes, Yates tries to block out the last time he drank kava, tries to think of this as an altogether different drink consumed by an altogether different person than the disillusioned, whisky-in-a-coconut-drinking, breast-puker of Déjà Vu, and it goes down fine.

After dinner they go back to the small tiki bar. While Jope serves and drinks with them, they press him for information on the area's other renowned breaks –Wilkes Right, Swimming Pools, Restaurants, Albert's Place. At one point Yates wants to know what the deal is with the motivational speaker Tony Robbins's decadent retreat on the other side of the passage, but the others either don't know who he's talking about or don't care, and the talk quickly returns to surfing and, again and again, to the legendary Cloudbreak, partly because when the swell is high enough the surfing there is as good as anywhere in the world, and partly because it is a forbidden break, off-limits to everyone except guests of the resort on Tavarua Island. So, understandably, when Jope tells them that because the resort is almost empty this week he might be able to bring them to Cloudbreak for a few hours tomorrow morning, it is all they can talk about.

"Can we go?" Marjorie's question surprises him. Marjorie, who twenty-four hours ago insisted she no longer surfed. She'd been talking with C-Mac and two of the American girls, and he'd been sitting quietly, listening to the others, watching the kava and the drinks sink in. He looks at Jope, who shrugs. "Cloudbreak is a little different. You got the reef snapping at your feet there. And if the end of today is a sign, it looks like the swell is getting agitated."

C-Mac weighs in. "It's a wild ride, Yates."

Yates's pride rises at the adolescent challenge. But before he can say, *Oh yeah, motherfucker,* Marjorie speaks. "We don't have to go. I can surf again tomorrow back at our place."

Yates smiles at her. Now he doesn't know what to say. He wants to go because of the challenge, and to shove C-Mac's face in it, even if he dies trying. But he can tell that it will be best for Marjorie if she went and he stayed behind. "You know, my back is a disaster. I had no right even trying Desperates. So I'm gonna pass on Cloudbreak for now. For ever, actually. Which means you're gonna have to get your mentoring from someone else tomorrow, C-Mac. But you've gotta go, Marjorie. Show these boys how it's done."

One of the Americans breaks out an acoustic guitar, and of course he starts playing Jack Johnson, and of course the handsome son-of-a-bitch is good. After a while Yates gets Jope's attention and persuades him to sneak off and shuttle him back to his island. No matter how good you feel about yourself, no matter how beautiful the setting, no matter how humble and selfless you have become or are trying to become, you can sit watching people younger than you are party without joining them, without trying to be like them, for only so long.

When he gets back onto the anonymous island, he lays on his cot and thinks about the way the others had all talked about the jolt of adrenaline, the rush they felt surfing breaks this challenging, this beautiful. But Yates can't relate. What he had felt the short time that he was on the water was fear. And he realizes that it isn't only on the water that he feels it. He feels it everywhere, every day. It just manifests itself differently. Closing his eyes he wonders if he'll ever be able to replace it with joy.

He doesn't hear the boat, or her entering the hut. He's been asleep for several hours and, when he feels her getting into his cot alongside him, he's not really sure where he is, or who is sidling up to him in the sticky darkness. She finds his hand and squeezes it with hers. He waits. For the other hand to reach for another part of him. For her lips. But nothing, for a long time. Long enough for him to figure out who she is, where he is. He reaches for her other hand, but it is wrapped around the hairbrush she had left in his hotel room in Johannesburg.

"How long have you had it?"

"Since I found it in my room."

"Why did you keep it?"

"To give it back to you. Or as a keepsake. Preferably the former."

She turns the brush handle around in her palm, touches the bristles with the fingers of her other hand. She smells like rum and coconut juice.

"What about Cloudbreak?"

She doesn't answer for a while. "You were jealous of him, weren't you?"

"Absolutely. But it made me feel good, that you enjoyed them."

"Good, and jealous."

"Correct. But mostly good."

"The emotionally scarred young woman being eased back into society. Getting the attention of a handsome young man unaware of her dark past."

"Surfing and spear-fishing her way back to health and happiness."

She laughs. Not as loud as she had earlier with C-Mac, but it is genuine. "How long are we going to stay here?"

"I don't know."

"Why don't you just do what they ask and be done with them?"

"If I knew it was one thing and then I'd be done with them, maybe I would. Plus, it matters that I take a stand. Maybe a month ago it wouldn't have. But right now it does."

"Avoiding them isn't necessarily a stand."

They're quiet again. For a few moments his whole body trembles, then it passes, like a fever shiver. When it stops, she leans on her side and rises up on an elbow. "What you asked about yesterday – I came here, I followed you, not because I cared for you, but because I had to leave. One summer I was surfing with my brother and the next he was dead, my parents were dead, and I was worse than dead. I was left alone. With nothing. One summer I was looking into universities, deciding between Medicine and Agriculture. The next I was alone. And the summer after that, Johannesburg."

"I don't know what to say. Other than I want you to be happy."

"But I don't feel that way about you now. I care about you. How much, or which way, I don't know. Leaving me with them, thinking that that would make me happy... I thought it would make me happy. But when you left, it made me sad. How I feel about you truly – it's more than caring. I don't know. Is it okay that I don't know for now?"

"It is. It's incredibly okay."

She leans forwards and kisses him. But rather than tasting rum and coconut and the soft lips of a beautiful woman, he tastes his own anxiety and desperation, and something that is much better than fear.

When she pulls back to look at him, to see what's wrong, he pulls her closer to him, touches her hair with his hand and kisses her forehead. "What?"

"I don't know. I always do the wrong thing. I just don't want to do the wrong thing with us."

After another pause, she says, "I spoke to Jope on the way back tonight, and he said he would take us to Cloudbreak tomorrow afternoon, without the others. If the swells cooperate."

On the 180th Meridian (or Thereabouts)

The Futurist's father died tomorrow. Or was it yesterday? He's not sure. The email from home is dated one day later than today, and because of the International Date Line's crooked path through Fiji, Yates is confused. Either way, it's too late.

He had always thought his mother would die first. After all, she was the smoker. She's had the strokes, the quadruple bypasses. The so-called sedentary lifestyle. But his father was always going. Always working. Not working doing the crap Yates did, but working with his hands. Building houses. Cutting trees. Paving roads. Since he retired ten years ago, his father spent a good part of almost every day preparing his house for his death. And ironically (and accidentally), this is how he died, making sure that the house he shared with his wife would be safe and secure when he was no longer there. It wasn't enough to redo the roof himself – the tarpaper, the flashing, the snow shield and the forty-year architectural shingles (because the thirty-year shingles were apparently too structurally suspect for the seventy-four-year-old couple). He had to do the gutters too. Vinyl gutters that some guy with a truck and a roller could have banged out in half a day – but he didn't know the contractors and therefore didn't trust them. He didn't want to shell out the extra three grand, didn't want them to wreck what he'd worked so hard perfecting.

So he died doing it himself. At first they thought he had just fallen, but when they found him, before he died, he told them it was his heart. Yates wonders if his father knew. If his father had tracked him down to say goodbye in his own way. Of course he had. His father never did anything on a whim. *I worry about your mother, she is lonely and your visits always seem to lift her spirits.* He had reached out to Yates, and the Futurist has missed the signs.

Before dawn, before he found out about his father, he got up to walk alone on the beach. Marjorie was asleep. A grey scrim of cloud muted the sunrise, and the wind had shifted and was pushing the mild swells back upon themselves. Having missed out on the sunrise he'd got up for, he walked back to the activity hut and broke out his laptop.

The emails started bad and got progressively worse.

Okay. We know for a fact that you are not in fucking Rio. Don't know what you are thinking, how you thought you could do this to us and possibly believe you could have any kind of life going forwards. Unless of course this is a simple misunderstanding. Perhaps you're in some other Rio. Or perhaps you decided to get an early jump on your imminent trip to Bas'ar, and you're holed up somewhere boning up on the Koran, burka dos and don'ts and how to say "phenomenal investment opportunity" in thirty-six languages. That must be it, right?
Sincerely,
Johnson (Johnson is on vacation this week)

Next came another note from Nostradamus.

Nostradamus knows that you are in Fiji. He also knows that you are with your South African whore-friend. And that you have really pissed off a lot of people, whom Nostradamus has decided to keep in the dark, for now, regarding your whereabouts. Nonetheless, I predict very bad things for the future of Yates. What do you predict? Or are you out of the business of Tomorrow? Are you no longer a Codifier of Cool, A Commissar of What's Next? You may not know this, but many of my predictions have not been seen by human eyes for many centuries. Some are kept in a papal vault, but others are simply unaccounted for. Missing. (Century VII, quatrains 43–100 for those keeping score at home). Missing, but they do exist. And some, Yates, are all about you. You'll see. But first, I'll leave you with an old favourite to contemplate on the flight to Bas'ar.

The Third Antichrist (hmmm, maybe you?)
Very soon annihilated...
The heretics are dead, captives exiled,
Blood-soaked human bodies, and a reddened, icy hail covering the earth.

–N-VIII-77

Two notes down was the message from home – from his neighbour's teenage son – actually about his father.

As he walks back to the hut, to tell Marjorie that he has to go, that she is welcome to stay or to come with him, he's already forgotten about the Johnsons and Bas'ar and Nostradamus. He's thinking about the stars he had seen in the southern sky these last few nights, about the note he never would have expected and about the note he never sent.

By late afternoon they are in a car on the main island, Viti Levu, on their way to Nadi Airport. Jope had shown up in his boat after breakfast to tell them that no one would be surfing today at Cloudbreak or anywhere else, and Yates told him that he had to leave the anonymous island and the nation of Fiji as soon as possible. Marjorie had helped him pack and had made them breakfast. She didn't ask him any questions about his plans, her plans, or theirs. She just went where he did. On the boat and now in the car she doesn't talk at all, but she stays close, and he feels better because she is near. They drive from the southern part of Nadi Bay to the airport along a road that passes through miles of sugar-cane fields. At an intersection Yates looks out of his rain-streaked window at a young man wiping his machete clean, a piece of cane dangling from his mouth, waiting for someone to tell him what to do next.

At the airport, Jope checks their bags and gets their tickets for the flight to LA and the connection to New York. Their Resnor connection accelerates the process. In the lounge at the gate, Jope and Marjorie sit away from Yates and talk quietly for a while. They exchange addresses and hugs. At the gate, Yates hugs Jope as well and hands him an envelope filled with American cash.

Marjorie takes the window seat, but she is asleep before they are even off the ground. As they ascend, he looks out at a sunset seascape silhouetting her face. He tries to identify the islands he had seen, the passages, even the Mamanuca Group. But there are hundreds of them now, and as they rise he concedes that he knows none of it and never will, and he thinks it's ironic and maybe even profound in some pretentious Icarus-like way that you can see the most islands just before you get too high to see any.

When the jet banks back to the right and the wings level out, he picks up the in-flight magazine and thumbs through an article on Fijian history. A woodcut gets his attention. It shows half a dozen canoes filled with warriors of the Yasawa Islands chasing Captain William

Bligh in his longboat in May 1789, right after the mutiny on his ship the *Bounty*. First a mutiny, then this, Yates thinks. But Bligh survived the mutiny and escaped from these warriors, and went on to live another thirty years. Quietly, he rips out the woodcut and scribbles a note on it that he will mail to Lauren during the stopover in LA.

Bula! from historic Fiji!

Homeland

He once wrote a novel about the future, in the tradition of H.G. Wells and Jules Verne and Ray Bradbury, when he was nine years old, and called it *Kinda Like Today, Only Better*. Once an administrative official at NASA called his house during dinner time to discuss his recent job application, when he was ten. Once, when his father noticed that he was reading a book about the 1938 World's Fair, he drove him to Spokane that so he could experience one for himself. Senior year in high school, he was voted Class Optimist.

There was a time when he believed. And not just because he wanted to believe, but because he really did believe. There was a time when he truly thought that things were always getting better, that the world was a remarkable place where fascinating things happened every second. He believed that science had a heart, that progress had a conscience and that true art happened in the last synapse before epiphany, in the unstoppable momentum of an original idea. And, for a while, others believed this too, because of him. It's not that he was in denial about the horrors of everyday life – the wars, the greed, the natural disasters, the backward-thinking morality of the masses. He just chose to seek out and revel in the progressive, in the enlightening, in the smallest thing that could spark a flint under the arse of change. Then there was a time when, although he still believed, he began to acknowledge the difficulties. He began to recognize that such grand dreams were not so easily achieved, that the obstacles standing in their way were not so easily overcome. And he began to acknowledge this in his speeches and presentations. He began to criticize the present and he warned of a more damaged tomorrow if we refused to change. He gave heads-ups and watch-outs, supported by facts and scientifically validated forecasts and cautionary tales.

When it was suggested to him that he might want to put a bit more of a smile back on his work, because clients were complaining, because people were asking for other speakers, his first reaction was to go harder the other way. To shove the idealistic truth in their faces and shock them into epiphany. But that didn't work at all. People didn't want wisdom, he soon discovered. They wanted shortcuts to getting more. For a while his clients, other than small liberal arts colleges, not-for-profits and those who hadn't done their homework, stopped asking for him altogether. His message didn't match the extravagant, NASDAQ-giddy times. There wasn't any momentum to it, any positive inevitabilities. It lacked anything close to a guarantee that the prosperity would never end. So he altered his approach again. He avoided the dismal truths, the warnings about doomsdays yet to come, and he tried to be encouraging. *We can do better*, was his new positive spin on it, his mantra. But they didn't buy that either. Clients found it patronizing, condescending. It came off more like a lecture than a speech. More like a reason to feel guilty than a reason to be excited. Finally the think tank threatened to drop him. The lecture agent stopped taking his calls. The press rarely mentioned him. So he changed again. He began telling people what they wanted to hear. He began to customize his optimism to specific industries, specific companies, specific versions of tomorrow. And this is important: he wasn't lying, at least at first. The main difference was that he was only telling the good parts, the truths they wanted to hear. The bad parts, he left out entirely. It was easy. Appearance after appearance, everyone ate it up and soon he was a bona-fide player again. He got a new lecture agent, the think tank gave him his own sub-brand. His appearance fees tripled and he was a rock star in the arena of what-if. Everything was great as long as he didn't think about it too much.

But he did. Eventually Lauren stopped listening to what he had to say, because it was all the same, all a bit too good. His father, who never took his job seriously, began to think that these prophecies were borderline delusional – at least that's what his mother told him. Blevins's reaction to the latest incarnation of Yates was to try to steer him back towards the material that had attracted him to Yates in the first place. But that didn't work, and for a while, until Johannesburg, Blevins questioned Yates less and less and could hardly look him in the eye when Yates asked his opinion of his latest insights. The only people who loved what Yates was saying were the people for whom he had less and less respect, including himself.

Then the stock market collapsed, the Internet frenzy cooled, and buildings and bombs began to fall, and he didn't have an answer. He didn't have any new wisdom or truth or reason to believe that he could honestly tell anyone any more. And the only way he could come up with a way to make people feel good, to tell them what they wanted to hear, was to start making things up.

His father would not have found humour in the fact that the news of his death came to his son via the Internet. His father wasn't exactly a Luddite, but he did hate the

Internet. And this wasn't because he was afraid of it, or didn't understand it. In fact he probably understood the science behind the Internet more than most (and with time he had even grudgingly acknowledged its practical and professional possibilities). What his father hated wasn't so much the Internet itself, but the hoopla that surrounded it, from the NASDAQ-IPO hysteria to the over-promises of the journalists, marketeers and politicians. Sure, he hated the dot and he hated the com. But most of all he hated the dot-commers themselves. He hated them and anyone who tried to exploit the technology by telling people that they had to have it, that it was going to change their lives for ever.

"No piece of wire or silicon is going to change one aspect of my life for a second, let alone for ever," he often said.

This view, not surprisingly, made for some disturbingly awkward pauses at the dinner table during Yates's visits home, when his mother would innocently turn to her Internet-rich, futurist son and ask, loud enough for her Depression-era, transistor-radio-listening husband to hear, "So how is work going? What's the next big thing?"

Twenty-seven hours later he is in a town car with Marjorie, driving east on the Pennsylvania Turnpike towards his childhood home. The busy highway reminds him of a conversation he'd had with this father several years ago. He had been trying to explain an aspect of his prognosticating methodology, something about the economy, but his father had seen right through it.

"All you have to do is look at the highway to see the state of the nation, to see all you need to know about leading economic indicators," he had said. "You can talk to all the analysts and trend-spotters you want, but the tractor trailers in the passing lane will tell you more than any *Wall Street Journal* or CNBC forecaster. You can see a recession right in your side-view mirror. A boom right in front of you. You'll see it in the absence of things. Wheels and mudflaps. Fat men with amphetamine eyes glaring down at you as you pass them on an incline. You'll see the state of the economy by the amount of taken stools at the counter of the truckstop diner. You'll see it in the lack or prevalence of particle board and fibre-optic cable on flatbeds. Concrete culverts, turbines, sections of modular homes. When you have a nice traffic-free weekday ride on an interstate, when no one's bearing down on you or boxing you in, when there's no fruit or helix screws or homogenized milk sprayed across five lanes, no refrigerated truck stuck in the underpass, when you don't hear the word *jackknifed* in the traffic report on the eights, that's when you start worrying about the economy, when you start thinking this might be a good time to sell, to get out, to switch to an interest-bearing money-market account."

Actually, his father had only said the first part, and though Yates had dismissed it when he had heard it, he later found a way to expand on that sentence and use the rest of the preceding riff at a dinner given by a hedge-fund manager for his top 100 clients. He never told his father that the hedge-funders had eaten it up, never told him that he often applied his common-sensical, homespun approach when addressing complex things, and that people liked it, and liked him because of it. He realizes now that to dismiss a thing so passionately, especially when it came to his father, was to validate it.

It is raining, and they are barely moving, merging from four lanes to one. Marjorie is in the back seat to his right, looking out of the window. "So this will be your first memory of the United States." He says. "Jet-lagged, stuck in traffic, in the rain, on your way to the funeral of a man you never knew."

"The traffic is picking up, I see sun peeking over the hills up ahead, and he is your father."

"And you and I go way back. Cumulatively, close to a week by now, right?"

She smiles. The driver sneaks a look at them in the mirror, tries to pretend he's not listening. "Less than a week, actually. But this is our third continent, which should count for something."

Yates nods, looks outside at the green hills and dairy farms of the Lehigh Valley. He asks the driver to take the next exit, tells him they might as well take the scenic route.

Marjorie turns to him and smiles. She's all for the scenic route. A truck driver waves them into the right lane and a clear path to the exit ramp. "I'd like you to tell me about your father."

Yates takes a deep breath and looks outside at a billboard for a democratic senator from Kansas who's considering making a run at the presidency in three and a half years. This morning, at the airport, he had picked up the *Pittsburgh Post Gazette* and had gone right to the obits, just to check. Of course, his father wasn't listed. Besides, who would've written it all down and made the call? Sixteen-year-old Phelam Gallagher? Maybe in the local paper there will be something. In the *Gazette* there had been two obits side by side that caught his attention. One was for an eighty-eight-year-old man who had spent two hours every weekday morning for the last twenty-three years standing on a street corner near an on-ramp to the 405 in Los Angeles, waving to commuters. He wasn't insane, wasn't particularly poor. He started doing it the day after he buried his wife, because he wanted to make people feel better, he told a reporter who had done a feature on him several years ago. Whenever someone smiled back, it made him feel better. The headline above his picture said, WILLIE ROBISON, ELICITOR OF SMILES, 88. The headline that accompanied the obituary of the billionaire next to him read, WALLACE SHIRER, 76, TELEMARKETING GURU.

Yates knows he's oversimplifying but still he wonders which of these lives his father would have approved of more, if at all. Then he wonders what his father would have wanted the headline on his obituary to read. His father was a builder, but not a particularly wealthy or prolific one. He built homes, one at a time. Over the years he'd been offered jobs as a project manager with large developers who had been buying up dairy farms and apple orchards in the valley and putting up hundreds of homes at a clip. But he could never tolerate shoddy construction techniques (he used to go on for hours, if anyone was willing to indulge him, about the difference between custom work and developer work) and he could never abide having someone he didn't respect telling him what to do, even if they were right. So he lived a modest life as the custom builder of one or two homes a year. He was a veteran of the Korean War, the proverbial loving husband and the father of one living son and one deceased, an older brother Yates had never met.

WILLIAM YATES, 74, HUSBAND AND FATHER, BUILDER OF CUSTOM HOMES

Yates thinks this is a headline that his father might find tolerable. But Yates can't help adding his own take on his father's obit: *war hero, hard-arse, perfectionist, champion of underdogs, unperturbed by the rich, outwardly simple, inwardly complex, and like every human being you ever loved, a complete fucking enigma.*

"He died in the town in which he was born," he finally says to Marjorie. "The only time he left the United States was to fight in Korea. An experience about which, predictably, he never spoke. He married his childhood next-door neighbour when he got back home, had a son who died in his sleep, before I was born, at the age of three. He taught himself to be a master carpenter and eventually built homes with meticulous, obsessive, loving care. He loved the Pittsburgh Pirates and the Steelers. He treated my mother with respect and, if not love, a certain modicum of devotion. He was not comfortable with success, his or others', and mine in particular. And I can truly say that I don't think he ever did a thing in his life that he was ashamed of."

Marjorie takes this in. They are moving away from the highway. Hundreds of brown-and-white dairy cows cover the rolling green fields on either side of the road. "I think this is a lovely place to have grown up," she says.

His mother is pulling weeds in front of the house when the town car pulls into the driveway. "I could have warned you about her," Yates says to Marjorie. "But it's not like it would have helped."

Helen Eismann Yates looks at them and waves, but she doesn't get up. Instead she goes back to weeding around the pink-and-white impatiens.

"She's adorable."

"Your word. Let's revisit its accuracy tomorrow." The driver pops the trunk. They get out and approach her.

"One second. I promised myself I'd finish this before you got here."

"I'll finish it later, Ma."

"Nonsense. I won't have you wasting your short visit weeding."

"Instead I should spend it watching you do it, right? Anyway, Mom, this is Marjorie, my wife."

This gets Helen Eismann Yates to her feet. Rather than looking for weeds she is already looking over Marjorie for the human equivalent. "Well... my goodness."

"Yeah, she's a keeper all right."

"I'm not his wife, Mrs. Yates. I'm Marjorie. A friend."

When his mother looks at him for confirmation, he winks.

"Even though we just met," his mother says, "I'm going to believe Marjorie here. Simply because she hasn't spent the last thirty-odd years lying to me."

It always unsettles him, the first few minutes back in the house. Then it usually gets worse. This time, the absence of his father and the presence of Marjorie make it exponentially worse, but he tries to act like he is fine. Breathing in a scent of place he could never describe but would recognize anywhere in the world, it occurs to him that for his entire adult life the concept of home has been alien to him. Over the years he has lived in more than a dozen apartments in five different cities, and has travelled an average of 150 days a year. Only when he walks through this door does it occur to him that this may be as close as he will ever again get to feeling like he has a home. So much has remained the same since his childhood that the smallest change stands out like a major renovation.

"What happened to the 'Washington Crossing the Delaware' print?" He's in the entry hall. He hasn't even put down his bags.

"I threw it out this morning. I know it was his favourite, but I hated it. Especially in the entry hall."

"The least you can do is bury it with him. He claimed that we had an ancestor in that boat."

She smiles. "Oh, yeah. The same ancestor that signed the Declaration of Independence, raised the flag on Iwo Jima and was sitting on the fifty-yard line for Franco Harris's Immaculate Reception."

Marjorie looks at Yates for help. She hopes they're not talking about a man who died two days ago, even though she knows they are. They make their way into the kitchen. Yates puts on a pot of tea and motions for Marjorie to sit at the table. Outside the kitchen window is a flat, vast, recently mowed back lawn, spotted with bird-feeders and gnomes and Adirondack chairs. In the far-right corner is a vegetable garden, rimmed with an eight-foot-high deer fence.

"Did you cut the lawn?"

"No. He did."

"Like he knew. I'm surprised he didn't build his own coffin."

"He died doing what he loved."

"Preparing his house for his death, right? What was he doing, the roof?"

"The roof."

Yates looks at Marjorie. I told you. "I thought he had finished the roof. That's what he'd written to me."

"He was done but he kept going up to look at it, under the guise of 'checking things out'. He wanted to see how it handled the first rain."

"Sunday?"

His mother shakes her head. "Monday. He had just gotten home from church."

"He went to church on a Monday?"

"Six days a week, actually."

"I don't believe it. He never even went on Sundays when we were growing up. When did he find God?"

His mother takes a sip of tea and looks out of the window. "I have a theory, that all old men find God when they can't get it up any more. What do you think, Marjorie?"

Marjorie doesn't know how to answer this, and Helen Eismann Yates doesn't bother to wait for one. "Anyway. You two go freshen up. Take a nap. Then I'll fix a late dinner for you. I want to hear all about everything, but first you have to excuse me. *Jeopardy*'s on."

After she's gone, Marjorie looks at Yates for an explanation. When one doesn't come, she says, "I can see where you get your sense of... your sense of..."

"Cynicism? Humour? The moment?"

"She sounds like she's handling it all rather well."

"You think she's being kind of harsh, right?"

"Well."

"That's how we deal with grief. The more outwardly flippant she becomes, the more inwardly devastated she is."

Perpetual Swing State

Dinner in front of a big screen in a little room. Bratwurst, potatoes au gratin, and a behind-the-scenes, making-of-reality-TV show about a reality TV show.

"If it's reality, why is he reading a teleprompter during an alleged argument with his wife?" Yates asks.

"Don't cast your cynicism on my guilty pleasures," his mother says. "Who cares what's real or fake."

"Yeah," Marjorie agrees. She knows this show. Likes it. Used to get it on the dish in Johannesburg.

Even though it's July, the commercial breaks are almost all political ads.

If it weren't for legislation passed by Anthony Capalbo, the animal who brutally raped and tortured my little Jenny would've still been behind bars.

Dan Kirk thinks it's a good idea to put chemical weapons into the hands of known terrorist organizations.

Beth Ortiz thinks she has what it takes to be President of the United States. So, apparently, does the off-the-books, sixteen-year-old "cabana boy" who, among other things, "trimmed the hedges" at her $2.4-million estate.

"How come there are so many political ads?" Marjorie asks. "I thought you just had a presidential election."

"We did, sweetie," Helen says. "But we live in a so-called

swing state. Half blue, half red. Our handful of electoral votes determined the last two presidencies, so both parties have decided that it's never too early to start trying to sway us."

"But these commercials are not on behalf of anyone. They're just character assassinations."

"Exactly. Phase one. The weeding out of the weak. The exposing of the corrupt, or at least the ones they've chosen to call corrupt. They sling the mud on TV while in phase two they woo us in person. In the past six months I've had no less than six senators and three governors knock on my door, including one who now resides at 1600 Pennsylvania Avenue. I've had strudel with left-leaning Academy Award nominees, merlot with Grammy winners, coffee with the Head of the NRA, strolls in the park with a gay, fascist Olympic gold-medal-winning decathlete, and a fireside chat – or argument, actually – with the Reverend Billy Graham Junior. Christ, you can't even think of going into a diner, a Kwiki Lube or an ice-cream parlour without one of them sidling up to you, making nice. They're starting to get like the deer. Cute at first, from a distance, but in reality a terrible, destructive nuisance."

Yates sits up. "Are you suggesting we thin out the herd?"

His mother's eyes widen. "Oh my goodness, no. At least not without a licence and the proper tags."

Marjorie puts her hand over her mouth to keep the food in, she's laughing so hard. Not so much at Yates, but at his mother. At first he doesn't get it, Marjorie's attraction to his mother, then he absolutely gets it, why a young woman whose family has been taken away from her might enjoy spending time with such a character.

After dinner Marjorie and his mother go into the kitchen to clean up, and don't come back for a while. They make tea and sit at the table, and from the snippets of conversation and laughter he overhears, Yates figures they've already revealed more about themselves to each other in an hour than Yates had known in a week, a lifetime. He sits in his father's chair, drinking lemonade, watching his father's team, the Pirates. He doesn't know any of the players any more. At one time he knew them all, mostly because he thought that it would please his father. His father's favourite player was number 21, Roberto Clemente. The first year Yates had followed him, 1971, Clemente was in decline, but still a star. Yates didn't get it, because at that point there were bigger stars on the Pirates. Like the larger-than-life home-run-hitter Willie Stargell. But his father maintained that Clemente was a complete player who knew his role and never made a mistake and excelled in ways that only aficionados of the game could appreciate. In this room, sitting next to his father, Yates had watched Clemente help the Pirates win the 1971 World Series and later get his 3,000th hit against the New York Mets at the end of the '72 season. That winter, on 31st December, Clemente was on a humanitarian aid mission on a DC-7 that crashed into the Caribbean en route to earthquake-stricken Nicaragua. The next day, when the story broke in the US, was the only time that Yates had seen his father cry, and it was in this room. He looks around the room at the familiar objects. The ashtray from a vacation at Caesars Palace. The wedding picture. The baby pictures. The glued-together lamp he broke chasing a Super Ball in sixth grade. The bookshelf with the Sidney Sheldons, the Leon Urises. And, in a round plastic holder on the top shelf of a pine corner hutch, a baseball, autographed by Roberto Clemente, to Yates's father. Yates picks it up, takes the ball out of the holder and decides that when the women in the kitchen stop whispering and laughing and unearthing truths about him that he'd rather forget, he will tell his mother that this ball he never gave a second thought to for the last twenty years, he now wants to keep.

He once had a distinct point of view. Once he wrote an article for *The Atlantic Monthly* castigating the administration of the moment for premeditated crimes against the environment, including irresponsible offshore drilling, ignoring rising emission levels and warming threats and undermining the Kyoto Agreement. Once he went to Africa, not on behalf of a corporation or government, but to raise awareness of AIDS and formulate a plan for the millions of people on that continent stricken with it. He once gave a commencement speech at the Harvard Business School about "Poverty in the Outer City", another at Grambling on "The Future of Slavery". He was once on the board of the Boys & Girls Clubs of America. He once appeared with Hanson in an MTV Rock the Vote promo. He once voted religiously and taught creative writing to disabled veterans. He once gave blood regularly, gave advice freely and gave a shit. Really.

Then he didn't.

They were never a physical family. Maybe a kiss hello for his mother after a separation of a month or more, or a reluctant yet crushing handshake from his father. Maybe. The fact that he hasn't kissed or even hugged his mother since he's been home is what Marjorie doesn't understand, what she asks him about in the back of the funeral parlour.

"It's the German part of us."

She doesn't accept his offer of an explanation. "I'm half-German. My family always kissed each other. On the farm, my brother kissed my father goodnight every day of his life."

"My father's brother once said the only time he wants

to touch another human is if he's making love to them or punching them."

"Wonderful. Is he coming, this man?"

Yates shakes his head. "He was beaten to death in a bar fight in South Philly."

Marjorie doesn't blink. "Perhaps he crossed the line with someone. An inappropriate tap on the shoulder, an over-zealous pat on the back."

They both laugh for a while, then stare at each other for a while. "Your brother," Yates begins. "He was on the farm that day too?"

"He was."

"Were you close?"

She doesn't answer. Doesn't have to. "He died," she says, "trying to protect me."

At first they are the only three people in the funeral parlour. Yates's mother is upset, because the owner had to unlock the door for them and was still setting up floral displays around the coffin. When he was done with the flowers, the director opened the coffin and Yates went with his mother to kneel and pray. He didn't plan on looking at all, he was basically going to try to squeeze out a prayer, but that's all he finds himself doing, looking at his embalmed father and wondering. What was his attraction to the stars? The comfort of being able to identify fixed points in the universe, or the possibilities that coursed across the sky in their wake? Was he really happy framing houses, mitring joints, doing the things that separate the ordinary from the custom-built, or did he have another, unrequited dream? How did the death of his first son change him? Why, after sixty years of not going to church at all, did he go almost every day of the week? And what in the summer of 1955 prompted a conservative, white, German-American carpenter to make a skinny, black, Puerto Rican, Spanish-speaking right-fielder his hero?

His mother has to nudge him to get up with her. "My knees," she explains. He stops to look at the collage on an easel that his mother and Marjorie had put together late last night. Then he moves on to the framed photos on a walnut sideboard. For a moment he loses his train of thought, and as he watches the mortician straining to light a candle on a high brass stick near the coffin, a million lights flash before his open eyes, a million more spark inside his head. His knees bend and his legs wobble and his head feels as if a sluice gate has been opened, draining its blood from a reservoir of consciousness to the dead lake-bed of his soul.

Before he even starts to fall, and surely he is on his way to a hard landing at the base of his father's coffin, Marjorie puts her hand on his shoulder, then under his arm and guides him into a chair. When he opens his eyes, Marjorie's face is inches from his.

"Tell me I didn't faint."

"You had a spell."

"I fainted in front of my old man. He'd be so proud."

"You don't hug or kiss. You just pass out in front of each other."

"Don't tell my mother."

"My God. I'll get you some water."

It's a pretty good turnout. Lots of people he'd forgotten about, people he'd known as a child who had been relegated to parental anecdote for the last twenty years. They know all about him. His travels. His notoriety. *Your father told me,* said Tony the barber. Y*our old man was always giving us updates about you,* said Gerard from the lumber yard. *He was so damned proud of you,* said Isaac, the well-driller. *Of course he did. Of course he was,* Yates thinks. *And I was proud of him, too. We just never bothered to tell each other.* After a while he gets up and goes outside to the parking lot for fresh air.

"Yo, Futurist."

He turns. It's Blevins. They stare at each other for a while before Yates approaches and extends his hand. "You didn't have to come all the way out here."

Blevins stares at the pavement as he answers. "Not a problem. I have a gig in Lancaster County on Friday."

"The Amish are into futurists?"

He looks up, frowns. "No. A high-school reunion. My other job. The one that still pays."

"I'm sorry about Johannesburg. I'm sorry about blowing you off so much. I've been... conflicted."

"You know, I said what I said because I cared. I cared about you, and what you could accomplish if you set your mind to it."

"I know. I know. I kind of drifted from doing some of the stuff that mattered."

Blevins's expression softens a bit. "You mean the stuff that made me want to work with you in the first place?" Yates nods and Blevins sizes him up for a while. "Any chance," Blevins continues, a little too optimistically, "that after you regroup, rethink things, you might go back to it, to doing it right?"

For a second he thinks of saying exactly what Blevins wants to hear: that there is indeed an extremely good chance that he'd go back to being the man that Blevins once believed in. But that would be a lie, and as easy as it would be, as pleasant as it would make this uncomfortable moment, he decides not to. Blevins deserves better.

"I can't do it, dude."

Hope turns to confusion and then anger.

"I'm gonna try something else."

"You're gonna quit."

"I don't have the spirit, Blevins. I don't have the religion. It helps to actually believe what you feel so passionately about, and I don't know what to believe any more. I'm tired. I hope you understand." Yates steps forwards to shake hands again, but Blevins takes a step back. "Look, I've got to get back. You comin' in?"

Blevins shakes his head. "I just wanted to stop by, pay my respects. See if, in light of things, you might have reconsidered, might have changed."

"Sorry to disappoint. Thank you for coming all the way out here, Blevins. I mean it."

Blevins reaches for his keys, clicks open his locks. "It's what people do, Yates."

When he goes back inside, he sees Marjorie against the far wall of the anteroom, talking to Lauren, who must have arrived while he was in the parking lot talking to Blevins. His first instinct is to go back outside and hop into his car and drive, but they both see him and are enjoying watching him squirm. On the way over he decides that a handshake will suffice, but as soon as he's within arm's reach, Lauren is hugging him.

"I'm sorry."

"Thanks for coming. It's a surprise."

"I told your mother I was coming."

"Did you call Blevins?"

"Who?"

"Ble— Never mind. Man, you look wonderful."

"Aren't you going to ask about Stephen?"

"Who?"

"The history teacher."

"No. I'm not. That would demonstrate that I'm still emotionally attached to you. That I still obsess about our failed relationship."

Marjorie bows her head, then looks up. "I think I will take a little walk."

As Marjorie leaves, Lauren watches, then says, "I like her. A little young for you, but she seems like she can handle it."

Yates considers trying to tell Lauren the truth about Marjorie, then lets it go. Let her think what she wants.

"Are you well otherwise?"

Yates shakes his head. "No. I am not."

"I got your gifts. They're very funny. I think they got to Stephen."

"That's a shame. You talk about him in past tense."

"We broke up."

"Really? I imagine I'm a tough act for anyone to follow."

"Maybe so. But he left me."

"I see. You could have made me feel good and told me you left him, because of me. Me and my funny gifts."

"I don't think that's what you wanted to hear anyway. I don't think you even know what you want to hear."

"Anyway, it was nice of you to come all this way."

"When your mother called, I had to come. For her. You know, she worries about you. We all do."

"I don't know what to say other than I'll try not to be the kind of person who makes people worry about them."

"That's it?"

"I don't know, Lauren. What am I supposed to say? That I'm angry? Heartbroken? The truth is we probably had no reason staying together other than the fact that we were relatively comfortable with each other. The only thing that sucks is that you realized it first, because I was too caught up being the monster I'd become. Listen, you were right to do what you did. You look great, and I want you to be happy."

She steps back and considers him. She hadn't expected this. "When are you coming out to San Diego again?"

"To try to rekindle our relationship or get my earthly possessions out of the apartment?"

Only two people who have lived together more than five years can stare at each other this long. At one point she looks like she might cry, at another like she might spit at him. In the end, Lauren smiles and says, "I don't know, Yates. Maybe we should just go out for a cup of coffee or something and take it from there."

If Lauren was the ghost of Yates past and Blevins was the ghost of Yates present, then Johnson, standing next to a pastor from his parent's church, talking like he's been in the parish for ever, is the ghost of Yates yet to come.

"Was that you who sent the horseshoe-shaped arrangement that looked like it was stolen from the winner's circle at Philadelphia Park?"

Johnson steps away from the Pastor and reaches to shake Yates's hand, but Yates offers no hand to shake. "No," Johnson says through a fake smile, "I'm the one who sent the fresh poppies from Bas'ar. I'm impressed that you recognize me, Yates."

"And I guess I'm impressed that you came all the way here to find me."

Yates says this as he starts back out to the parking lot. Johnson combined with the people inside is too much to handle.

"Actually, I took my kids to Hershey Park for the weekend. I was in the neighbourhood, so to speak."

"Listen, I'm going to have to take a rain check on the Middle Eastern vacation. Maybe there's some local tradeoff we can negotiate."

"Like a gig in Cabo, or Montreal? Something more accessible, something a bit less volatile?"

"Yeah."

"Not a chance."

"I'm not going to Bas'ar, Johnson."

Johnson looks around. The funeral parlour is next to a Carvel and a Blockbuster. It is staggeringly hot in the parking lot. "Bas'ar can't be much worse than this shithole."

"Destination Capitalization will do just fine without me."

"Perhaps it will, but we had an agreement, and I have guaranteed your attendance to people whose happiness is directly linked to my livelihood. My success."

"I'm not going to say it again..."

Johnson shoves Yates against the hood of an SUV and mashes his right forearm against his throat. "I know you're not gonna say it again. Because you will fucking go to fucking Bas'ar tomorrow afternoon, and here's why. We will share the Vespa tape with everyone from Interpol to the lowest-level traffic warden in Milan. We will leak it to the networks, the Internet, Al fucking Jazeera. You will not even be able to get a speaking gig in front of Cub Scout Pack 81. And if you run, no place on the planet will be remote enough for you. It's not a very good time to be a fugitive terrorist, Yates." When Johnson finally eases his forearm off Yates's throat, Yates shoves him away.

"I don't give a shit. Share the tape. Leak it. I did nothing and I'll do everything I can to take you down with me. I should have told you to fuck off from the start."

Johnson stares at him, gives a tiny nod. "I see you have your South African girlfriend with you."

"She's got nothing to do with us."

"She's a convicted criminal, you know. And she's wanted for additional crimes in Johannesburg. Prostitution. Terrorism-related activities. Perhaps drug possession. I can make a few calls and have her extradited within the hour. Believe me, Yates, she will go away for a long time, and the penal system there is no picnic."

"She's a goddamn kid."

Johnson shrugs. "Apparently she's not too young for you."

Yates stares at Johnson long enough to realize that punching him will not help. He drops his hands to his sides to control himself. "If I go, I want you to promise that you will leave her alone, that you'll let her stay here in America as long as she wants."

"You act as if I'm with the INS."

"You will leave her alone. And when this is over, when Destination Capitalization is done, then we are done too."

Johnson's cellphone buzzes. He takes it off his belt clip, checks to see who's calling and puts it back. "Fine," he finally says. "We leave her alone. Marry the bitch, for all I care. But here's how it's gonna go down tomorrow: after the funeral, let's say 3 p.m., a car will be in your mother's driveway to take you to JFK, where you'll catch an evening flight to Kuwait. In Kuwait you'll be met by a chaperone, and I imagine you'll bum a ride on a C-130 for a desert shuttle that will get you into Bas'ar International by nightfall. Once there, you'll be briefed, given some talking points, some safety tips and a schedule of events and interviews at which your enthusiastic participation will be required."

"What about the war?"

"What war?"

"The civil unrest. The blood in the streets. The clerics versus the mullahs versus the sheiks. The jihadis versus the revolutionaries versus the students. The Kurds versus the Sunnis versus the Shiites versus all things American. What about that?"

"It will all shake out. First of all there was no war. There was a peaceful political transition, and now it is time for the seeds of economic recovery to be planted."

"Your seeds. Your soil."

"Our interests. Plus, you won't be in Bas'ar City proper. You're gonna be at the airport, which is a veritable fortress."

"Thanks, I feel much better now." Marjorie is at the door, waving him inside. "Now, if it's alright with you, I'm going to say goodbye to my father."

Johnson gives a dismissive wave. "Go ahead. One thing. Don't try to run anywhere tonight. Maybe you'll get away for a while, but we'll catch up with you, with both of you, and do all of the horrible things I just talked about. I'm sorry it's come to this, Yates. Now, go inside. I've got to get back to the theme park."

Inside, in the receiving room, Marjorie tells him they are about to begin the service. Then she asks, "Who was that man? It looked like you were fighting."

"Him? He handles my speaking engagements. We had a disagreement about the logistics of my next trip."

"Where are you going?"

"That's what we were trying to figure out."

"When?"

"Not sure. Soon."

"Do you want me to come with you?"

Yates forces a smile. "I do," he says. "That would be nice, but it may prove difficult."

By the time Yates returns to his seat in front of the casket, the Pastor is just about finished with his eulogy.

Graveside

It's just four of them at the grave, five if you count his father. Yates, his mother, Marjorie and the Pastor. The coffin is already in the ground. The Pastor peeks down into the grave as if he wants to make sure the casket is in there. As he leans over the edge, Yates does all he can to fight the temptation to push him in. A car stops on the access road and two old men in VFW hats get out, one cradling a folded flag. They apologize for being late. They've been lost. When they all take their positions and the Pastor breaks open his Bible, Yates makes a show of putting his arm around his mother, the dedicated son, the rock, here to give loving support to those who need it most. But his mother feels like she needs about as much support as a marble column and, when no one is looking, she shrugs his arm off and takes a half-step to her left, towards Marjorie.

Earlier, his mother asked him to say a few words at the funeral parlour and, though it was barely two minutes long, it was the most difficult speech he had ever given. Not because of his emotional state, which was clearly unstable, but because he felt compelled to tell the truth, because the subject was his father. So he told the bit about the seventy-four-year-old who needed a forty-year shingle. He told them about his father's fascination with the night sky. About custom-built versus slapped-together. About how the things that his father refused to build said more about him than the things he built. He told them that his father did not believe in compromise and, other than the person standing here talking to you right now, there was no part of his life, nothing he ever did, that he could ever be ashamed of. He also told them about his father's love of Roberto Clemente, a man who lost his life trying to help others.

Last night, after the wake, after he had said goodbye to Blevins, Lauren and assorted members of the Knights of Columbus, the American Legion, the VFW, the Volunteer Fire Department and every plumber, carpenter, mason and electrician in town over the age of sixty, they went home, and again had dinner in front of the television. Because he had been at his father's wake, because he had seen his ex-live-in girlfriend for the first time since she had left him, and because he had scuffled in a funeral-parlour parking lot with a clandestine, psychotic corporate spy who blackmailed him into going to a newborn country in flames, Yates was pretty well fried and had wanted to go straight to bed. But because he knew what lay ahead of him, and that he might not see his mother and Marjorie for a long time, he stayed with them and watched *Jeopardy*, watched *Entertainment Tonight* and watched *Dart on the Map*, a show where for a half-hour every week they show a live camera feed from a different place on earth, and people watch by the tens of millions, hoping for something horrible to happen.

This week, the location was Rio.

When his mother got up to check on the apple pie, he looked at Marjorie. Before he left, he had to know. "What happened in Johannesburg? Why didn't you come back?"

She sighed, shook her head. She was in his father's chair in a T-shirt and shorts, with her legs crossed in the lotus position. "They stopped me," she said. "The

CBD people. When you gave the wrong speech, they were furious. They asked me what I knew. Then you did something else, went to someone's room and did something that I knew nothing about. They wanted to know who you had seen, what you were up to. Again I told them I didn't know, which was true. They slapped me but I said nothing. Then, when you called and told me to come with you, they were listening, and when I hung up they slapped me some more."

"I'm sorry. Were you going to come before they hurt you?"

"Oh, Yates. I don't know. It was inevitable that I'd get in some kind of trouble with them. With someone like them. I told you before, I had to leave. I'm lucky that you were there to help. That I ended up here."

"I feel lucky too."

Later, Marjorie went into the kitchen and told his mother that she insisted on doing the dishes. When his mother came back into the TV room, Yates turned up the TV volume and leant close to her. "I have to go away tomorrow. Right after the funeral."

"Will she go with you?"

He shook his head. "She can't. If she does, she can get in trouble, and she's seen enough trouble."

"She told me. So you're not going to tell her?"

"She'd come."

"Do you love her?"

"Enough not to want her to do something that might get her in trouble."

His mother looked at the TV for a while, at the place on the shelf where the Roberto Clemente ball used to be. "So what do you want me to do when she asks where you are?"

"Tell her that I had to go away on an emergency and that I want her to stay and take care of you for a while."

"I don't need taking care of."

"I know that," he said. "If anything, I'd like you to take care of her for a while."

In truth, he hoped that the two women, neither of whom would ever admit to needing care, would take care of each other.

In the afternoon, before he left for the funeral, his mother knocked on his door. When he opened it, she held out a watch, a black-banded, gold-cased Longines from the 1950s. His father's.

"I set it the way he always did," she said. "Ten minutes fast." Then she dropped it into the palm of her son, the Futurist.

Destination Bas'ar

On the plane – the first of three, an Air France Boeing 777 heading to Paris – he looks at the "official website" for Destination Bas'ar, or Destination Capitalization; the title flip-flops throughout the link, which is to be expected for an event that's been cancelled and rescheduled four times since Bas'ar became a nation or had nationhood thrust upon it, depending upon where you sit at the UN Security Council table. The home page calls it "an historic event, bringing together the international *privet sektor* business community with their sub-contractors and ministries, showing the world that Bas'ar is *open for business* – at the fairgrounds adjacent to Bas'ar International Airport". Yates tries to imagine what kind of fairs they could have possibly had at the so-called fairgrounds – Arts and Crafts? Renaissance? – since the airport is a recently built US military airstrip some fifteen miles out in the desert from bombed-out Bas'ar City. For a while he skims over the site, noting the list of exhibitors, the myriad ministries and commissions, the shifting members of the governing council, a message from the President of the United States on top of one from the Prime Minister of Bas'ar, a thousand variations on the statement that this is about so much more than oil, and five pages validating the credentials of the professional security force charged with keeping the Expo safe. Where one page dedicated to security measures would have given Yates faint reassurance, each successive page scares more and more of the living shit out of him.

During the changeover in Charles De Gaulle, he stretches his legs, buys a cup of tea and listens to a woman tell a man, "I am not celebrating your misfortune. But I am pleased that something happened to you that is finally beyond *your* control, because my life has always been beyond my control." In the otherwise empty men's room, he hears a man in a closed stall say, in French, "No one ever dies in Disney World, have you noticed?"

Paris to Kuwait. He tries to bone up on the region, on Islam, on hegemony. He reads paperbacks by Thomas Friedman, Bernard Lewis, Chomsky. When this thoroughly depresses him, he switches to science fiction, stories by Philip K. Dick. He escapes, but not far enough. Alcohol is a possibility, but he won't let himself start, primarily because he wants to keep that option in reserve. He knows it's only going to get worse. Even though he dreads it, he checks his email every half-hour. So far, no word from Nostradamus or the Johnsons, who must have received word that he got in their car and made the plane. And no word from Marjorie, who will be furious with him for leaving without saying goodbye. For suggesting that she accompany his mother to the pharmacy, because "she seems like she could use the company". For leaving her in a place that is his idea of safe.

The only email of note comes from Campbell, offering condolences and regrets, telling him that he might have a lead regarding Nostradamus and begging Yates to come back to visit him in Ilulissat, which he admits he is too scared to leave.

At 6 p.m. local time, he lands at Kuwait International Airport. It's pretty much what he thought it would be

– rich people in robes and lots of men with guns in a small, immaculate, well-air-conditioned terminal. They issue him a visa on the spot, and he's met on the other side of customs by a muscular American man with a crew cut named Forrester, who insists that he's not with the military, that he works for the company helping to run the Expo.

Outside, the sun is almost down, but it is still more than a hundred and ten degrees. They get into a silver Chevy SUV that has been security-modified, with armoured skin and bulletproof glass. Every now and then Forrester says something and Yates starts to answer, only to realize that Forrester's not talking to him, but into a tiny mouthpiece to one of his non-military co-workers. For a while they are the only car on the highway that cuts across the desert. This is fortunate, because at one point Forrester is talking to base, unwrapping a KitKat bar and checking out his nostril hair in the mirror while driving at more than 180 miles per hour.

There is no cursory wave-through at the gate to the Ali Salem US Air Force Base. The guards check out Forrester and ask Yates for ID, for his story, and to get out of the SUV, which they search inside and out. Near the runway, in a large storage hangar, Forrester leaves him with another man named Intrary, who looks exactly like Forrester. Yates shakes Intrary's hand and is tempted to give Forrester a great big goodbye hug, just to see, but decides not to.

"We had you scheduled to hop on a C-130 at eleven hundred," Intrary says. "But there's a British Tornado heading over to Bas'ar in half an hour to pick up some big shot. I think I might be able to get you to hitch a ride on it, if you don't mind the Brits."

"Don't mind at all," says Yates. "C-130s, Tornados, Brits, mercenaries. All the same to me."

"Good. If they're cool with it, and because of where you're all headed, I believe they will be, then you're in for some fun, dude."

* * *

The biggest difference between a C-130 and a Tornado GR4, Yates discovers, is about a thousand miles an hour. While the C-130 is a staggeringly large cargo transport that lumbers through the sky filled with things like tanks and shipping containers, the RAF's Tornado GR4 is a two-seat, supersonic attack aircraft with a maximum speed of 1,453 miles per hour, or Mach 2.2, the pilot is telling him in his headphones. "We have a Mauser 27-millimetre cannon, cruise missiles, Paveway laser and GPS-guided bombs."

"This is reassuring, I think," Yates says. His fingers have clawed into the trousers of his flight suit and are scraping thighbone. "Have you tried them out lately?"

They bank hard left, and Yates feels a series of chiropractic pops in his neck. "Just about every day, sir," explains the pilot. "But not tonight. Tonight I'm strictly a taxi driver."

"Supersonic taxi driver."

"No need to break the sound barrier tonight, sir. Tonight we're just meandering along just above fifteen thousand feet, just out of range of the surface-to-air ordnance."

When he finally gets up the nerve to look out of the cockpit window, Yates sees the sun setting behind a red desert floor that is only a few hundred feet beneath them. Slowly they bank back to level, and then he is jolted forwards as the jet decelerates and the swing-wings move into position, further slowing the jet as it prepares to land on the longer of Bas'ar International's two short runways.

From take-off to touchdown they were in the air for a total of five minutes.

If they were to tell him he was at a base in the States, at Los Alamitos in California or Nellis in Nevada, he'd believe them, because Bas'ar International is basically two runways, a terminal/conference centre that used to be a prison and hundreds of tan military-style buildings, tents and Quonset huts in the desert. Sure, there are native "Bas'arians", as Yates decides to call them. But clearly they are the safe ones, the American-approved, capitalization-friendly ones. And they are in the minority. Just about everyone else seems to be American: American security, American paramilitary, American business and American "Advisors".

"Where are the world-famous fairgrounds that I read so much about?" Yates is walking with his new chaperone, Dewayne Dreiser, across a barren patch of desert that connects the runways and the retrofitted conference centre.

Dreiser doesn't break stride, doesn't smile as he answers. "From what I've heard they weren't so much a fairground as a place where public stonings were conducted. The motherfuckers would drive out of the city with their white pickups filled to the brim with their version of tailgaters to watch some infidel – or some poor bitch who failed her virginity test – be on the receiving end of a few hundred badly thrown stones. I think they played some soccer here at one time, too."

Yates grunts. "And all along I had imagined colourful big-top circus tents. Clowns and jugglers."

"It's subjective," Dreiser adds. "One man's fairground is another man's execution pit. Either way, it's all pretty festive, right?"

Because he is a VIP, Yates gets his own room, and a double at that, in the prison. Since the liberation, the bars have been removed from the cells, and the Arabic pleas for mercy and declarations of revenge that had been scrawled on the walls have been painted over. They've closed the rooms in with plasterboard and installed locking doors. Down the hall is a public bath and shower.

"It's kind of primitive, isn't it?"

Dreiser frowns. "Six months ago it was a prison. If it's a real problem, you're welcome to stay at one of the former four-star hotels in downtown Bas'ar City with the so-called real journalists. With the price on an American head down to under twenty-five thousand, they're taking fewer hostages these days, and some of those are even being released."

"Do you have a schedule for me? Do you know when or where I'm supposed to give my speech?"

"Like in a plush auditorium or something? Shit, what you're gonna be doing here is sound bites and photo ops. Canned stuff for the electronic media to be distributed by the Freedom Channel."

"Amanda Glowers' outfit?"

"You got it. She's already here."

"But no formal speech."

"No formal nothing. You're not here for the benefit of the other people crazy enough to be here. You're here to let the rest of the world know that we're coming back, that we're open for business. To shout from what's left of the rooftops, 'Open up your motherfucking chequebooks, because everything's just peachy in beautiful downtown Bas'ar.'"

"Fifty miles away."

"Twelve, actually. But it might as well be a hundred, the way we've got this place fortified. Anyway. It's all about the illusion of progress, the cock-tease of profit."

"So I'm not going to be visiting Bas'ar City proper?"

"Oh yeah," Dreiser says. "We'll be taking a field trip to see some of the sites, manufacture some photo ops. You, standing in front of the new Ministry of Construction. The future site of the Ministry of Arts and Culture. Of course, the Bradleys, the armour and your heavily armed escorts will be discreetly positioned out of frame." Dreiser hands Yates a folder filled with press releases with the Destination Bas'ar logo on the top. They are all dated tomorrow and later, and Yates sees upon reading them that each has at least one glowing testimonial, or breathless endorsement of Bas'ar's commercial viability, present and future, attributed to Yates.

"I give quite the tasty sound bite."

Dreiser smiles, nods. "Gives one chills, the prescient eloquence."

"I particularly like the part where they call me a cutting-edge, world-renowned futurist."

"The coiner of the phrase."

"But no reference to the Coalition of the Clueless?"

Dreiser shakes his head. "Too sensitive. Too open to interpretation. One faction wanted to play it up, because they felt that the extreme level of frankness and cynicism of that harangue would only lend credibility to your statements here, but somebody shot it down."

Because he is hungry, Dreiser completes Yates's tour by way of pointing at, rather than walking to, supposed places of interest. In addition to the converted jail cell rooms, there is a cafeteria, a business centre, a recreation room with darts, ping-pong, table football and two pool tables. And, a short walk away on the top floor of what had been an air-traffic control tower under the past regime, is the most popular destination in the entire complex, a cocktail lounge with panoramic views of the greater Bas'ar City metropolitan area, open at night only to high-level security personnel, "advisors", friendly politicians, select journalists and VIP civilians, like Yates.

"The perks never cease."

"Get some sleep, or get some dinner before they close the cafeteria. Maybe I'll meet you over there later for a drink or two."

Air Traffic Out of Control

Yates ignores the suggestion of food and sleep, and once Dreiser leaves he heads downstairs, and outside and across the former stoning fairgrounds towards the tower bar. Since that night at Resnor's in Fiji, since he has reconnected with Marjorie, he has been making an effort not to drink, but what are the options here? Playing table football with a spy? Masturbating in a room in which men once waited to be stoned to death? There are probably websites dedicated to both, men for whom such opportunities are the stuff of fantasy, but for Yates it's much easier simply to ease himself off the wagon and onto a bar stool.

At the bottom of the tower he's stopped by two men in tan baseball caps and black golf shirts with automatic weapons. On the closed steel fire door behind them is an elaborately painted sign for the tower lounge that reads AIR TRAFFIC OUT OF CONTROL! Yates has no formal credentials yet, but apparently the guards have some kind of list, and he's on it.

On the other side of the steel door and up three flights of stairs, a velvet burgundy curtain opens upon another world. He had expected a dingy, expat, *Casablanca*-esque, last-helicopter-out-of-Saigon kind of vibe, or some raucous, *fin du monde*, rock-'n'-roll, denial-fuelled excess. Instead he sees a tastefully lit room with plush velvet couches and lounge chairs, a circular black veneered bar and an energetic yet soothing kind of house music not unlike the music that played in the lobby of his Milan hotel. The bar, his destination of choice, is filled mostly with men, but with more women than he'd expected. So he settles for an empty seat on a couch that is one of three forming a horseshoe around a table covered with beer bottles, martini glasses and candles.

"Have a seat, friend," one of the men on the couch across from Yates says, after Yates has already had one. The man is wearing a short-sleeved, yellow-flowered surfer shirt that leaves his enormous, veiny arms exposed.

"Thanks. Do I have to go up to the bar, or will someone come around?"

"Oh, someone will come around all right," the same man says, and the others in the horseshoe, three more men and a woman, break into laughter. "*Garçon,*" says the man, snapping his finger at a waitress, then looking at Yates for his order.

"Bourbon," Yates says. "Maker's Mark, on the rocks, if you got it." This elicits more laughter.

"Oh, they got it, man. They got it." He reaches across the table to shake Yates's hand. "Martell."

"Yates."

"Mr Yates, this is Jablonski, Speros, Gonzales and Mrs Eileen Quinn."

"Take notes," the man identified as Speros jokes, "because there will be a test."

Yates laughs along with the others at the worn-out joke he's heard too many times at too many meetings. But Martell interrupts. "So, take it."

"Excuse me?"

"Take the test. Give us your answers."

Yates, still smiling, looks at the others for help, but they're no longer smiling.

"I mean it," Martell says. "Take the name test now.

And if you fail" – he pulls back his untucked shirt, giving Yates a glimpse of the holstered nine-millimetre on his hip – "I'll fucking kill you."

Yates stares at Martell, trying to determine if he just has an abominable sense of humour, is a legitimate psychopath, or both. "Let's see," Yates says, just as his bourbon arrives, which buys him a few seconds. He points first at Jablonski, and makes his way around the horseshoe to Martell. "You are the ex-CIA lackey who puffed up his credentials to get a job with Bechtel; you (Speros) are the one with a Ph.D. in Geology and a minor in Advanced Game Theory who has somehow managed to parlay his rudimentary knowledge of Arabic into a high-paying consultancy with a conservative think tank; you (Gonzales) are part of the public-relations firm whose primary task is to convince the world that this is clearly not about oil; you (Mrs Eileen Quinn) are a graduate of the Condoleezza Rice school of world domination, and are here to make sure that the temporary Governing Council doesn't do too much governing; and you (Martell) are either a second-rate comedian here with the USO troupe because you can't land a gig in the States or a high-testosterone, greenie-popping mercenary with questionable taste in fashion." He raises his drink to the group and waits to be shot or thrown through the tower window. Not caring any more has its privileges. "So, how'd I do?"

Martell lets his shirt tail drop back over the pistol and smiles. When he begins to clap, the others join him. "Holy shit, Yates," he says. "Where'd you learn to talk that kind of extemporaneous shit? What line of business you in?"

Yates takes a drink, his first in a week, and it tastes way too good. "I'm a futurist, Martell."

No one seems to know if Yates is serious or not, or what a futurist does, or what one is doing on a couch in a lounge called Air Traffic Out of Control in Greater Bas'ar. Martell, for now, doesn't seem to care, either. He raises his glass in tribute. "To the Futurist."

After that, thankfully, they go back to their conversations. Yates sits back, drinks and listens. For a while Jablonski gives a synopsis of the local politics. What the Kurds are looking for. The fate of the Governing Council. Which mullah is on the rise. The differences between a Shiite and a Sunni. A fundamentalist and a jihadi. They listen with lessening intensity as his synopsis approaches dissertation length. When he's finally done, he takes a long sip of his martini and says, "Or maybe it's the other way round."

At one point another man joins them. He says he recognizes Quinn from the Al-Rasheed hotel in Baghdad, and later asks Speros if the company he's with is a subsidiary of Halliburton. Speros looks to Martell, who does his patented "Let's make the stranger uncomfortable" laugh. "Brother," he says, "at the end of the day, all God's creatures are a subsidiary of Halliburton."

Soon after, Gonzales looks at his watch and says to Eileen Quinn, "Well, well. It's almost time."

She checks her watch – it's 8:59 Bas'ar standard time – then nods assent and adjusts her position on the couch to give her an unobstructed view through the large tower window facing east. A minute later there is a bright orange flash in the eastern sky, followed by an iridescent web of tracers.

"Here we go," Martell says, as a series of much larger flashes sear the horizon, rattling the windows of the tower. He raises his glass once again, and the others raise their glasses as well. "To the peaceful transfer of power."

"Here, here!"

For the next several minutes all conversation stops, and they watch until they become desensitized.

Half an hour later, with Amanda Glowers, it's as if they're meeting during a break-out session of an innovation conference at the Arizona Biltmore. No mention of

Johannesburg or the Johnsons. Or their panoramic view of the continuing phantom military activity. She does say that she's here to help with the media, but she doesn't say much more. He can tell that she would never have come to this couch, to this part of the room, if she had seen his face in the darkness. Now that she's recruited him, now that she's got him involved in this mess, she seems to be having a hard time looking him in the eyes. "I'm sure we'll see each other tomorrow, for the press junket," she says, averting her gaze, looking much older than the Amanda Glowers of Johannesburg, before heading off to look for a more forgiving horseshoe.

Now Dreiser appears with the Johnson who didn't take his family to Hershey. They are standing at the bar, and Dreiser motions for Yates to join them.

"You're in real shit now," Johnson says.

"Indeed," Yates says, sipping his fourth – no, fifth – bourbon on an empty stomach.

"You're finally getting a taste of it."

"I've tasted shit before," Yates says. "All kinds of it, for many years."

"I'm talking about reality. Not Milan, Fiji. Fucking Iceland."

"Greenland."

"They're not real. This is real."

Yates looks around the air-traffic control tower cum moody Tribeca lounge, then outside at the nocturnal destruction of a newly consecrated city. "Yup. This is about as real as it gets."

"Dreiser showed you around alright?"

"Yeah. I love my cell. The only thing missing is the threat of shower rape, unless you guys are holding out on me."

Johnson either doesn't get or chooses to ignore the attitude. "The thing about tomorrow is to project stability.

Try to get your patter down to ten-second bites. Read your quotes in your press releases and spit them back out so it sounds natural. If you don't get it right, don't worry, we'll just do another take, but it would help to be prepared. We've got a shitload of stuff booked for tomorrow."

"Gotcha. So this is what's gonna pave the way for capitalization, a bunch of paid-for testimonials?"

Dreiser laughs. "It's one of many ways. And if they don't work, we'll just have to create some situations beyond the private sector that might get us some outside help."

Yates looks at Dreiser. He wants some examples, but Johnson cuts him off. "I suggest you lay off the Maker's Mark for a while, Yates, and get some rest."

Yates looks at Johnson and Dreiser, then at his half-filled drink. He puts his glass on the bar, pushes it away, "What was I thinking? You're right, man. I'm beat. I'm gonna watch the fireworks display for a bit, then I'm gonna crash." When Johnson and Yates walk through the curtain to leave, Yates reaches back across the bar and grabs his drink. Then, when he catches the bartender's eye, he makes a series of gestures between himself, the glass and a bottle on the top shelf. Back me up.

On the way out he stops, because he thinks he sees Blevins watching the two big-screen TVs in the back corner of the room. On one is a WWF Smackdown, and on the other is the space hotel, which apparently has faltered again and is about to come back into the earth's atmosphere.

He's curious about the space hotel, and about what Blevins is doing here, but not so curious that he wants to walk back across the room, past Amanda Glowers and Martell's gang, and subject himself to Blevins, who will only try his best to make Yates feel worse than he already does. If in fact this is Blevins that he's looking at. No one notices when he puts his empty glass on the bar and slips through the velvet curtain.

Junket

Back in his room, he picks up the space-hotel coverage online and lets it stream in the upper-right corner of his screen while he checks his email. Lauren says she's thinking of him. Missing him. *Which is to be expected,* he thinks, *now that her boyfriend has dumped her, now that she feels guilty because my father died, and now that she's had a good look at Marjorie – all of which makes me a slightly less pathetic, slightly more sympathetic, slightly more desirable character. Then again she might just be trying to be friendly.* He click-drags into his reply a logo from Destination Bas'ar Expo and a picture of two Bas'arians toeing a ceremonial spade into the desert earth, and writes:

> *Greetings from the Cradle of Civilization! When I get back, after performing this final despicable act of a shameless career, I'll visit, and hopefully we can talk – after which you will probably realize that you really didn't miss me (or at least that you were missing a long-gone version of me/us) and that you made a damned smart move a few weeks ago. A move that, combined with a lot of other unpleasant things, gave me the first of several wake-up calls. So far, I've heeded none of them. But I'm starting to stir. I'm a little drowsy, a little jet-lagged, and yes, kind of buzzed, but for the first time in a long time my eyes are definitely open.*

He likes the Cradle of Civilization concept so much that he sends a similar note with the photo attachment to Campbell before going back to his other messages. Now the streaming space-hotel video is showing on a split screen. On the left is an earth-based view of the empty night sky over the Indian Ocean, and on the right is the empty cockpit of the sinking spacecraft, which is minutes away from entering the earth's atmosphere.

He opens a short note from Nostradamus:

Did you know that Nostradamus predicted his own death?
How do you see yourself dying, Yates?
Quietly in your sleep?
Or wide-awake and screaming?

He's staring at these words when the chutoy tone sounds. Someone's instant-messaging him. Marjorie.

–Where are you?
–I am in the recently created nation of Bas'ar.
–???
–I had to come. To fulfil a contractual obligation. It should take about a week. But after this, I'm done. And things will be fine.
–Is it dangerous?
–Not at all.
–That entire country is dangerous. Why didn't you tell me?
–Because you would have wanted to come.
–Your mother thinks you are at a conference in Orlando.
–Sometimes I do, too.
–What you said in Fiji, I've been thinking.
–Whatever I said, I meant. Which doesn't necessarily mean that I understand it.
–My reasons for leaving Johannesburg... for leaving South Africa, have changed. I wanted to get out. Then I had to get out. Then I wanted to be where you are. At first it was a

matter of survival. Then selfishness. And now it's something more. I feel like my reasons for leaving change every day and I imagine they will continue to change. So if you need to know every bit of my story, I don't know if I'll ever be able to tell you. There are parts I never want to think about again. And if you need to know my reasons, my true motivations, I can't be sure. I can only tell you what I feel at the moment. And when I do choose to tell you anything, it will be the truth. But what I don't want is to be a parasite. Or a mercy case.
–Don't think that for a second.
–I don't know what to think, Yates. I don't want to be some little kept woman nervously waiting with your mother – who, incidentally, I adore – for the return of a man I don't really know.
–First of all, you are not kept. I imagine the only act you've been forced to perform is to watch Antiques Road Show *every Wednesday night. If you don't want to stay, if you have a plan, if you want to find what makes you happy, then go. I will help you do whatever it is you want to do with your life, in whatever way I can, when I get back.*
–Which is when?
–Good question. I'm hoping soon. Do you miss me?

As he waits for a response that isn't going to come, he clicks to make the streaming space video fill his screen. After a while the reception on the cockpit cam gets fuzzy, flickers to black, then turns finally to snow, to white noise. Then, seconds later on the earth-based screen, dim sparks fizz in the starless sky, remnant bits of failed science, the debris of misguided ambition and blind hubris, barely sparking and briefly falling, but not quite reaching the sea. When the sparks disappear, the view quickly cuts to a full screen of the night sky, some producer somewhere hustling to capture more, hoping that it will be spectacular. But it's not. It's done.

As the camera stays locked on the empty sky and the

IM quadrant in the upper-right corner idles on the precipice of a reply, Yates picks up his orientation packet, flips past the illustrated booklet on Muslim etiquette and settles on a one-sheeter that outlines what to do in the event of a poisonous gas attack.

He falls asleep before the next email lands in his life. Marked urgent, from Campbell, titled: *I know who Nostradamus is.*

"We provide this community with everything, from people, contacts, intelligence, crushed ice, salt and pepper, hydro-electric power, mail delivery and auto parts to grain, concrete anti-terrorism barricades and no-tears shampoo. It is profit that brings us here. A cost-plus contract. Because it's dangerous, there is more profit. This is what democracy is all about, am I not right?" This is Yates's breakfast companion in the cafeteria, Roger Something, who won't divulge the name of his company. Yates is still half drunk, half asleep, still wearing the clothes he passed out in last night. Dreiser finally had to drag him out of bed to take him to breakfast without changing or showering or checking his email.

"And you're not connected to the government?" Yates asks.

"Fuck no. We are not spies or soldiers or politicians. We are businessmen and women. We outsource for war, peace, democracy, revolution – at the highest attainable profit, of course."

"Of course."

"Why are you here, Mr Yates?"

He looks down at his bacon and scrambled eggs. Good question. "To validate the hypothesis," he finally answers.

"Pardon?"

"To sign the certificate of authenticity. To say, *Absolutely, I believe that there will be a Baby Gap in downtown Bas'ar City before the year is out.*"

Rather than be offended, Roger Something-or-other plays along. "A Wal-Mart in the outlying suburbs."

"An upscale gentlemen's club near the airport, with a wet-burka contest every Wednesday, sponsored by Budweiser."

The man reaches across the table and gives Yates a high five. "That's what we're talkin' about."

Yates doesn't notice Blevins until he puts his tray down on the table. "I thought I saw you last night at the bar."

"Yup," Blevins says. "I thought that was you going out of your way to avoid me."

"What are you doing here?"

"I thought you retired."

"I did."

"An offer you couldn't refuse, eh?"

"What about you?"

"Believe it or not, I was invited. You may have noticed they're not exactly turning people away at the credentials booth. Plus, now and then someone actually thinks of me, especially if they can't get you first. In fact, with you out of the picture I think I'll make a decent living off your scraps."

"What happened to the sympathetic associate who was at my father's wake?"

Blevins stops buttering his toast and looks at Yates. "See the space hotel re-entry last night?"

Yates lies, shakes his head. But Blevins is looking at him like he doesn't believe him.

"What a shame, what those poor people went through. So, what are they paying you to sell what's left of your soul here, Yates? "

"Don't make me cry, Blevins."

It turns out that the business centre, the orientation centre, the conference centre and the cafeteria for Destination Bas'ar are all the same place. After breakfast they just slide the tables around and hang white posters from them. Ministry of Construction. Ministry of Finance. Ministry of Information. Ministry of Housing. Conspicuous by its absence, Yates thinks, is the Ministry of Oil.

They affix curtains, pieces of canvas and colourful tapestries to the block walls to present a more telegenic backdrop. There are four "reporters". One is a beautiful young Frenchwoman, one a beautiful young Arab woman and one Yates recognizes as a fallen game-show host from the late '90s. He recalls some controversy involving the designer drug ecstasy and the on-camera, prime-time, sweeps-week boast that he was going to make Alex Trebek his bitch. At first Yates doesn't recognize the fourth reporter, a handsome young man in a network-anchor-style suit, who's having make-up dabbed onto his forehead. But when the man sees Yates looking his way, he waves and makes a show of pointing to the buttons on his suit. Chandler shrugs – which Yates interprets as *It's slightly better than death, right?*

Give Amanda Glowers credit, she runs an efficient junket. The "reporters" take turns at each remote, and the "guests" are shuttled through, a new one every five minutes. Here's Yates at the satellite campus of the Ministry of Education. "The day is not far off when the University of Bas'ar will be synonymous with the world's great institutions of higher learning – Oxford, Harvard, MIT." At the Ministry of Housing: "The homes of tomorrow are being built today right here in God's country. I mean Allah's country. One more time, on two. The homes of tomorrow are being built right here, today, in beautiful Bas'ar." And so on. If it wasn't all such a spectacular lie, so patently wrong, it would be easy.

"What if a real journalist tried to crash this party?" he asks Amanda Glowers, on his way to a segment with the Ministry of Film.

"Oh, they've tried," she answers. "We placate some of the more tenacious ones with the occasional premeditated diversionary scoop."

"Meaning?"

"We send them into the city. The war zone. To get them out of our hair."

"I'm curious," Yates says. "What crime against humanity did you commit to get sucked into this mess?"

Glowers narrows her eyes. "What are you talking about?"

"This mess. This massive fucking money-grab."

"You think they could manage this themselves? They need this help. The Governing Council is a bunch of exiles, cons and criminals."

"Put in place by whom?"

"They don't even govern. They jet to reconstruction conferences around the world while we do the work."

"Out of pure altruistic goodwill, of course."

She plays with her hair, tilts her head. "You should be careful, Yates. I say this because I like you. Think whatever you want, but what we're doing here is better than declaring war. And much more popular in the polls."

"Why declare war when you can have them fight each other? When we can set up the conflict, finance both sides, exploit the chaos and let big business play the role of the conquering army by throwing an 'Expo' on the 'fairgrounds'?"

"When did you become such a bleeding-heart weenie? I had you pegged for a hardcore cynic. Besides, the Head of the Coalition of the Clueless ought to know nothing is that simple."

"You know, in the tower bar last night I thought I was gonna deal with a bunch of rah-rah delusional types who drank the freedom Kool Aid, but instead I hit a wall of fatalistic cynicism that made even me blush."

"Don't go all mushy, Yates. Mushy doesn't have much of a shelf life over here."

"You didn't answer my question."

"Honey," Amanda Glowers says. "I was the CEO of the second-biggest advertising agency in the world. *Advertising*. I had the US Army for a client. Raytheon. Global pharma companies. You act like I spent the last fifty years in a fucking convent." She turns to the cameraman standing behind her and says, "Now let's roll some goddamn tape and move on."

As soon as the red light goes on and the cameraman points at him, Yates turns away from Amanda Glowers, smiles into the camera and says, "The independent film movement in Bas'ar is absolutely thriving, teeming with young would-be Scorseses. And there is already talk within the Ministry of Film of having an annual festival right here that will hold its own with your Sundance, your Cannes."

When the camera stops rolling, he looks at Glowers and says, "The only young film-makers they have in this country are videotaping suicide bombers in ski masks standing in front of a silk jihadi flag."

She pretends she doesn't hear him. He checks his watch. Ten minutes fast, even here. "Come on," Amanda calls to all of them. "We're losing light."

Delegation of Denial

On the tarmac it is 121 diesel-clouded degrees, and the only movement of air is the occasional toxic breeze from the west that reeks of the city's perpetually smouldering fires. There are dozens of idling vehicles lined up in front of the cafeteria: armour-fitted, machine-gun-mounted Humvees, military-grade Bradleys, two M113 armoured tracks and six silver SUVs pimped-out with 50-calibre Brownings and tinted glass. Everywhere there are tobacco-chewing, ball-scratching swaggering men in jumpsuits and tan baseball caps, Kevlar vests and Oakley wraparounds. Some carry holstered pistols, Berettas and SIG-Sauers, one even has an old Walther PPK, but most are armed like action heroes, with everything from M4 carbines with attachable grenade launchers, to Mossberg 590 pump-action, urban-warfare shotguns, and Barrett .50-calibre sniper rifles. Out of sight, in the back of the trucks, is the higher-powered stuff, just in case.

Inside, in the air-conditioned holding area, Yates waits with the others for the signal to head out to their designated vehicles with the film crew, the other phoney experts and reporters, the business types and paid-for politicians, all forming what Johnson is calling the "Delegation", with an absolutely straight face.

"This ought to be interesting." It's Blevins. He's wearing a flak jacket and a helmet and drinking a Peach Snapple. Yates shakes his head. Yes. No. Something. For a second he thinks he recognizes Martell from the tower bar loading some kind of ordnance into the back of an SUV, but he can't be sure. By the front door a Jordanian "businessman" is pacing, smoking, waiting for the old Fokker out of Kuwait City to land. And in the back of the holding area, Expo personnel are doing their best to shield the others from a female CARE worker who is trying to comfort another, younger female relief worker who is three stages into a nervous breakdown. But they can't hide her shrieks. Somebody outside gets a signal from someone else, and waves at the members of the delegation. "We got us a convoy," Blevins says, standing up and tightening the strap on his helmet.

Yates stands and looks at him. Blevins grins. Yates has never seen Blevins grin. He's seen him smile before, but nothing that's ever creeped him out like this, nothing like this close-mouthed, goofy-eyed grin that borders on a smirk. "Are you carrying a pistol, Blevins?"

Blevins winks, nods, shows some teeth. "I'm carrying a lot of shit, Yates."

He once saw a prototype for an Internet tool that could give you the global cool quotient, the intellectual, cultural and spiritual Q-score of any given word or idea at that exact nanosecond. When he was eleven, he built a precise scale replica of Jefferson's Monticello using only natural materials, right down to the slave quarters.

Through the first gate and into the desert. Yates is sitting next to Blevins in the back of a silver Chevy SUV that has a manned .50-calibre machine gun mounted on a swivel where the sunroof used to be. He sees now that he was right, that it was Martell on the tarmac, because now Martell's in the front passenger seat, looking at a map, chewing a combination of regular-flavour Bazooka bubble gum and freeze-dried coffee crystals. Martell turns to him when he's done with the map. "Looky here, if it isn't the fucking Futurist."

"At your service."

"They should do a comic book based very fucking loosely on you, called – let's see – *The Futurist*! Of course you'd need a uniform. Maybe tights and a blue cape with a big F-U on the back."

"He'd need a nemesis," Blevins says, a little too loudly.

Yates looks at him, decides to go along with it. "The Evil History Major. Father Time. The Pastist."

Martell ignores him. "And some kind of special powers. What are your special powers, Yates?"

While Yates thinks, Blevins answers for him. "He has the uncanny and often unconscious ability to avert failure, to avert disaster, to avert his eyes from doing the right thing and still come out smelling like a rose."

Yates looks at Blevins for an explanation for this latest outburst, but only gets a variation on his initial stupid grin.

Martell asks, "But can he prevent disaster, the Futurist?"

Blevins takes this one, too. "No. His gift is to dodge disaster and, more often than not, benefit from it. Am I not correct, Yates?"

"Sure. Although today I have to admit I'm questioning this power, the disaster-avoidance ability. Today, it feels kind of diminished."

"Psychic kryptonite," says Blevins, who is sweating profusely, even in the air-conditioned truck.

"Well, I suggest you pull every trick in your cartoon-superhero arsenal to replenish those powers, dude. Because despite the rich Cuban-cigar smoke those suits have been blowing up your ass, we're heading into one fucked-up little patch of planet earth."

Yates nods, wonders if Martell had scripted his crazy-warrior bit. He half-expects him to put in a Wagner CD and break into an *Apocalypse Now* napalm-in-the-morning routine, but thankfully he's back looking at the map, listening to the convoy leader on his headphones.

Past rows of coiled wire, past concrete barricades, past two Abrams tanks, a mobile missile unit under camo netting. The airport perimeter is a barren, flat stretch of hard-packed, garbage-strewn land. To make it harder for insurgents to hide, every tree and palm bush for miles has been razed. When they pass the last checkpoint, the convoy speeds up considerably, and when he looks ahead, through the dust and the smoke and the glare, Yates thinks he can see the jagged escarpments of civilization in the distance.

"Cutaneous."

Yates looks at Blevins. "What?"

"Cutaneous. Remember when that word held so much power. How it scared the crap out of everyone with a mailbox?"

Yates has no answer. He wonders what anthrax, cutaneous or otherwise has to do with anything.

"Cutaneous. Seems almost quaint now, doesn't it Yates?"

The Futurist was never cutting edge or far ahead of the curve. He was often just a few minutes in front of the pack, a couple of seconds ahead of the global Zeitgeist, or at least of the middle-American one. His gift was to be able to see that something was going to be big in a mainstream way months and sometimes years before your hipsters, your early adapters, your so-called thought leaders embraced it. But his real talent was holding on to this information until the time was right, knowing the exact moment at which to drop it into the flabby lap of a mass-market, mall-addicted America that wanted to be a fraction of an inch above average, not so much ahead of the times as just about keeping up with them. He knew when it was the absolute best time to deem that which had long been cool to cool people *cool* for the rest of us.

White Datsun pickups and white Toyota 4Runners kicking up desert dust. Just far away enough to keep you from panicking, yet just close enough to make you think. Like Indians shadowing wagon trains in bad westerns. Buildings taking shape in the heat-blurred air. Rambo in the sunroof pumps off a few bursts of the Browning, at nothing, causing Blevins to spill Snapple all over his Kevlar. Closer to the city, light traffic. More trucks. American cars from another millennium. A Grenada. A Pacer. A Cordoba. A Pinto. "A fucking Pinto! Sweet!" Martell exclaims, pointing at a 1976 lime-green model with a shattered hatchback window.

Yates sits up, lowers his sunglasses. "I guess they still haven't gotten the recall letter about the exploding gas tanks. They're taking an awfully big chance."

"What's the deal with the '70s cars?" Rambo shouts.

"Maybe it was someone in Detroit's idea of a joke. Payback for the fucking energy crisis." Martell.

Yates sees a red AMC Gremlin, circa 1976, and says. "No wonder they hate us."

The charred shell of a Russian-made tank two generations removed from military relevance. Goats in the passing lane. A billboard in Arabic for *Seinfeld*, the final season, now available on DVD. Off the road at the base of a berm, a woman stops picking through a pile of clothes too ragged even for the homeless and watches them pass. The blank stare of a country at war with too many versions of itself.

One of his tricks had been to take the obvious, the popular, often true perception of the masses, and flip it. *As technology becomes more ingrained in our lives, people will become more cynical.* Bullshit, he'd say. I see the return of the old time. Of comfort food. Of handshakes that trump instant messages. Or he would fuse the old with the new and predict a nation that will crave anything that combines the handcrafted with modern applications. Ergonomically correct kitchen utensils with old-world materials. Houses with quaint front porches wired with T1 lines. Anything that combines leather, rare wood and silicon. Not necessarily true, but what they wanted to hear.

A quick stop at a tributary that supposedly, somewhere, flows into the Tigris. Yates can't help but think that this is where the Futurist will meet his fate, in the cradle of civilization. They stay in their SUV while a crew gets out of another truck to set up a quick shot. He sees a man in the white jacket of a scientist. An environmentalist, or maybe a site manager for a proposed hydroelectric dam, Yates thinks. Then he sees Chandler dressed like a network news reporter on Viagra. Khaki vest, wind blowing his fabulous hair, a fake network logo on his mike. First Chandler asks the guy a couple of fluff questions. Then they film the guy kneeling streamside with an upside-down, bullet-riddled Ford Windstar just out of frame. The guy dips his hand into the brown muck, tastes it and smiles to the camera, to Chandler, to the rest of the planet, like it's Evian. When the camera cuts away, he spits it out, wipes his mouth.

"I'm welling up with pride," Blevins says as they watch. "How about you, Yates?"

They pull back onto the road and cross a structurally suspect bridge into the city. Everything is boarded up, bullet-pocked, bomb-damaged. There are signs of people everywhere, just no people. As they turn and go the wrong way on an empty avenue, Martell turns to Yates and says, "You're on deck, pretty boy. Apparently our location scouts have found a building sound enough to be the site of our thriving Internet café."

People found him handsome, but not so handsome as to be a threat, to be someone you'd resent. Older executives embraced his wide-eyed, innocent optimism, treated him like the son they wished they'd had (instead of the petulant prick they had sent to boarding school while they spent the last thirty years reading conference reports in business class). But to younger audiences he was a fast-talking, all-knowing, self-deprecating wise-arse with a heart, a winking cynic launching endless sound bites and pop-culture asides and then taking them down like clay pigeons. Later, his white friends who saw him in action with the old and the young, with men and women, would tease, call him a chameleon, an evangelist, a televisionary.

His black friends called him a blue-eyed devil.

It takes a while to set this one up. They have to pay some locals to be extras. They have to position the monitors, the laptops with wires connected to nowhere. A healthy tech infrastructure is a critical part of the message they want to get out. Martell is outside with the others, forming a perimeter, scanning the surrounding rooftops. A young woman in a burka is placing teacups on the counters. A production assistant is checking the light meter. In the truck, Blevins is drumming his fingers on his thighs, looking out of his window in the opposite direction at a group of young children playing in a pile of rubble.

"You okay?"

This startles Blevins. Spooks him, Yates thinks. "Yeah. I'm fine. Why would I not be fine in such a wonderful place, at such a wonderful time, Yates? What we're witnessing is the proverbial tipping point, right?"

"What I don't get is why you came here. I mean even today, this strange little excursion."

Blevins looks back out of the window. With the puffy vest and the oversized helmet he looks about twelve years old. "I wanted to see what it was like, Yates. I already saw what it was like at the airstrip. All the bullshit there. Now I wanted to see what it was like here, to see the latest incarnation of you in action."

"And?"

Blevins considers Yates, and for a moment his face relaxes. The grin, the smirk, the sweat, the tension goes away. He almost looks lucid. "Not everything's about a paycheck. Or a kickback. I thought maybe I could learn something from the experience."

"And do what? Design a class reunion around it?"

Martell knocks on the window. They have the shot set up, they're ready to roll. Yates gets out of the truck and walks into the café. A production assistant tries to dab his forehead with make-up, but he waves her off. He sits at the stool they've set up, picks up a local newspaper in one hand, the teacup in the other, as if this has been a part of his routine for ever. Then he lowers the cup and looks at the camera lens as though he is looking into the eyes of a long-lost, filthy-rich multinational business associate.

Even the cameraman – a bitter, skinny Brit who claims to have worked for the BBC – is impressed by the ease with which, unscripted and unprompted, the Futurist lays it out there. *This is just one of the myriad high-tech, Wi-Fi outposts popping up in this boom town. Forget Silicon Valley – this city, this country, is a veritable digital phoenix rising from the ashes.* He talks about the benefit of not having a burdensome legacy of a telecom system in place, how much easier it is to start fresh with bleeding-edge technology. He talks about the thousands of online bloggers in Bas'ar who once represented the only way to get real news out of the oppressed country, now at the forefront of the new openness sweeping the nation. Now they lose the microphone and get some B-roll footage of Yates pretending to surf the Internet on a dead laptop, of Yates sipping tea with a group of young Bas'arians acting like net geeks, of Yates shaking hands as if closing a deal with a man in a borrowed suit and tie. And finally, here is Yates standing in the café doorway, trying to ignore the men with guns, the bombed-out devastation just out of camera frame, looking out up at the endless sky.

"Got it?"

"Yup," says the cameraman.

To Martell he says, "So that's it then, we go back?"

Martell looks around, shakes his head. "They just called from back at the Expo. They want to grab one more location with you in it. The future site of the Ministry of Communication."

"Jesus Christ."

"That's it. Go there, then if you want you're on the next flight out."

Once, when he first started in the business, he quoted the writer Max Dublin in a speech at a venture-capitalist gathering in San Jose. "It is myopic and evasive to forget that most questions that can be posed about the future can more meaningfully and forcefully be posed about the present. If we used only the knowledge we now have, and used it only for the good, we could have heaven on earth, without one further innovation or discovery, and thereby create a better world than any of our false prophets are capable of envisioning. It is a matter not of ingenuity but of character, and it is the key to any and all possible good futures." When he was finished, his sponsor pulled him aside and said he had already complained to Yates's boss. Said, "You're lucky I'm even gonna pay your honorarium. No one wants to hear that pragmatic bullshit here." He never used the Dublin quote again. Stopped giving attribution to the thoughts of others soon after, and never looked back.

"So tell me about this Ministry of Communication."

Martell shakes his head, fiddles with his headset. "I'll see if they know. Otherwise you're gonna have to wing it."

"Welcome to the Future home of Al Jazeera II. Of the Freedom Channel. Of *Late Night with Mullah Bob*."

"I said I don't fucking know."

Yates looks at Blevins. He hasn't got out of the truck since they left the airport. "So what do you think?"

"I think we're all going to hell."

They drive into a roundabout. The trucks at the front of the convoy, the Bradleys, the Humvees, the armoured tracks, peel off to the right. But their SUV continues around the circle and turns right two streets later. "Where're they all going?"

"Back to the Expo," Martell says. "Relax. We're out of the hot zone."

Yates looks out of the back window, around the legs of the sun-roof gunner. Except for one Humvee, all of the other trucks are gone as well. He looks at Blevins to see what he thinks, but Blevins is still looking out of the window, mumbling, more pasty than sweaty now.

The two vehicles drive on back streets through a neighbourhood that seems to have escaped the violence that has gutted much of the city. Men sitting at street-side tables. Robed women shopping at market stalls. More children than Yates has seen in a long time, since before Johannesburg. It takes him by surprise – the energy of the place, the smiles – until they see the trucks recklessly speeding through their neighbourhood, their world. But it only lasts for a few blocks. Soon there are no more stores, and those doors that are still intact are closed, and the street merchants, the bustling women and children, are gone. The driver has to stop more than once so that Martell can get his bearings on the map.

"I thought you guys had GPS."

Martell turns to bark something back at Yates, then thinks better of it. "Make a left up there, by the crater," he tells the driver. Soon they come upon the concrete ruins of a row of warehouses. "This is it."

"But..." the driver begins.

"Stop the fucking truck," Martell says. "This is the place."

Yates turns around and watches the second vehicle, the Humvee, back up and swing around to the other side of the warehouse and out of sight. Martell gets out. For the first time he has his M4 in the ready position. He waves for his driver to get out of the truck, then tells the machine gunner to get down and grab an M4 as well.

"We're gonna check things out, make sure everything's cool and help them set up," he tells Yates and Blevins. "Sit tight in the truck till we come back."

Yates nods. Blevins doesn't seem to have been listening. As the three heavily armed men walk through the sun-blasted rubble towards the other side of the warehouses, the Futurist has a premonition about what's going to happen next.

Missing Quatrains

> *"By fire he will destroy their city,*
> *A cold and cruel heart,*
> *Blood will pour,*
> *Mercy to none."*

At first Yates doesn't process the words. He's too busy worrying about where Martell has gone off to. Then he realizes what he's just heard. "For God's sake, Blevins. Who put you up to this?"

> *"The Young Lion will overcome the older one*
> *On the field of combat in single battle."*

"Oh hell, Blevins. You're Nostradamus?"

Blevins nods. "Except the Mabus part. They stole that. Exploited it to meet their needs."

"Do you mind if I ask why?"

"Why I fucked with you? You don't even know?"

Yates shrugs, shakes his head. "Jealousy?"

"Jealous? Of you? God, Yates. It's because you are so fucking oblivious."

"To what?"

"See what I mean? To the well-being of others. To the rest of the world. To what you've become. You think you're this happening, worldly, caring guy, but you couldn't be more out of touch, more self-absorbed."

"This was enough of a reason to stalk me, to torment me?"

"If it would have resulted in you changing, in doing good again, sure. I still held out hope. Even at the wake I thought I'd give you one more chance. But then this. This is worse than being indifferent to what you once cared about. You betrayed it."

"So what are you going to do, kill me?"

Blevins looks at the gun at his side as if this is the first time such a thought occurred to him.

"If you're going to kill me I suggest you act quickly, because I have a feeling someone else is gonna steal your thunder in the next few minutes."

Blevins looks outside, then back at Yates. "I'm not here to kill you, Yates. "I'm here to condemn you. To damn you. For selling out. For switching sides."

"I'm on nobody's side. I did this because they made me. They blackmailed me. After this, I'm done."

"You should have left after Johannesburg, but you couldn't help yourself. I laughed when they gave you that phoney assignment. Travel around the world to find out why people hate America, when all you had to do is look at yourself, because you're it, dude. Never has someone capable of doing so much more done progressively less. A formerly admirable, socially conscientious, forward-thinking intellectual. Beacon of hope to the disenfranchised, supporter of the underdog, an enemy of injustice, ignorance and intolerance who has been corrupted by his own power, who has twisted his own cultural mojo and betrayed his once well-intentioned and considerable charms and used them as a cold business tool, as a profit centre run by a fallen man who has mutated himself into a quick-to-judge, dismissive, self-centred, self-righteous, self-appointed master of a universe he no longer cares about."

"That's a bit harsher than *oblivious*."

"I know about Milan too. I have the video."

Yates opens the door.

"Where are you going?"

"The video will mean nothing if we're already dead. We'd better find them."

Blevins gets out and begins to follow Yates along the same path Martell and his men had taken. "You picked a hell of a place to damn me."

"I think it's the perfect place. The most preposterous, morally compromised, socially devastated place in the world. It transcends corruption, and you're at its despicable, profit-grabbing epicentre."

"That way." Yates walks into the rubble of a warehouse on the other side of the street. He looks inside and sees no sign of the others. "What about the Clueless speech? People seemed to respond to that."

"Oh please. That was basically rationalizing inertia. Making it cool to be ignorant, acceptable to be disengaged." They walk through the spot where a door used to be and stop in the shade beside what's left of an interior concrete wall. As Yates peeks around the corner, he motions for Blevins to stand against the wall and be quiet, but Blevins can't stop speaking. "More and more I tried to influence you, to get you back to doing the things we used to care about, saying the things you used to believe in, the constitution on which our relationship was founded. But you marginalized me. Smirked at me. Pretended you didn't see me. You left me at the Arrivals gate. The smart, socially responsible man whom I once aspired to be like began to treat me like a third-world nation at the G8 Summit and flinched as if he were being molested when I had the gall to beam something into his laptop that didn't have to do with money."

"So that's when you digitally raped me, isn't it? When you stole all my data, my passwords."

"When I got full access inside the decaying mind of

the Futurist? Yup. At first, I did it out of curiosity. But then it all opened up – Lauren, the soccer riot, the space hotel and then these rancid corporate snakes – it was too easy, the number of ways that I could fuck with you. But after a while I realized that wasn't satisfying enough; I finally realized that fucking with you wasn't going to help anyone."

Seeing no one at either end of the street, Yates decides to walk towards the next building. "But you saw that they blackmailed me. That I would never do shit like this. They threatened to send Marjorie back to some Johannesburg prison."

"I don't buy that. From the beginning you could have taken a stand, had the backbone to say no. You may think you took a stand with your supposedly brave speech. You may think you set yourself up to crawl off stage and feel sorry for yourself with a shred of dignity. But what you really did is create a romantic exit that would get your conscience off the hook. But, ironically, it didn't. And you didn't have the good sense to stop there. You decided, when approached by the snakes, *Why not sell out all the way? Why not bring everything down – principles, relationships, nations?* Because quietly bringing yourself down wasn't satisfying enough for a man with your ego. Then you go to fucking Greenland as if to remind everyone that there's an even more obscene squanderer of talent in the world."

"Campbell? He's harmless."

"Children are harmless. Flowers are harmless. He is infinitely worse than harmless, because he has the resources to do the most. Like you, he has everything but a purpose in life, everything except the courage to do something for the good of someone besides himself."

"Some people may have all that, but find the responsibility of applying it to be a burden."

Blevins waves him off. "It's funny how it only becomes

a burden when it applies to the well-being of others. By the way, he knows."

"Campbell? About you?"

"He called me last night and told me he was going to tell you. Which he did. He emailed you just after two. But you didn't open it. Too drunk, I imagine."

Yates stops. He's certain that this is where the other truck had stopped, but he sees no sign of it now. "Let's go back."

"Why?"

"They're gone."

"Why?"

"I think it's safe to say that leaving us wasn't an oversight. Your prophecies may prove to be more prescient than you could have imagined."

Blevins looks at him, wary but curious. Yates turns and starts to walk. After they cross back through the bombed-out warehouse and he sees the truck again, Yates stops and looks at Blevins. "You're right."

Blevins waits for the rest.

"I should have quit. Or at least I should have stopped feeling sorry for myself and actually tried to turn it around. To do the right thing, even if it was as a son, or a friend."

Blevins starts to say something, then stops.

"Ironically, that is what I promised myself I'd do if I ever made it back from here. Help my mother. Help Marjorie. Figure out a way to do something good on a less preposterous level again."

Rather than calm Blevins, some aspect of this last sentence enrages him all over again. He starts to take a swing at Yates, but Yates catches his fist and pushes Blevins back against what is left of a wall. With his armed subdued, Blevins starts to kick at Yates, and the two tumble to the ground. It takes a while for Yates to roll away from the wall and get Blevins in a cradle hold, with his arms looped under a thigh and around the back of Blevins's neck. They stay like that for almost a minute, sweating and panting, with Yates trying not to vomit. Just when Yates thinks it might be okay to release his grip, Blevins starts to thrash again, and Yates has to muscle up all over again. During the second pause, Yates hears the whine of an engine. He lifts his head and cocks his ear towards the sound. When Blevins starts to struggle again, Yates slams his back into the hard earth. "Shhhh. You hear that?"

"What?"

Yates releases Blevins and stands up.

Blevins thinks Yates is messing with him, but he hears it too. It is an engine. He gets up, too. "Are they coming back?"

Yates moves out onto the road for a better look. The only direction Martell could be coming from is the south or the west, he thinks. But this engine is coming from the north. "I don't think it's them."

"Then who is it? I mean, why would they abandon us? It makes no sense."

To Yates it does. The Expo has been a disaster. The country is devastated, in ruins, unfit for anything close to normal living conditions, let alone corporate investment. He thinks of what Johnson had told him several times, *We are not "with" any administration in any official capacity other than when our corporate interests often intersect with whatever interest that administration might have... sometimes these interests need to be nudged, nuanced and occasionally pushed so that they intersect with more frequency and transparent.* He thinks of Dreiser's slip in the tower bar last night: *If they don't work, we'll just have to create some situations beyond the private sector that might get us some outside help.* Like the assassination of a dedicated, well-known American citizen.

"They're gonna have us killed, Blevins."

Blevins comes up alongside him and they stare out at nothing. "Why?"

"They played me. Set me up to feed their machine. So if I were to die here, it will actually please them, give them a nice piece of propaganda."

As Blevins tries to comprehend this, Yates starts to walk towards the SUV.

"We've gotta get out of here." He jogs across the road to the SUV and looks in the back hatch window, then in the driver's side window. The idiots left the keys and an M4. He takes the M4 and lays it in the passenger seat. As Blevins walks across the street, Yates hears the rising diesel churn of the approaching truck.

"You sure they're not coming back for us?"

Yates scrambles into the driver's seat, turns over the ignition. "Get in the truck, Blevins. They're coming to kill us." The truck is already moving as Blevins steps onto the sideboard. Yates has the accelerator floored by the time Blevins shuts the passenger side door. Blevins looks at the M4, then at Yates. He looks back to see if anyone is coming. Nothing yet. Yates races the truck down the narrow street, looking for an avenue, a way out.

"They set us up, Blevins. Or at least they set me up. The death of a semi-prominent, superficially loyal, yet increasingly irritating American businessman suddenly represents a lot more PR value to them then some insidious sound bites." He turns right down a vacant residential street. "Though, come to think of it, they have the sound bites, too, which would make my passing all the more tragic."

While Blevins tries to process this, they hear the distant popping of automatic weapons. Yates looks in the mirror and sees a white pickup truck making the same turn he'd just made, a hundred yards back. He floors the SUV again, heads down the centre of the empty street and then makes a sharp left next to a bombed-out electronics store, then another quick left at an abandoned Burger King.

Blevins slouches in the passenger seat. "Why don't we just surrender?"

"Because they've been paid to kill us. Telling them that you're a liberal democrat, that you're anti-war, anti-globalization, that you actually supported the Kyoto Agreement isn't gonna be enough." He turns right into a narrow side street lined with still-standing residential buildings through which the truck can barely pass. A woman is looking out her second-storey window at them. A teenage boy on a rooftop looks down at them and pulls out his cellphone. A spotter. "Shit!" Yates slams on the brakes. "Can you drive?" Yates is already outside, opening the back door.

Blevins slides over. "Where?"

"Go. I don't know. Just go!" He climbs into the back seat and up through the sunroof. He spins the Browning around, facing backwards. He yells, "Maybe if we can get downtown, near the hotels, the journalists..."

"What?"

"Nothing. Go!" As the truck swerves around a corner, Yates strains to understand the features of the mounted machine gun, tries to figure the thing out. He aims at the sky and pulls the trigger, but nothing happens

Blevins swerves out of the narrow single-lane and onto a two-lane avenue with a barrier island in the centre. "Which way?"

Yates looks left and right. In the distance to the right he sees through the haze the outline of a tall building. Maybe one of the hotels. He bends down and yells inside, "Right-right-right!" As they're turning, Yates sees the white truck careen out onto the avenue two streets back on their left. He again hears the pop of small arms fire. He squints to get a bearing on the truck, but it is coming right out of the setting sun and he loses sight of everything. He pivots back around and yells, "Head towards that building," pointing at what he hopes is a hotel. "Any route you want, but keep heading back that way."

"What about the airfield? Back to the Expo?" Two minutes ago, Blevins was slouched in the passenger seat, humiliated, caught up in his own convictions, but now he is crying, his hands shaking so much they pulse off the wheel as if it is electronically charged.

Yates looks back. "They're trying to kill us! Just aim for the fucking hotel!" He climbs back up through the sunroof and grabs the Browning, swivels it towards the oncoming truck. He tries to fire it again and nothing happens. But just his presence on the roof, his bumbling, overly demonstrative swinging of the gun, has an effect. The truck, which had got within a block of them, eases back, and for the next few moments the small-arms fire ceases. As they get further away from the slowing truck, Yates wonders why they hadn't done a cleaner job of ambushing him and Blevins. He thinks of Martell, jacked up on God knows what, repeatedly looking at the map, and figures that Martell dropped them off at the wrong place, and that if it wasn't for the incompetence of Martell, in all likelihood they'd be dead. These guys are just paid killers, he thinks. Not suicide bombers or jihadis. They didn't expect a chase or somebody manning a roof-mounted machine gun. He turns around and sees the hotel looming larger, maybe a dozen blocks away, and suddenly it occurs to him that, more than anything, he wants to live, wants to make it out of this so desperately it even surprises himself. *You don't want to die after all, do you?* He immediately begins to make a series of pledges to himself. *If we get out of this, I will definitely make changes, I'll live an exemplary life, I'll be less cynical, more truthful. I'll be the son my mother deserves, the friend that Marjorie needs, I'll forgive*

Blevins, apologize to Lauren and try to give Campbell the psychological help and friendship he deserves. I'll be neither an optimist nor a pessimist, just a well-intentioned realist. I'll engage in the act of living and, whenever possible, I will do whatever I can to do the right thing. Whatever that is.

To his surprise, the white truck makes another run at them. Bullets whiz overhead. When a round shatters the back window, Yates drops back inside and lays flat on the back seat. Blevins begins to scream and pound on the steering wheel. "I can't believe I'm gonna die with you! I don't wanna die with you!"

"Then stop crying and drive!"

"I hate you."

Yates slowly sits up and peeks over the top of the headrest and through where the rear window had been. He can see the faces of his attackers – young, afraid, angry. For a moment, lying back down and closing his eyes and giving up becomes the most favoured option, but he doesn't take it. Instead he continues to rise up through the open roof. He rights the Browning and squeezes the trigger but it doesn't fire, the kick doesn't come. He swivels it back and forth, hoping that the broad gesture will be enough to slow their pursuit, but this time they keep coming. They either know what's up, that the gun is jammed or that the man operating it is clueless, or someone got on their arse about backing off the first time. A burst of automatic fire rips up the sheet metal in the back of the SUV. Yates smacks the side of the gun as hard as he can. He jiggles the ammunition, searches frantically to find a way to make it fire. They're less than half a block away now, hanging out of the white truck training their guns on Yates. When more bullets tear into the truck, he realizes he has no choice but to climb onto the roof and try to free up the gun. Fully exposed, sitting on the edge of the roof, he jiggles the ammo belts and runs his hands along the barrel until he locates a switch that may or may not be the safety. Just as Blevins swerves hard to the right, Yates squeezes the trigger. The solitary burst rips into the front grill of the white truck, a white Datsun. Then the window shatters and the Datsun fishtails and rides up the kerb and onto the centre island. A few seconds later it rights itself, squares itself off on the avenue.

But Yates sees none of it. The force of the burst, combined with his precarious seat on the edge of the roof, kicks him backwards. His unsecured legs come up through the open roof, and he topples feet first over the side and onto the road. He rolls to a stop and looks up, waiting for the truck to approach again, but it is up on the centre median, its front end smashed into a concrete divider. In the opposite direction, the brake lights on the SUV flash on, and for a moment it looks like Blevins is going to back up to save him. Yates tries to stand up to wave, but his right leg gives out, so he begins to wave and shout from a sitting position. When the brake lights go off, he waits to see the white reverse lights, but they never go on. Instead, the SUV begins slowly to move away.

Yates makes himself stand, and is yelling louder now, begging Blevins, then cursing him when the ground beneath the right front tyre of the SUV erupts in a fountain of rock and flame. The SUV twists back and upwards through the bone-dry air, bursting into flame before crashing down onto the empty avenue. The concussion of the blast knocks Yates back. He lands hard at the base of what was once a fountain. He rolls and looks back, waiting for the white truck to come again to finish him off, but there is no truck, no sign of life other than his own. He forces himself to stand again and he looks around. Four blocks from the hotel – their only chance of asylum – and Yates is sure now that it *is* the hotel, because he recognizes the gilded façade from the news. He begins to limp towards the upside-down, burning Chevy. Rounds from the Browning continue to go off, triggered by the flame. To the men in the white truck around the corner, the report of the Browning sounds like the return fire of a fierce and determined opponent. It is enough to make them give up their pursuit. To the people watching from the upper floors of the hotel, it looks nothing less than heroic, the tall man limping towards the burning vehicle in which his comrade's life hangs in the balance, unfazed by the rogue rounds tearing the air around him. But Yates is oblivious to the bullets, unaware of the risk: the blast and the concussion from his fall has rendered him all but deaf, and the primary reason he's walking towards the SUV is because it's on the way to the hotel.

To his surprise, Blevins is alive. All blood and splintered bone beneath the waist. Blevins, who fifteen minutes ago wouldn't have minded seeing Yates get fragged. He tries the driver's side door, but it is stuck, so he kicks in the window with his good leg.

"You're alive because you're incompetent. Because you're a fucking coward." Yates looks at Blevins, imagines that he's making some sort of apology, some weepy expression of his gratitude, but he can't be sure, because he can't hear. "You should be the one who's dying."

"Don't worry about it, buddy," Yates says. "You can thank me later." He reaches in and grabs Blevins by the shoulder loops of his Kevlar vest.

Blevins screams for him to go away, tries to wave him off. "I hate you!" As Yates tilts his shoulders to fit through the window frame, Blevins takes a swing at him, clips him in the chin. He falls back, catches himself and stares at Blevins for a while, finally realizing what's going on.

This time, as he strains to pull Blevins out, he can't help but think of the Italian boy at the *gelateria* in Milan, and wonder why so many people would rather die than be saved by the likes of him.

The Land of What's Next

There will be a journalist. And a photographer. And the picture of the bloodied American carrying his critically wounded, would-be protégé and one-time stalker on his shoulders as gunfire tears the surrounding air apart will be released into the digital universe before they strap the first IV tube into him for the flight to Heidelberg.

He will be temporarily famous.

He will be treated by the world's best doctors and his prognosis will be excellent. He will be greeted by a crowd at Dulles. Interviewed by the networks. Given a Presidential Medal of Freedom. He will be debriefed by the government. Then, unofficially, by some others. And as long as he behaves, he will be left alone.

For months, he will be held up as an example of all that is still right about America, at home and abroad. He will call the person who the media tended to neglect in all of this, the one-legged futurist Marco Blevins, a true American hero.

Then, for the rest of his life, he will be unavailable for comment.

He will give up drinking on six different occasions, gain and lose fifteen pounds twelve different times. After a series of awkward exchanges, ill-timed starts and stops, years of friendship and abandonment and watching each other fail at love with others, he will seek out Marjorie, and she will give him a chance.

The event that will prompt their reunion and lead to their true expression of love for each other will be his mother's wake.

He will be the catalyst behind an intervention in Greenland that, for a while, will be successful.

He will be approached by a group of national political leaders and asked to run for Congress, but he will respectfully decline.

He'll get a titanium knee, and will have rotator cuff surgery and corrective laser vision.

He will take up golf and pretend for a while that he likes it, and that he likes the people in his weekly foursome.

He will stop voting, stop reading the newspapers, stop calling people just to check in.

Other than Marjorie and Campbell, he will never have another real friend again.

For eighteen months they will live in South Africa, only to realize it is a terrible mistake.

He will get into a fist fight with another parent at his daughter's soccer game.

He'll have some road-rage issues.

He will be a loving but inconsistent father, a distant but generous grandfather.

He will take a prescription drug specifically *because* of its possible side effects.

He will have a kidney scare, a cancer scare, a fucking quadruple-bypass scare.

Twenty-six years later, he will run into one of the Johnsons in the floor-and-tile section of a Home Depot in Marco Island, Florida. Yates's last words to him will be, "What's it supposed to be like tomorrow?"

Often, late at night, he will find himself walking the floors of an empty house, thinking of Leonardo and

Judas, of a fuel-soaked American flag, a teenage girl on a Vespa and Roberto Clemente.

At the strangest times, he will start to tear up.

Eventually he will move to a retirement community and discover that twenty years earlier his wife had an affair with a man he never met. He will never mention this to her, even when she calls him a heartless son-of-a-bitch for not going to her Timeless Tap and Ballroom Dancing Classes. If anything, he will understand.

He will write a novel based on the novel he had written as a child. And he will write his memoirs. But he will share them with no one.

And some nights he will walk outside and away from the street lights of his planned-community town home and he will look at the sky, and he will think of the sky over Johannesburg and Greenland, Milan and Fiji, Pennsylvania and the nation formerly known as Bas'ar and he will think of how, in that last moment before he collapsed with Blevins on his shoulders, when he looked up at the gorgeous sky and that gilded hotel façade, his last thought was a wonder.

He will.

Then again, maybe not.